D0115790

Playing with the Grown-ups

By the Same Author

THE MAN WITH THE DANCING EYES

Playing with the Grown-ups

SOPHIE DAHL

BLOOMSBURY

First published 2007

Bloomsbury Publishing Plc,
36 Soho Square,
London W1D 3QY

www.bloomsbury.com

A CIP catalogue record for this book
is available from the British Library

ISBN 978-0-7475-7777-5

10 9 8 7 6 5 4 3 2 1

Typeset by Hewer Text UK Ltd, Edinburgh
Printed by Clays Ltd, St Ives plc

The pages of this book are printed on
100% Ancient-Forest Friendly Paper

The papers on which this book is printed are manufactured from a
composition of © 1996 Forest Stewardship Council A.C. (FSC)
approved and post-consumer waste recycled materials. The FSC
promotes environmentally appropriate, socially beneficial and
economically viable management of the world's forests.

For Daniel 'Catcher' Baker, who
raised high the roof beams and
saw it as a book before I ever could;
with love, as ever, and the biggest
thank you, pure and true. S.D.

'One sees clearly only with the heart. Anything essential is invisible to the eyes.'

–Antoine de Saint-Exupéry, *The Little Prince*

Chapter One

The phone is ringing. In her sleep Kitty hears her own voice on the answering machine, husky, as her husband laughs at the serious tone of her message in the background. Then there is the beep, and another voice, a voice tinged with a panic that is familiar.

'Kitty, it's Violet. I'm sorry to ring you in the middle of the night, but it's Mummy. Something's happened.'

She sits up, scrabbles for the phone in the dark.

'Violet?' she says.

She packs methodically, already in a different place, distancing herself from her bedroom, the cartoonish skyline that she has loved from the moment she first saw it as a little girl. The city is sleeping, although it has the reputation of being one that never sleeps.

She looks at her husband's broad back, every inch of which she cherishes.

'Coffee,' he says as greeting, disappearing to their kitchen.

She laughs. She has always been able to wake, her brain engaged from the moment she opens her eyes. He needs to be cajoled from sleep, with coffee and tendresse, something she has joked with his mother about. His mother maintains it's a Southern affliction, a by-product of sugary heat, dawns so hot they make the pavement steam.

'The sleepy South', his mother calls it.

They sit next to each other at the round walnut table. He drinks coffee and she drinks tea.

'What time is it?' he says. 'I feel like we only just went to bed.'

'It's four-thirty,' she answers. 'The flight's at seven.'

'You're sure you don't want me to come? I can figure it out. I hate the thought of you being there on your own.'

'I won't be on my own. The others are all there. I'll be fine. It's what I'm good at, remember? Good in a crisis, that's me.' She smiles at him.

'I don't think crisis management suits you. You were made for calm. You're my little Buddha.' He cups her stomach gently.

'At least her timing was good. Three months more and I couldn't have got on a plane if I'd wanted to.' She looks at her belly with rue. 'Poor baby. There she was minding her own business in New York, and now look. Let's hope it's character building, and I won't have scarred her for life before she's even out of the womb.'

At Kennedy she turns to him.

'Mark?' she says. 'About the baby . . . You don't think I'll damage her before she's even left the gate? I wanted it all to be so perfect.'

He wraps her in his arms.

'What's perfect, Kitty? Life is flawed. She has to meet

her loopy relations sometime. Why not now? Life is full of imperfect, my old sweetheart. Just say the word and I'll park the car and get on that plane with you.'

'I'll be fine. You can't take the time if we want a summer holiday,' she says, gathering herself.

As he drives away she looks at him from the kerb like a child with big serious eyes, and he feels his heart lurch.

She steadies herself, places her hand on her stomach as if for luck, and walks into the terminal, her overnight bag hanging from her arm like a charm.

Her grandfather, Bestepapa, had hands that were true as butcher's blocks, and his voice was like the beginnings of a bonfire.

'Will you be QUIET, small child?' he roared, his huge hand banging on the wooden table, a full stop to the meandering chat around him. 'A hen house; I live in a hen house! All of you women talk too much . . . peck, peck at my poor ears! Men do not like this endless feminine banter. Men like women with MYSTERY, don't you know?'

Starling chatter lulled, the chorus (Kitty's mother, aunts and grandmother) practised looking like enigmatic women with secrets, until someone, likely her Aunt Elsie, spoiled it by laughing.

'Sexist,' Kitty muttered, her second favourite word. Since she turned eleven it had been replaced by 'alacrity'.

Her mother and her younger sisters were considered to be spectacular beauties. Not just valley beautiful, but beautiful all the way to London. The telephone rang for them incessantly.

'WHO is it? Which one do you want? Speak up, young man. How do you think I can bloody help you if I can't bloody hear you?' Bestepapa made a distinctly unhelpful face. 'Ah. You want Marina. Well, you'll have to call back, we're about to have dinner.' He finished with his antidote to lecherous pursuit: 'She does have children, you know.'

Kitty thought the routine was riotously funny. Her mother and her aunts did not.

Her mother said, 'You know, Papa, you can't keep us here for ever.'

'But I can try,' he answered. 'You're safe here.'

One out-of-wedlock baby born to his eldest teenage daughter was quite enough for him. Kitty saw it in the grim set of his mouth as he hung up the phone.

'Why is she crying now?' he asked her grandmother who was stroking her mother's shuddering back as Kitty watched from the hall.

'She is sad, Harald,' Bestemama answered, always with Scandinavian simplicity.

'Well, what does she have to be sad about, woman?! She is beautiful and she has this one, and the other two . . .' He motioned angrily in Kitty's direction. 'Give her a gin and tonic, and let's be done with the tears. Exhausting stuff, all of this crying.'

Marina flashed him a look of sodden fury.

'Come on, you,' he said to Kitty. 'I've had enough of this. Let's take Ibsen for a walk in the bluebell woods.'

Ibsen was his mongrel, fast as a blade. His sleepy-eyed demeanour belied a sly murderous instinct. The farmer at the top of the lane crossed himself when he saw him.

'Do I have to wear shoes, Bestepapa?' Kitty said.

'No. It's good to harden up your feet for the summer.'

He loped out of the front door, sighing as his hip gave a twinge of protest. Kitty skittled out after him like a shadow.

'What are you reading at school?' he asked her. She was in the third-form reading group, though she was in the juniors.

'*Go Ask Alice*,' Kitty said. 'It's about a teenage drug addict.'

He grimaced.

'No lovely Fitzgerald? No Steinbeck?'

'I think they're trying to warn us against perilous ways,' she said, rolling her eyes to indicate that she thought perilous ways were beneath her.

'I had an aunt who was a drug addict in Sweden. Well, actually a pair of aunts. Opium smokers the both of them, raddled their brains . . . Never understood it myself. I'd much rather have a lovely gin and tonic any day.'

'So would I,' Kitty said.

'That's the stuff.' He leaned on his stick, and they walked in warm silence up to the woods, Ibsen hungrily regarding the chickens, who gazed at him, their black eyes sharp like stones.

Hay House was the very centre of Kitty's universe. She grew up with the fields in her eyes and the woods in her nose. Her mother said Hay was her Never Never Land, and why would she ever need somewhere else? A house with a mortgage, and a roof that might one day fall in? Kitty thought it sounded horrible, and understood her mother's choice to stay at Hay in their whitewashed cottage in the garden with the yellow roses that hugged the outside wall, falling asleep under a roof that was as sturdy as their Irish nanny, Nora.

Kitty's brother and sister, Sam and Violet, were twins. They had a different father. Theirs was a magician called Barry. Kitty's was the husband of someone who wasn't her mother and his name was Mr Fitzgerald.

She heard the grown-ups say her mother was his kept woman, which didn't make sense to Kitty, because he hadn't kept her. He paid for Kitty's school, and sent her vast amounts of pocket money which she never knew what to do with.

Her mother called Mr Fitzgerald her 'one great big love'. Their affair began when she was very young but because he absolutely couldn't marry her (the contributing factor being Mrs Fitzgerald, a solid pre-nuptial agreement, and the iron grip of the Vatican on his conscience), he was perfectly happy when she gave birth to Kitty (Mrs Fitzgerald was unable to have babies) and because of having 'pots of money' (said in a whisper) he was perfectly happy to give her mother some of it.

It was an arrangement that worked, at least for them. Kitty read *Daddy Long Legs* and thought it might be about her. She was compelled by shadowy, mysterious men; in particular, detectives.

When she watched her favourite programme, *Bergerac*, on television, she couldn't decide whether she wanted him to be her father, or kiss her passionately, as they chased criminals together. It was what Bestepapa called 'a conflict of interest'.

Nora came into Kitty's life when she was six months old, and her mother had banged the door shut on her affair with Mr Fitzgerald. Her mother said Nora saved her life at this time. She did not say how but Kitty knew it must be true, because Nora was the kindest person in the world and very tolerant. Her mother made Nora laugh mostly, but when she made her angry, by having 'FANCIES', such as, 'Nora, I think we should all go and live in the medina in Marrakech,' or, 'Nora let's give the children a firework party just because it's Monday, and they do hate Monday,' Nora went silent and pursed her lips and refused to leave her room. Her mother left flowers outside in the hall and made butterscotch Angel Delight to curry Nora's favour. In general this worked.

When her mother ran off with Barry the magician and married him after three weeks, Nora was so angry she didn't address one single word to Marina for a whole month. Kitty knew this was torture, because Nora's silence was more powerful then any shouting, or the infinitely preferable quick sting of a smack. When she was spectacularly bad, within five minutes she wished she hadn't been, because to be put in Nora's Coventry for fifteen minutes was to sit in a cold damp room with no light. Kitty was very well behaved.

Nora was tiny like Tinkerbell with steel-blue eyes and the softest earlobes you would ever touch. She was exceedingly good at crossword puzzles and even better as a secret keeper. Unlike her mother, who couldn't keep a secret to save her life, though she tried.

Kitty never saw Nora cry, not even when their dog Pelly died. She grew quiet instead. When they went to smart places, she wore pearls and a splash of Ma Griffe and navy-blue jumpers from Marks & Spencer with brown slip-on shoes. She said they were practical. Her mother sometimes called her 'the husband'. 'I don't know,' she said when someone asked her something. 'You'll have to ask the husband – she rules this roost.' Kitty sort of knew that this was true.

Sam and Violet were seven years younger than Kitty, who didn't count them in the grand scheme of things, because she thought them babyish and beneath her, in the way that older children do.

Her mother met Barry the magician on a rainy day at Kitty's friend Bella's sixth birthday party in Shropshire. She was married to him for one year. He had brown velvet eyes, a thirst for whisky, and was always broke. His final trick was to leave her mother with a great bellyful of twins. When Sam and Violet were born, he joined the circus and Kitty's mother said she couldn't cope with his 'wandering ways'. In the end, he went off with a woman lion tamer named Lou with strong-woman thighs. Her mother snorted whenever Lou or her thighs were mentioned.

Sam and Violet's childhood was from a Victorian children's book. They went to nursery and finger-painted and sang, appearing neatly before supper in the big house, scrubbed and sweet, their round faces a canvas for the shower of kisses poured forth by the grown-ups. Kitty was allowed to have supper at the big table, and they ate in the playroom. Bestepapa thought babies and small children were tiresome, and complained often that girl babies shrieked like fishwives. He said, 'They're all right in small measures, but definitely small.'

Bestepapa adored Nora, and was the only person that dared to question her on salacious matters; the rest of them feared her wrath too much.

'Have you had lovers, Nora?' he asked one night, slurping his oxtail stew with marathon gulps.

Everyone held their breath waiting for the tight-lipped-Nora rage that was bound to follow.

Nora smiled a slow, secret smile.

'Ooh yes, Mr Larsen, of course I have.'

This was news to Kitty. She imagined Nora a sacred vessel that none had sailed in. She envisaged an anonymous manly hand, creeping swarthily through Nora's steely curls. It made her feel anxious.

'And how many lovers have you had?' Bestepapa's eyes, bright and Arctic-blue, beamed into her.

Bestemama started to cough, and asked whether anyone thought it was hot.

Nora fanned her hand airily.

'I'm never hot, Mrs Larsen. Going back to your question, Mr Larsen, which is obviously not one for small company, I'd say yes. Then I'd tell you to mind your own beeswax. All right?'

Bestepapa roared with laughter.

'Good show,' he said. 'Good show.'

Nora smiled again; her foreign, girlish smile and Kitty was plagued by thoughts of her in amorous clinches with every man in the village.

Before she went to bed Kitty was allowed to watch half an hour of television with Nora in her little sitting room. Nora was the programme dictator. She liked videos from the *National Geographic* and things about history. Kitty thought Nora was the cleverest person she knew.

'Nora?' Nora had painted her nails maroon, and Kitty knew this was new evidence of her femme fatale status.

'Yes, Kitty?'

'You're not planning to run away, are you?'

'Oh, no imminent plans. I'll tell you when I am. If Sam and Violet give more trouble like they did tonight over bedtime, I may.'

'No, but you're not going to run off with Gareth Jackson from the farm, are you? Because I think he likes you. When he talks to you he goes bright red like a big fat sunburnt bum.'

'Is that what you think?' Nora's eyes twinkled.

Kitty nodded.

'No. I'm going to stay and look after you lot till you're big, if you haven't sent me to an early grave.'

She smiled, and wiping the frown from Kitty's forehead with a finger, said, 'Oh you've got your mother's imagination, that's for sure.'

Kitty loved being told she had the traits of her mother, even if they were small.

Her mother was a beauty, a painter, and a weeper. She lived with alacrity. She spent her life being photographed by many exotic-sounding people, and people bought her paintings for amounts of money that Kitty could not comprehend. She wept about five times a week, though not quite as much in the summer. If Ibsen got at the chickens or she saw a starving child on the news, she was prone for days, and Bestemama went to great lengths to hide the newspaper from her in the morning. After an outburst of weeping, Bestemama made Marina rest in a darkened room, and then she took her for a long walk in the woods, just the two of them. She called her tender-hearted.

When she was on her best form, Marina was Kitty's most favourite thing. At school they were asked to write a list of their favourite things, and hers was all about her mother. Her mother loved to laugh as much as she loved to cry. She took her on outings to antique-clothes shops, where they tried on tea-stained wedding dresses and tiaras. In the garden they had a christening for Kitty's doll, Jumble Sale, where her mother was the vicar, baptising Jumble Sale in the bird bath, and Nora was the godmother, even though she was an atheist.

On Sundays, if it was warm, her mother took her for picnics on the hill by Hay House, a hill that looked out to for ever. When she smiled at her, Kitty felt like she was the only person in the entire world, because her mother's smile covered her from head to toe. Marina's smile reached past her eyes way up into her golden crown of hair. Everyone said she should have been a film star.

In the summer they lay in the garden with lemon juice on their hair to bleach it blonder. She showed Kitty the exact tree in the bluebell woods where Richard McDonald the doctor's son had pressed her up into the bark and kissed her when she was twelve.

She taught her, over miniature cups of coffee, thick with milk and sugar, how to do the twist in her studio. Her studio was at the edge of the orchard, and it was yet another facet of Hay House's magic, filled with silk butterflies and orchids, old love letters, and postcards from people who knew her so well they didn't sign their names. To be invited in was a treat, to be drenched in a world that reeked of her mystery. Kitty got the same feeling she had at church when they went at Easter or Christmas. Sometimes when her mother was up in London, Kitty stole in like a ghost, breathing in the air so still and full of her.

Bestepapa bought Hay House from a farmer in the fifties for £500. Then it was a simple Georgian farmhouse, but over the years he and Morris, his oldest friend and gardener, had added to it with higgledy-piggledy ambition, so it resembled a doll's house that had been placed as an afterthought by a giant amongst long outbuildings and crazed half-finished pathways and mazes.

The house was surrounded by ancient orchards whose sturdy trees were made for climbing. There was an aviary in the main garden, home to a rainbow of sherbet-coloured canaries who keened lovingly when Bestepapa came to shut them up at dusk.

Kitty's school was a sixteen-minute walk down the lane, a walk that she loved most in the winter where, still bathed in the porridgy half-light of morning, she walked feeling that she was the first to see the world as it was just shaking awake. Stepping firmly on the frost, in her red winter boots, she was the first to hear the longing whistle of the train as it flew over the bridge, the first to hear the neighbour's car splutter alive in protest at the cold, Classic FM sending her on her crackling way.

Kitty liked school. Her mother and her aunts were legend in the village and some of this stardust by association rubbed its coppery sheen on her, even though she had glasses, and unlike her mother she could not play netball, or, like Ingrid and Elsie, win a prize for the high jump. She did have her mother's eyes, silvery grey, and a fortune teller at the village fête once told Kitty they would get her in trouble. She hoped so. She felt a pretender to the family glamour, even when girls from the fifth form showed her a picture in *Vogue*, her mother gazing soulfully out of its pages, her sadness palpable perhaps only to her oldest child.

Her illegitimacy too, was a badge of separation, though not one that she could divine. The absence of her father, given his marital status, was not something that she questioned – she had Bestepapa and Bergerac. The girls at school found it ceaselessly fascinating, so Kitty answered their questions with studied affront, because she realised early on that it was considered a social hindrance to have an unmarried mother. She manufactured hysteria when Katrina Donnelly called her a bastard after fouling her in netball as the other girls stared on in mawkish sympathy waiting for her tears.

When her mother wasn't prone, painting, or in London, she waited for Kitty by the gate after school. She wore vintage thirties chiffon dresses, her long pale legs and knickers whispers through the fabric. Her short scarlet nails and gypsy hoops cemented her fate: she was a magnet for the pursed lips and scorching eyes of other mothers and the slavish open-mouthed worship of their daughters.

If her mother was up in London Elsie and Ingrid would dress Kitty up and smuggle her into the pub. They had done this since she was small and they barely qualified for pub drinking themselves. Elsie was seventeen to Kitty's eleven, Ingrid eighteen. Her mother was twenty-seven.

Walking down the lane holding her hands, they told her

who they fancied. In the dark their blonde hair glinted and swirled behind them like mist. They shared a B & H, but Ingrid got angry with Elsie and said that she was disgusting because she always 'bum-sucked' cigarettes.

'Who do you fancy, Kitten?'

'Don't be stupid,' she said gloomily. 'I go to school with girls.'

'What about that heavenly boy with acne in the chemist's . . . I know you love him.' Elsie dug her in the ribs.

'Shut up,' Kitty said. Her neck was hot in the dark.

She liked the fuggy pub. They made steak sandwiches and crispy chips, and she was allowed Appletise in the bottle with a straw.

'Stop,' Kitty said. 'One moment. I have a pain in my ovaries. A serious pain. I think I have to go back to the house, and get one of my sanitary towels.'

'Not this again,' Ingrid said. 'Kitty, you do not have your period, OK? Just stop it. You probably won't get it for another two years. You're completely flat-chested. Why do you want it so badly? It's really strange. When you get it you'll be sorry: it's not fun.'

'I think I have it, I do. I can feel things moving inside me, and I have a cramp.'

'We're going to ignore you if you carry on. It's called the curse not the blessing. I'll bet you your pocket money it's not. Are you willing to take a bet?'

'No,' Kitty said.

'Would you like to go to another school? Boarding school, like we did?' Elsie asked.

'Don't think so. Maybe, if there were boys.'

* * *

Boarding school was a topic of tired discussion at Hay House. Kitty had wriggled out of it for years. The others had all gone from eight to sixteen. Kitty knew secretly that one of the reasons her mother wanted her to go was so she could go up to London and not feel guilty. If she was away at school, she wouldn't be there to stare at her mother with accusing eyes when she came back the next day from a party.

Her mother sat huddled in the sitting room with Elsie and Ingrid, their hushed voices and squawks of laughter wafting under the door as Kitty eavesdropped.

'God, I want to move to New York,' her mother said. 'What can I do here? There's nothing to do, I'll be stuck here for ever with you and the bloody chickens.'

Kitty ran into the room, scandalised.

'There's me!' she shouted. 'I'm here! Don't forget me! And there's everything to do, the walks and the woods and the canaries and the mornings . . .' She realised that she couldn't think of anything else and began to cry.

Marina pulled her into a familiar softness that smelled of Mitsouko and Marlboro Reds.

'Hush, hush, sweet girl, I would never leave you anywhere. Come and sit on my lap. I was just talking . . . being a silly chatty mummy . . . Whilst I realise that Hay is joy for you, my little bird, sometimes I get a bit bored here.'

'It should be INSPIRING to you, you're a painter. No one else is bored, just YOU.'

'I am,' Elsie said.

'I want to move to Paris,' Ingrid said.

'Well, I don't understand you – I think you're all horrible and disloyal to the lovely place where you were born!'

They laughed and fluttered about Kitty, plastering scented kisses on her head, their soft hands pulling her this way and that, until, sated with love and ravenous, she ran to the kitchen to pester Bestepapa for one of his bacon and marmalade sandwiches, feeling that things were restored to their rightful order.

Kitty always measured the passing of time by the calendar of her birthday, which fell, inevitably, like a spent plum, during the first week of the autumn term. The Larsens were big on birthdays, and from the moment she woke, Kitty was treated like a queen. Her mother brought her breakfast in bed, and she had been there for each and every birthday of Kitty's small life.

It was the one day of the year Kitty was officially allowed coffee, and it arrived in a great oversized cup, so sweet it made her grimace, then smile, and her mother sat on her bed and told her, each year, the story of the day she was born. Kitty loved the story of her beginning; it reminded of her of Bestepapa's Viking stories:

> My waters broke at three in the morning. I had been ready for your arrival for weeks, and my suitcase sat at the end of my bed neatly packed, so nothing halted my trip to the hospital. I knocked on Bestepapa and Bestemama's door, with a navy-blue pea coat on top of my nightie, and I said, 'The baby's coming.' Bestepapa leapt out of bed, and he was as agitated as I was calm. Bestemama kissed my stomach for luck (she had

to stay to look after Elsie and Ingrid) and we said goodbye.

When we walked outside, everything seemed electric. The moon lit up the garden so we could follow the path to the car. It was an Indian summer that year, and everything was still in bloom, and I remember thinking that the roses had never looked more voluptuous, or smelled quite as beautiful. The night was so thick and alive with magic it was tangible. As we were getting into the car, the canaries, in the silence of the garden, sang out, as though they were heralding the beginning of your journey, and wishing us well.

We drove to Oxford, Bestepapa and I, listening to Duke Ellington and eating boiled sweets. Just before we got there my contractions became closer and closer together, so sharp they took my breath away.

Bestepapa had smuggled a bottle of champagne into the waiting room, and he paced there for seven hours, as I screamed and pushed, pushed and screamed and the world was nothing but you and me, and this extraordinary, other-worldly pain, but it kept reminding me how alive I was, how very much I wanted you, and I called out for Bestemama as you were pulled out by forceps that looked like medieval instruments of torture. You screamed, outraged that you were in this cold place of strip-lights and intrusion. They placed you in my arms. You had barely any hair, and because of the forceps, your little nose was squashed to one side of your face, as though you had been in a boxing match. But when I looked at you, I had never seen such perfection, or felt such an all-consuming love. I was on fire with love for you.

The doctor went into the hall to tell Bestepapa that you were born and he shouted and hooted so much they had sternly to tell him to shut up. He came in and he held you in his huge hands like you were a baby butterfly, crying big salty tears that fell on your face. You seemed undisturbed by all of the commotion, and Bestepapa declared you, in a choking voice, 'A GOOD EGG.'

Her mother cleared her throat.

'Well, birthday girl.' She stroked Kitty's hair back from her eyes. 'You know the rest.'

Having feasted on the rich tale of her existence, Kitty got ready for the spare banality of school. Ingrid and Elsie took her shopping in the afternoon, and there was a big birthday supper, whose menu she was allowed to dictate, like a miniature gourmand with an eye for excess.

Her mother came back from one of her London trips flushed and dizzy. Kitty presumed she had met a man and took up her watchpost outside the sitting room.

'Who is he?' asked Ingrid.

'It's God. I've found God,' Marina said serenely.

There was silence as her sisters waited for the punchline.

'I always felt like something was missing. I've ached my entire life; except when I was pregnant.'

This was news to Kitty. She wondered if a lifelong ache was like the flu. It sounded painful.

'But I've found God and now I feel whole.'

Elsie's giggle broke the spell.

'That's classic! Woohoo, God! . . . You are joking?' she asked nervously.

Kitty heard a match being struck, the measured drag of a cigarette.

'No, Lillian Rhodes invited me to what I thought was a yoga class, this teacher they've all been banging on about, and I went in exercise clothes to this house in Victoria, and I was sort of dreading it, and I was meant to meet Lola and the Baron for dinner after at La Famiglia. When I walked in, incense was burning and there was a circle of people sitting at the feet of this, this, being. Everyone looked so happy and full of love. No one was judging anyone . . . I sat down and HE looked at me, a look of utter compassion. I felt like a boulder rolled aside and my heart opened when I sat at the Guru's feet and received his blessing. I can't really explain it, except to say I felt like I had come home.'

'Fantastic. Far out. So you're in love with a guru, very sixties of you, Marina,' yawned Ingrid. 'How was Peter's party? Has the Baron said anything about me?'

Kitty could tell from the silence that her mother was giving them a withering look. She bit her thumbnail.

'Marina, can you get us tickets for the Rolling Stones?'

They were dismissing this as one of her mother's whims.

But now Marina had purpose, and carried herself as though she contained the secret of bliss. Kitty found it all infuriating. Her new mother didn't swear and smiled beatifically whenever Kitty misbehaved. Her new mother got up early and sat crossed-legged in the dining room deep in prayer.

'Can you try to be quiet? I'm meditating,' she said with the smile that Kitty was certain she'd copied from the photograph of Mother Teresa that was stuck on her bathroom mirror.

'Well, WE are trying to make breakfast,' Bestemama said tolerantly.

'Bugger off, Buddha!' was Bestepapa's response.

Now Marina did not cry, as she'd done before, she looked at her family as though she pitied their souls, hoping for their liberation.

'Bloody Maggie T,' Nora said, watching the news. 'Who does she think she is?'

'I'm sure she's filled with God's love, Nora, like the rest of us,' Marina said, blissfully smoking a cheroot.

'I'll show you God's love, woman. That smile you're wearing is giving me the heebie-jeebies,' Kitty heard Nora mutter under her breath as she flew out of the room to put the eggs on for tea.

Marina bowed her head.

The thin end of the wedge was at six o'clock, Bestepapa's sacred gin and tonic hour, where nightly he hummed tunelessly to Beethoven's Seventh, and imbibed like a bootlegger. Kitty sat next to him and did her homework and he let her have one sip of his drink, a big one.

They were just settling into their ritual when across the Beethoven came the mystical throb of a sitar followed by a mournful wail from her mother. Kitty thought that maybe she was crying, and became heartened.

'Come with me.' Bestepapa gave Kitty a look that promised trouble. A recklessness came over her and itched like a rash.

They crept up the stairs along the hall which reeked of incense, stopping in Ingrid and Elsie's bathroom and applying orange lipstick to the spot between their eyes. Bestepapa looked deranged, and Kitty gasped with pleasure at his theatrical touch.

'You're brilliant!' she said.

'Shush.' He winked, holding his finger to his lips.

Opening the study door, Bestepapa sprang in whirling like a dervish as she tried to keep up, doing an impromptu belly dance, rolling her white tummy in and out with the music. They clapped their palms together in a spontaneous Hindu high five.

Her mother opened one eye and glared at them.

'It's fine,' she said. 'Laugh at me. It's your dharma. Though frankly, Kitty, I expect more of you. I thought you were interested in other cultures, but it would seem that's not the case.'

'It was just a joke.'

Kitty began to feel unsure, but Bestepapa gave another giant hip roll, and she laughed out loud at his defiance, leaving her mother to sweep out, without deigning to acknowledge them, the religious philistines.

Bestemama was up within minutes.

'Honestly, Harald,' she said. 'You of all people should be pleased Marina's found something that makes her happy, and encouraging Kitty to join you in mocking her is unforgivable. It demoralises her.'

Bestepapa tried his hardest to look contrite.

Bestemama stumped downstairs, each footfall a stamp of disgrace, and once he was sure she was gone, Bestepapa held his hands to his heart coyly and whispered,

'OMmmmm,' releasing a giant fart that sounded like a duck quacking.

'That showed her what we think of mumbo jumbo gumbo.'

Kitty promptly fell on the floor, convulsed with laughter, blue spectacles steamed up from her exertions.

Unlike her mother's other phases – astrology, the fit-for-life diet, runes and knitting – which waned and flickered like the rain in May, this one had staying power. Every evening her mother drove to London for 'Satsang with Swami-ji'. She said that the Guru normally lived in Pennsylvania but was on a 'tour of compassion' in London. Kitty conjured up the Guru healing the sick, on a tour bus wearing a conductor's hat and a navy-blue dress.

She wondered what exactly her mother did with Swami-ji, and her head spun with the limited tabloid knowledge she had of Rajneesh and his Rolls-Royces, the jolly round Maharishi with the Beatles. She lay awake long into the night, and she felt jealous of her mother's newfound happiness. Nothing was certain any more. Her mother ate greying macrobiotic food that she bought at Holland & Barrett up in London, and spurned Bestemama's meatballs.

'Her favourite since childhood!' said Bestepapa, his voice rising with indignation.

Sam and Violet rejected Marina's efforts to teach them Hindi chants in the bath.

'Humpty Dumpty!' they shouted, drenching her with soapy water.

Elsie and Ingrid were equally glum about the whole

thing, and they lay with Kitty in the sitting room, waiting for Marina to come home, like the long-suffering wives of a prophet. They chain-smoked menthols, because they thought they were sophisticated and, if feeling particularly laconic, let Kitty have a hasty baby puff. They watched *Doctor Who*, which gave Kitty nightmares; she dreamed of her mother riding a Dalek in a crimson sari, evil grinning monkeys perched beside her.

Although she was calm like the desert, Marina, who Kitty felt was only half hers to begin with, seemed to be slipping quietly away. Since she was small, Kitty had suspected that her mother was really a changeling who had been left in the garden one night by a bearded witch who stole her from the fairies and hid her for safekeeping at Hay House. She knew the crone would return one bad day to claim her. That day seemed to have arrived. But instead of the twisted thorny figure of Kitty's nightmares, her mother's spiriter was a man, a reedy Indian man in his fifties, with kind eyes and feet like wrinkled walnut shells.

In the photographs her mother had peppered around her bedroom Swami-ji looked benevolent, but Kitty knew it was all an act. She did some detective work to catch him in his sorcery before it was too late.

'Mummy, has the Swami bloke ever said something secret to you, and told you not to tell anyone else, no matter who?' She tried to say this casually, as they walked up the lane.

'You are intuitive, Kitty,' her mother said. 'It's SWAMI-JI. "Bloke" is disrespectful. Yes, my mantra. This is a special thing you say over and over again when you meditate.

Each devotee of Swami-ji has a mantra that belongs just to them.'

Kitty's stomach started somersaulting but she tried to look calm.

'Are you allowed to tell me your mantra?'

'No,' her mother said smiling. 'One day when you meet him, Swami-ji will give you your very own.'

'Please tell me. I swear on my life I won't tell anyone,' Kitty said, wheedling. She knew that if her mother told her the spell would be broken.

'No. I can't.' Marina was final. 'Now stop it, please.'

'Please tell me, PLEEEAASSE; you're the best mother in the world . . .' Kitty smiled and shook her arm.

'No. Why am I not allowed to have anything of my own, just one thing? I don't have to share everything.'

Kitty didn't understand her, and it made her angry.

'I think the Swami man – ji, is . . .' She searched for the word, and then shouted it: 'SHIT.'

The word hung pleasurably in the empty lane. Her mother was silent, and for the first time since her spiritual awakening, she looked angry. This gave Kitty a small fleeting pinch of victory. She did think Swami-ji was shit; he was making her life unbearable. The truth was out.

Her mother grabbed her arm tightly.

'What has Bestepapa been saying to you?' she asked in a voice like tar.

Kitty wriggled away and glared at her.

'I can think someone's shit on my own and I can walk home on my own,' she said, running up the hill towards Hay House.

She left her mother standing frozen, like Lot's wife in scripture class.

Her mother stayed in her studio for two days. She appeared briefly to take Sam and Violet to nursery, and to kiss them goodnight after their bath. Kitty decided that maybe they were quite fun after all, and sat on the bathroom floor and watched as Nora sponged their funny little twiglet arms and legs.

When her mother saw her, she said hello politely as though Kitty were an acquaintance at a cocktail party. Kitty longed to say sorry, but her mother was a fortress whose walls she could not penetrate. Instead Kitty smiled at her extra hard, so she would know. Her cheeks hurt with the effort.

Nora passed Kitty a Quality Street, a caramel, her favourite.

'You can pick the programme,' she said. 'I think *Grease* is on Channel 4.'

'Nora, can I ask you something?'

'What is it, Pest?'

'I know I'm big, but can I sleep in your bed?'

Nora radiated heat from her flannel nightdress, and Kitty pressed her feet against her soft shins. Nora fell asleep tickling her arm, and Kitty marvelled for the umpteenth time how the small form of Nora was capable of producing such industrial noise in sleep. She whistled and gnashed her teeth; she fought unseen sleep burglars with her small fists. Finally she stilled and emitted deep rumbling contented snores.

'Sleeping with you is like sleeping with a washing machine,' Kitty whispered happily.

Nora gave a warm snore in response.

When Kitty was sure Nora was fully steeped in sleep, she slipped into Marina's bedroom and wedged herself in amongst her pillows, awkwardly trying to fit her body in the imprint of her mother's. Swami-ji stared at Kitty accusingly from the bedside tables. 'I'm sorry,' she said to him firmly, 'but she's my mother. Not yours.' She crossed her fingers superstitiously, and turned all of his pictures face down.

'Won't you come to London with me, Mama, to meet him?' Marina asked. 'Please, I think it could change your life.'

Kitty saw Bestemama shake her head.

'What makes you think my life needs to be changed, Marina? Answer me that. I'm happy.'

'How do you know?' her mother said. 'How can you know anything until you've tried it?'

'I just know, Marina,' Bestemama said with a stark sigh.

When her mother asked her to meditate with her in the studio, Kitty was thrilled. They sat cross-legged on the floor in the dark, and they shut their eyes.

'Clear your mind of all wandering thoughts,' her mother whispered, her voice sounding like the lady vicar's from *Songs of Praise*. 'Be still and allow the grace of God and the Guru to wash over you like water.'

Kitty tried. Every time she was nearly still a thought would pop into her head and flood it with disturbance.

'What's for supper?' her head said. 'Be quiet,' Kitty told it silently. 'Katrina Donnelly has ginger hair, which means her pubes must match, and Miss Jackson is a lesbian,' her head answered. It was exhausting. She tried to think pure thoughts. Instead her head swam with images of buxom page-three girls. Kitty was hungry. She knew they had been there for hours. Her bottom hurt. She opened one eye. Her mother sat glowing like a pearl in the dark.

'Mummy?' she said in a hushed voice.

Marina looked like a statue. She didn't answer.

'Mummy?' Kitty felt frightened. Maybe she'd fallen into a religious coma.

She poked her in the arm. After she'd poked for three minutes her mother said, 'What is it, darling?' She looked at Kitty in confusion, her silver eyes glazed.

'I think we've been here for HOURS. We've missed supper, what will I eat? I think it's definitely past my bedtime.' Her mother looked down at her watch, a Patek Philippe, a present from Mr Fitzgerald.

'Kitty, we've been here for ten minutes. Why don't you go to the big house and I'll see you down there in a few hours.' She said this kindly.

'Do you know what?' Kitty told the canaries in the garden. 'Soon I will be able to meditate for two whole hours.'

'Who are you talking to, Kit?' Elsie came out of the laundry room.

'To the canaries. I think they're listening.'

'Lord, you're odd,' Elsie said.

To Kitty Saturday mornings meant chocolate croissants with strawberry jam which she wasn't allowed during the week because, according to Bestemama, 'Flour cements the bowels.'

She was savouring her croissant with great oozing pleasure when her mother walked in, dangling her car keys.

'I'll be back in a minute,' Marina said, not addressing anyone in particular. 'I'm going to pick up a friend from the train station.'

'Who, darling?' asked Bestemama, hiding the *Telegraph* on her lap.

'Just a friend from London.' She sailed out, her chiffon billowing behind her like a flag.

'Will you bring me some rhubarb and custards?' Kitty shouted after her.

Nora took Violet and Sam up to the farm to feed the chickens, so Bestepapa could have his 'hour of peace'. He smoked his pipe, looking fondly at a picture of Nelson Mandela in the paper.

'Brave fellow, that one. Don't know about the wife though. Seems a bit suspicious if you ask me.'

'We weren't,' said Ingrid, glancing up from the *Tatler*. 'Mama, do you think I'd make a good marchioness? The Marquess of Blandford is looking for a wife.'

'No marriage yet, please,' Bestemama said. 'You need to concentrate on your career.'

'Hear hear,' said Bestepapa. 'What do you want a marquess for anyway? Find a man who is good with his hands like Morris.'

Elsie snorted.

'Maybe it's Mr Fitzgerald that's coming from London,' Kitty said, wiggling in her chair.

Elsie snorted again.

'Don't hold your breath,' she said.

Forty minutes later, they heard her mother's car crunching on the gravel, followed by footsteps on the garden path. The front door opened.

'Did you bring me my sweets?' Kitty called.

'No,' her mother said. 'But Shanti bought you all some prasad to eat.'

Lurching behind Marina was a lumbering pink woman in a gold sari with violently yellow hair. In one hand she held a tambourine. The woman wore anklets on her surprisingly small feet, that swung with little bells as she walked, announcing the arrival of a much more delicate sort of a person than she was. She carried a lumpy bag made from hemp, and Kitty realised that if 'prasad' came from that bag, she probably didn't want to eat it.

'Namaste,' Shanti said, hands folded reverently, her body wobbling, a great pink trifle. She hit the tambourine for emphasis.

Bestepapa looked confused, Bestemama furious and Elsie spat out a mouthful of crunchy nut cornflakes, which hit Ingrid's arm.

'Yuck,' Ingrid said. And it was unclear to which particular thing she was referring.

Shanti seemed unperturbed by the reaction her appearance had provoked.

'I am the director of Swami-ji's spiritual centre in London. I think you know that we have become a big part of Lakshmi's life – oh sorry! You will all still know her as Marina, more on that later – a big part of Marina's life, and she ours. We thought that you might perhaps be . . .' She searched for a word. 'RESISTANT to the idea of us. Lakshmi speaks so highly of you all, and wanted me to visit with you so I could . . . explain our philosophy, and I thought if Mohammed can't come to the mountain . . .'

'The mountain will come to Mohammed!' Marina finished the sentence, and clapped her hands like a four-year-old.

'Lakshmi wants me to give you the chance of spiritual redemption.' Shanti winked.

'Who's this Lakshmi type she keeps talking about?' Bestepapa whispered to Kitty.

'I think she means Mummy, but I'm not sure,' she hissed back through her teeth.

'Would your guest like a cup of tea, Marina?' Bestemama asked stiffly, unable, it seemed, to address the hulking stranger in gold.

'Not to bother,' Shanti chuckled. 'I bring my own; goat's milk is still hard to come by in most households . . . Fresh chai. Would you like to try some?' She pulled out a thermos from the lumpy bag and sat down, uninvited, next to Bestepapa, who edged away from her as though she carried a virulent strain of disease. Marina sat next to Kitty and patted her. She sat very quietly so she wouldn't be asked to leave.

'Would you like to take the stage, Lakshmi, or should I?' Shanti asked her mother in a confidential voice.

'I think I can start.'

Shanti gave her what was obviously a Sanskrit thumbs-up.

Her mother took a deep breath.

'I've made a lot of decisions recently, life-altering decisions, which have not been easy. I have prayed a lot, and sought the guidance of elders from my spiritual community.'

Here Shanti shot the Larsens a syrupy smile.

'And I hope, as I have, that you will come to a peace and understanding about them. Firstly, I have changed my name to the spiritual name of Lakshmi, the goddess of abundance.'

Ingrid and Elsie stared dumbly, in disbelief.

'I understand it may take some getting used to . . . Secondly I have decided that in order to practise my spirituality freely, when Swami-ji goes back to America in September I will follow. I'm going to live in New York so I can be closer to his ashram in Pennsylvania, but so I can also carry on with my painting. I've already found a gallery there that wants to represent me.'

'What about your children, Marina?' Bestemama whispered, pale-faced, her hands scratching in the air.

'Violet and Sam and Nora will come with me, but I've decided it would be too disruptive to Kitty's education at this stage to put her in a foreign school system. So I've started looking at boarding schools in England.'

Kitty shut her eyes and held her breath. If I can hold my breath and keep my eyes shut for two minutes, she thought, when I open them everything will be normal and this will all have been a horrible joke.

She heard Bestepapa say in a strangled voice, 'Kitty must stay here. This is her home.'

She started counting, one elephant, two elephant, squeezing her eyes so tightly that not a glimmer of light penetrated them. Her lungs felt like they would burst.

When she was at ninety-seven seconds she heard her

mother say, 'Swami-ji thinks Kitty should stay in England. Not here, but at boarding school. He has given his blessing.'

Kitty heard Shanti warble, 'Swami-ji knows best.'

She thought she was going to die, right there in the dining room with her eyes shut and her family gathered around her.

She cried out, 'But he doesn't even know me! How can he know what's best?'

Her mother turned and stroked her face tenderly.

'I know it doesn't make sense now, darling. I know this is a shock. I know it may seem selfish. But I'm doing what in my heart I know is best. Best for all of us. I promise you, it WILL make huge sense when you are a grown-up.'

After that there was more shouting. Shanti shuffled out towards the garden, dabbing at her moist face with a tissue. Her mother said awful things to Bestepapa. She said he was controlling, that he was incapable of showing his love, that she was a grown woman and that he had ruined every relationship with a man she'd ever had.

She started crying when she said, 'I would have had a chance with Fitzgerald if it wasn't for you. He would have left his wife. He loved me, he really, really loved me. You frightened him away. You threatened him. Kitty could have had a father, you bastard.'

Bestemama sprang up like a lioness.

'What did you say?' She spoke just above a whisper, but it filled the room like a scream.

'He's ruined my life,' her mother said in a child's voice.

'You are a fantasist, Marina, if you think any of what

you're saying is true.' She looked as if she were seven feet tall. Her whole body radiated with anger. 'Your father has worked hard his entire life to make sure you girls are secure. He has given you EVERYTHING. But it's never enough for you. Nothing is ever enough. What more could we have done? Answer me that. You have been pandered to and indulged more than anyone else in this house. And this is how you respond to us? With this poison? Your father is TIRED, Marina. He has fought in a war. He built this house with his hands. You are exhausting him with all of this.'

Kitty looked at Bestepapa's hands, as though she was seeing them for the first time. They were long and limply mottled with age. They were tired hands. She had never noticed before.

Elsie and Ingrid flanked Bestepapa's chair. Marina and Kitty sat alone at the other end of the table. Kitty saw they were now two separate families. She did not want her mother to cry, but she did not want to see Bestepapa folded in, as though he had been shot. She certainly did not want to go to boarding school. The shouting continued, unabated.

Kitty took her mother's hand.

'Mummy didn't mean it!' she said. 'She's just upset, aren't you? Mummy?'

There was a palpable shift in the room. In a breath, Bestemama took Bestepapa to his bedroom to lie down. Ingrid and Elsie muttered something about going to the village, and sped off in Ingrid's MG, leaving Kitty and Marina alone in the dining room.

Her mother looked into her eyes.

'You're my best girl, you know that, don't you?' Her voice, though it still quavered, was strong. 'From now on it's you and me, kiddo. That is – if you don't mind, of course.' She smiled at her.

Although Kitty thought this sounded potentially lonely, a thrill passed through her at the thought of being just the two of them against the world. She forgot the existence of everyone else, the looming prospect of boarding school and separation, a sea of separation.

'I don't mind,' she said, and she smiled back.

She calls her Aunt Elsie from inside the duty-free shop as she toys half-heartedly with miracle wrinkle creams. Elsie is up at 6 a.m.; her Pilates teacher comes to her immaculate apartment at 6.30 every morning.

'Oh Kit-kat,' she says. Her voice is still laced with hills and home, although she has lived in New York for fifteen years. She lives on Park Avenue in an apartment with silent polished floors.

Elsie's first apartment, on Elizabeth Street, would in its entirety fit into her present sitting room. Kitty remembers lying with Elsie on the cream sofa in the little flat, watching reruns of *Full House* on Sunday mornings; Elsie drinking coffee with smudged eyes, saying she was going to marry John Stamos one day soon. At night Kitty could hear her aunt's every footfall, padding over uneven floorboards, as she double locked the front door to keep them safe, blew out all the candles, turned off the lights, slipping into her bedroom, with a creaky twitch of the door. Through the thin walls that divided them, Joni Mitchell sang them both to sleep.

Now Elsie is married to an Italian sculptor, and they have two brown-eyed sons, who call her 'Mommy'. Kitty laughs at this, as Elsie seems shocked that she could have birthed a child with brown eyes AND an American inflection. Over a recent empathetic cup of tea, Kitty said gently, 'Did you really think they would come out with English accents? You do live in New York.'

'Well, I did rather, darling. I thought they'd pick it up from me. I thought it might be genetic.'

At which they looked at each other and fell about.

Kitty has absent-mindedly applied half of the make-up counter to her face. She catches sight of her panda-bear eyes in the mirror. 'Oh shit,' she says, wiping off lavender eye shadow with furious fingers.

'Do you have a warm coat?' says Elsie, interrupting her theatrics with reason. 'I was just there for the collections; it's freezing.'

'I'm wearing a warm coat, one you'd approve of. It's cashmere, but I look like a nursery pudding spilling out of it, it's so tight now.' Kitty looks at her body with mild affection. It is a stranger's body.

'Yum! Nursery puddings, like one of Nora's. She made the best rice pudding I've ever eaten. You will take care of yourself, won't you?'

'I will, Else. Lots of love,' Kitty says, rubbing away the last stubborn streak.

On the plane the stewardess's chatter calms her.

'Have you been on holiday?' she asks, hearing Kitty's accent, handing her an extra blanket.

'No, I live in New York. I'm going to visit my family.'

'That's nice, lucky you. Are you going to see your mum and dad before you have the baby?' she says, casting her eyes down at Kitty's stomach.

'Yes,' Kitty says, because that way it is easier.

Chapter Two

'I just need distance,' her mother said, frowning. 'Bestemama and Bestepapa don't understand the mechanics of change. I suppose it's their age, though one would expect a bit more from Elsie and Ingrid. Amazing that we're related to a bunch of such narrow-minded people.'

'You're having distance,' Kitty said. 'You're moving to New York.'

They were packing her mother's suitcase. Kitty put a silk shirt in the suitcase, and took it out again when her mother wasn't looking.

'Emotional distance,' she said. 'Until they recognise my choice as being positive.'

In which case, Kitty felt, the distance was going to last a very, very long time.

'I don't mind if YOU speak to them. They're still your grandparents,' she added. 'I'm not asking you to choose or anything.'

'Will you come back for Christmas?' Kitty said.

'Yes. I will – or you'll come to me.'

'Where will I sleep?'

'In the bedroom I'll make for you.'

'All right. Do you think Mr Fitzgerald will write to me at school?' Kitty asked, making a face at Swami-ji's photograph over her mother's shoulder as Marina wrapped him tenderly in a cashmere shawl.

'Yes. I'll ask him. He should.' She turned, and placed her hands on Kitty's cheek. 'I think it will be easier for you to have more of a relationship with him when you're a bit older. Do you know what I mean? I know that's not necessarily what's right, but it's just the way it is now, Magpie. That is the mystery of God's grace. I understand that it's desperately confusing though . . .'

'Because of his wife?' Kitty asked.

'Well, yes, sort of. I think the whole thing makes him feel guilty.'

'You mean me?' Kitty found it difficult to believe someone who had not even met her could feel guilty about her from afar.

'No, darling, not you. The whole thing is just rather complicated.'

'I hate complicated. I like everything to be simple, and straightforward.'

Her mother kissed her.

'I know you do. Which is one of the reasons you're going to Dourfield – it's a lot more simple.'

Her mother's god-daughter, Evie, was one of the reasons Dourfield had been chosen. Evie had been at Dourfield since she was seven. Before school started Kitty had only met her twice in her life. They had a strained tea the week before school, up in London, at Evie's big house in Chelsea Green. Evie was impish and wore Levi 501s, and Kitty had felt like a moron in her stripy jumper dress and her mother's fake pearl earrings, which had looked so bold and cool when she'd put them on in the morning.

They sat in Evie's room, which had a double bed with a canopy and her own television.

'What music do you like?' Evie asked Kitty, surveying her stripes and earrings in a way that was not covetous.

'Ella Fitzgerald, Billie Holiday . . .' Kitty racked her brains trying to think of something she'd seen on *Top of the Pops*, because Evie looked at her blankly.

'Who?' she said, wrinkling her little nose.

'Oh!' Kitty said. 'I know! I like Seal. I think he's really handsome.'

'He's black,' Evie said flatly, as if this ruled him out. 'With creepy scars. What about Bros?'

Kitty remembered a pair of skinny blond boys who wore leather jackets.

'Uh . . . Yeah, I like them too.'

Evie pointed to a poster on her wall.

'I'm going to marry Matt,' she said confidently. 'I'll be Mrs Goss. By the way,' she added, 'you're not going to bring clothes like that to Dourfield, are you? Because people will think you're really WEIRD.'

'My jeans are in the wash,' Kitty lied, because she didn't own a pair of jeans. She wore Elsie and Ingrid's hand-me-downs, and her mother's costume jewellery. Her love for all things shiny had earned her the family moniker of 'Magpie'.

When they left, her mother said to Evie, after giving her a beautiful necklace of dusty bottle-green beads, which Kitty instinctively knew she would cast to the back of a dark drawer, 'You will look after Kitty, won't you, Evie my darling?'

'Yes, Marina.' Evie smiled sweetly and Kitty's mother squeezed her gratefully, which annoyed Kitty.

When they were in the car she gave a sigh of relief.

'I feel a lot better,' she said. 'You'll have a friend.'

Kitty looked at her in disbelief. Which part of the equation didn't she get? Her mother had to be truly gormless if she thought that a 501-wearing, Bros-loving, pixie girl and she were going to be bosom buddies. Kitty raised an eyebrow meaningfully.

'Don't be such a worry wart,' her mother said. 'You'll be fine.'

'That's what you think. And she's a racist,' Kitty said, shooting her mother a nasty look through her glasses.

Ingrid and Elsie left for Paris the day before she left for Dourfield. Ingrid gave Kitty her most treasured possession, a soft T-shirt that said 'Never mind the bollocks'. She wrapped it up in tissue paper and left it on the top of her school trunk. It hadn't been washed, and it smelled of her Rive Gauche and clean hair. Elsie wrote her a note that said 'If you want to run away you can come and live with us,' and stuck silver star stickers on the envelope. Kitty thought of them, wearing ballet shoes, drinking *café au lait*, eating baby bites of delicate French pastries, their blonde hair swinging as they shimmied down the rue de L'Université.

On Sunday night, Elkie Brooks sang on the radio as they turned into Willow Road, the street that housed Dourfield

School. If the next song is by James Taylor, Kitty said to herself, then we'll turn around and go home. It will be a test. There was no next song though. It was a phone-in for the saddest love story; Barbara from Epping won.

They unpacked her trunk, watched the parents mill around uncomfortably drinking tea and eating digestive biscuits, making small talk with the eager house-parents.

Trying to postpone the terrible, inevitable departure, she kept stalling her mother.

'Come and look at the bathroom – there are four little baths all neat in a row!' Kitty was gay, a hostess.

'We saw it together before. I should really make a move, my darling,' her mother answered.

They had walked into the garden of the boarding house. Kitty could hear children outside the stone walls playing 'Mother May I' on the street. She thought irrationally, I will never be able to play again. The sun was going down. She tugged at her blazer. They made their way to her mother's red Beetle. A scarlet letter in a sea of Volvos.

Her mother opened the door and kissed her head.

'Mummy, please don't leave me here,' Kitty said urgently. 'You can't. Please let me come back to Hay with you.' Snot and tears were pouring down her face but Kitty didn't care.

Marina started to cry too.

'Goodbye, Kitty. You'll be all right. I promise.'

She navigated her limbs into the small car and shut the door.

Kitty longed to throw herself at the car but the other parents were watching and she wanted them to think she was brave. She watched as the car pulled out of the driveway, disappearing behind the wrought-iron gate.

Lying in a room full of strangers, shivering in her foreign sheets, in her checked pyjamas with their scratchy nametag, she was too ashamed to cry. She wondered if Bestemama and Bestepapa were thinking of her. They would be finishing supper now, in the all-pervading silence that had descended since her mother's departure. Marina's studio was stripped to an old bleached shell. There was nothing left of her at Hay but the views she once loved.

The lights were turned out, a blissful nod to succumb privately to the tears that had been pricking at her eyes, for hours. She held her breath so she wouldn't make a noise that was audible, and buried her face in her pillow. She wanted to run away, but she realised she was in the middle of nowhere, the nearest train station twenty-five miles away. Her hand scrunched up in the sheets by her side. She felt something brush against it that could have been a ghost, or a moth. Kitty thought the dormitory was haunted and more tears came.

Seconds later she was clasped by a hot little hand, and Evie's voice whispered, 'Don't cry, Kitty, the first night is always horrible, but you'll get used to it. I did.' And she held Kitty's hand tightly in the dark, so tightly she could feel Evie's pulse beating steadily against her own, calming like the hands of a clock.

In the morning Kitty smiled at her shyly.

'Why are you looking at me like that? Are you spastic or something?'

The dorm was frigid with cold; Evie was putting on her tights and vest under the sheets.

'Just because your mother's my godmother, does not mean we have to be friends.' She said it loudly, so the other girls heard.

Kitty quickly recognised what Evie was offering her. She would be an ally only in the dark.

On the day she was twelve, there was no breakfast in bed. Kitty woke in her narrow bed as the electric overhead light flickered on to illuminate the other nine narrow beds in the room.

'Up you get.' The strident voice of the housemistress Mrs Phelan rang out.

There was a thin chorus of dissonance.

Kitty didn't tell anyone it was her birthday. She got up and went over to the sink in the corner of the big hospital white room to see whether her face looked any older. It didn't, but there were the scarlet beginnings of a spot between her eyebrows. 'A bindi spot', her mother would have called it. She realised grimly that this and the two straggling hairs under her left armpit was the puberty she longed for, the thought of which, along with her mother, made her eyes well. She wanted to ring and tell her mother, but they weren't allowed to speak on the phone for the first two weeks so the boarders could 'adjust'.

Kitty brushed her teeth and washed her face with the facewash her mother had bought from Boots the Chemist's. She then stroked cucumber water on the way Marina had shown her, which made the other girls laugh. They said she was like an old lady. 'Be sure to do your neck and décolleté,' her mother had said the night before she left, as they were packing her trunk. 'Then you'll always have beautiful skin.'

'Like yours?' Kitty said.

'I have never in my life gone to sleep without washing my face,' her mother said. 'Not even if I was raddled with exhaustion.'

In the dining hall, Kitty stood in line with Rosaria and Olivia. Kitty knew from the moment she saw her that she would love Rosaria, who was tiny and ferocious with the biggest cackling laugh she'd ever heard. It was like the rattle of a machine gun. She could swear fluently in Italian, and her eyes were green like the orchard at Hay. Olivia was quieter and more reserved but she had a dark wryness to her which Kitty trusted, because it reminded her of Bestemama. Olivia was tall like her, with size seven feet. Rosaria was a size three. They were all in the same form. Rosaria and Kitty had been placed in the bottom stream for maths, and the top for English. Olivia was in the top stream for everything. They were in different dorms.

The eggs swam in a silver tray of grease, and the sausages lay anaemic next to forlorn hash browns. Vegetarianism was now a viable prospect, she thought.

She sat down at one of the long wooden tables with Rosaria and Olivia. The day was grey like the Lifebuoy soap in the girls' bathroom.

'Ugh.' Rosaria looked at her fried eggs sadly. 'Do you think they're trying to fatten us up and give us spots so no one will ever fancy us and we will remain pure and unsullied till the sixth form?'

A shudder went through Kitty. I can't stay here till the sixth form. Be calm, she told herself. It's like Nora says, 'This too shall pass.' Nora would have been taking Sam and Violet to nursery right now, warm in the smoky fug of her Golf, listening to Radio 4 as Sam and Violet chattered in the back. But now Nora was in New York, taking Sam and Violet to kindergarten in a yellow taxi. Nora was probably living in a constant state of fear due to muggers and 'the immigration'. Could she buy Angel Delight in Manhattan? Kitty doubted it. I could get her some with my pocket money, she thought, and send it to her when I have my first exeat: from 12 p.m. Saturday to 6 p.m. Sunday. That was six weeks away. The trees at Hay would be practically naked by then.

She had imagined boarding school as *Mallory Towers* and *The Twins at Saint Clare's* peppered with a bit of *Grease*. She'd thought she could start her own gang and they'd wear pink satin jackets at weekends. Kitty hoped she'd have a boy from the wrong side of the tracks, and second-skin leggings. She made the fatal mistake of confiding this to Evie and her group by the pond after lacrosse.

She sat with Veronica, Evie's best friend, Imogen Holliday, the prettiest girl in the school, and Rosaria and Olivia. She was good at telling the spookiest ghost stories, and she told three in succession that made them squeal. Kitty miscalculated. She took their post-story pleasure to mean that the forum was now hers for the taking.

'I've got an idea,' she said quickly, high with a sense of belonging.

'Yeah?' Evie yawned.

'You know in *Grease* – the film *Grease* – how they have a gang of girls?'

'Yeah.' Evie looked over at Veronica.

'Well, I thought we could, you know, do it here. We could make pink jackets and stuff.'

Rosaria shook her head and gave Kitty a look of sympathy, which made her heart sink.

'YOU want to start a gang?' Evie gave a yowl of laughter. 'Like in *Grease*? Uh, how old are you?'

'Twelve,' she said, ploughing on. 'You could be the leader.'

'If we were to have a gang, you mong, WHICH we never would, but IF we were, A, you wouldn't be in it. And B, Imo would be the leader because she's the prettiest.'

Imogen opened her big eyes.

'I don't want to be in a gang.' She sounded worried.

Evie sighed with exasperation.

'There is NO gang, Imogen,' she said.

Evie and Veronica proceeded to spend the next forty minutes pointing at Kitty, and howling 'Pink ladies!' or taking her glasses, and throwing them in the pond where they floated on a light layer of scum. She discovered a sad social truth that day. Court jesters jest, they don't come up with the ideas.

When all the other girls were unpacking with their mothers, her mother had tried to put a picture of Swami-ji on her bedside locker.

'Please don't do that,' Kitty yelped.

'No one's going to notice,' her mother said. 'He can watch over you, protect you.'

'Honestly, it's fine.' Kitty saw Evie look over slyly. 'I'll put him on my pinboard later. Then he can watch over everyone.' She smiled.

'That's a lovely idea,' her mother said.

Everyone thought she was odd: she felt it.

Kitty stared out of the window in the biology lab, wondering if she had the guts to run away. She thought it would make them worried then angry at home, remembering then that home was fragmented.

A Madonna song played in her head: 'If I ran away, I'd never have the strength to go very far.'

Madonna knew what it was like. She understood. Perhaps she could adopt me and I could be her back-up dancer, Kitty thought. Her brain filled with scenes of transatlantic glamour.

'Are you eating, Kitty?' Mr Ridgeley the biology master sounded concerned.

The class was silent. She thought about it. No, for once she was not consumed by the thought of food. Kitty gave what she thought was a pathos-filled face, the face of a hungry urchin.

'No. I haven't been very hungry.' Her voice wobbled in the warmth of his concern.

'I meant, are you chewing gum? The chewing of gum is not permitted in my lab. Your nutritional habits are not my concern. They are the territory of matron. Now, spit it out, please.'

Kitty gave him an injured look and spat out her Bubblicious in the bin. If Madonna had heard I wasn't eating, she thought, SHE would have cooked me a Philly cheese steak, and after eating and giggling, we would have broken out into an impromptu rendition of 'Holiday', followed by shopping for ra-ra skirts on Broadway.

Bestemama and Bestepapa came to take her out on Saturday after games. She sat by the gates keeping watch for the old regal BMW.

Ibsen howled with excitement when he saw her, his jowls swaying from left to right, his tongue lolling like a madman's. Kitty dived into the car on top of him.

'Have you spoken to Mummy?' It fell out of her mouth automatically.

Bestepapa made a bitter peppery noise.

'No, darling, we haven't. Do you remember that we decided it was probably better to let her get settled in New York, and speak to her when everything is a bit clearer?' Smiling at her, Bestemama's face became a mask of reassurance. Kitty preferred Bestepapa's grimace.

They went to a little hotel in the town, and she ordered a Coke. It tasted forbidden and ambrosial.

'Is the food at your prison FILTHY?' Bestepapa smeared a scone with jam, and passed it to her.

'Filthy. You'd hate it. Greasy fried eggs, baked beans, lumpy cardboard porridge and gammon and pineapple.'

'Dis-gusting. Can you smuggle in contraband?'

'I baked you a belated birthday cake, polenta and lemon.' Bestemama handed Kitty a tin with roses on it.

After tea, up on the top of the hill above the town, they surveyed the sea of green, fields filled with water from the recent rains. Ibsen pulled on his lead looking longingly at the sheep. Kitty pretended they were just visiting, and for a moment she appreciated everything around her, the damp air, the cathedral that rose below, mothers and fathers walking with their families.

'It is beautiful here,' Bestemama said.

'It is, but not beautiful like Hay,' Kitty replied grudgingly.

'We could kidnap her, or pretend she has appendicitis,' Bestepapa said as they pulled into the driveway of Dourfield.

'Enough, you silly man. We'll see her very soon.' Bestemama held Kitty tightly as she kissed her goodbye, filling her nose with rosewater and Pond's cold cream.

'Don't let the buggers get you down!' Bestepapa shouted as they drove off into the fog that had descended.

'Uh yuck, why can't your family give you chocolate cake for your birthday like everyone else?' Evie gave Bestemama's cake a sneer, the Goss boys pouting from her T-shirt.

'Lemon cake is delicious, try it.' Kitty proffered a slice.

Evie took a bite and spat it out on the floor.

'Rank,' she said. 'On MY birthday my mother orders a cake from Fortnum & Mason, a chocolate one, which everyone likes. Oh well, not everyone can have a mother as perfect as mine, and I suppose yours is pretty, which makes up for a lot. Funny, you don't look anything like her, do you? Your sister does. Maybe you're adopted.'

Nora had instructed her sister Molly in Dublin to send Kitty *Bunty*. At Hay, Nora bought it for her every Monday from Cutler's the newsagent's. Now she was gone, Molly sent a tightly rolled copy of *Bunty* to Dourfield religiously once a week. Kitty had never before valued her privacy, or questioned the things she read or watched because she just did them. They were a given. Now reading *Bunty* was symbolic of not quite rightness. Cool girls did not read *Bunty*. They read *Just 17, Mizz* or *Smash Hits*. Kitty was resentful of Molly for sending it to her, then filled with self-loathing for being so ungrateful for the precision of her neat brown packages, whose each arrival spelled social doom.

At the end of each day they had to put their knickers in a big open basket that sat, till morning, in the corner of the room. Kitty sincerely hoped that she did not start her period at school, where everyone would know before she could even tell her mother. She knew she wasn't being paranoid either; she had already heard the Chinese whispers. 'Laura Hall's started, she's had it since she was nine and she's got double D boobs.' Laura Hall's knickers lay, a scarlet announcement in the basket amongst their childish whites.

Even going to the loo was a potential minefield. She could not linger for hours with a book like she did at home. She had to run in furtively whilst the others were doing prep, because Evie was legend for standing on the cistern in the adjacent stall, peering over the wall and taking photographs of people unawares, which she then passed round the school. Kitty had seen a few of these gory documentations. Small heads bowed in concentration, innocently minding their own business. She sat there rigid with fear, listening intently to every suspicious footfall outside. Her eyes round and raised to the horrible open roof of the stall, in case of an ambush. This was a recipe for terrible constipation and frayed nerves.

* * *

She woke struggling, her feet and arms greeted by the cold air of the dormitory, and as the covers were rudely pulled off her she could feel sharp little fingers, the swishing of hair, and muted giggles all around.

'One, two, three, bog flush!' She heard Veronica, her voice high, quivering with pack excitement.

'You've got to be joking. Get off me.' Kitty aimed a kick, and made contact with a soft stomach.

'She's going to be a difficult one, Evie. Come on, pull.'

'Stop it,' Imogen murmured across the room from the safety of her bed, voice muffled by sleep.

Kitty was outraged. Bog flushing was what they did to pasty first formers, too thin and weak to protest. Like a lynch mob in the night, they came, Evie and Veronica, with their omnipresent third wheel Susanna, carting the victim from the privacy of sleep, across the hall, into the bathroom, until turned upside down like a corkscrew, the girl was plunged unceremoniously into the lavatory bowl, as it was flushed over her head. They called it 'christening'.

She was not going to be bog flushed.

'What the hell are you doing?' she asked as they carried her across the darkened room.

'You think you're so perfect. You're so prissy, with your little books you read before you go to sleep, and your posh voice. We're going to show you that you're not so perfect after all.' Veronica's doughy hand clung to her ankle.

'I don't think I'm perfect, you stupid bitch. My voice is the same as your voice. I don't even want to be here.'

'Exactly,' Veronica said.

She let them carry her like a plank of wood into the bathroom. She struggled a little bit to lull them into complacency. Then, as they made an awkward procession into the stall, Kitty began to fight. She scratched Veronica in the eye, and kicked her legs out like an Olympic swimmer. Susanna had her in a headlock, and Kitty bit her freckled arm as hard as she could.

'You animal!' Susanna said, dropping her against the porcelain.

Kitty did the things she was taught not to do as a toddler. She bit, she scratched, she kicked, she spat. She wanted to kill all three of them.

'This isn't fun any more,' Evie said. She stood back panting. 'You're being a psycho. Stop it.' Kitty stood up and she laughed.

'If you ever try to do that to me again, I'll curse you. That Indian man on my pinboard is a dark master. He can curse you by just thinking your names. I'll make sure he has them. We can start now . . .' She took a deep breath and whispered dramatically, 'I call on you, Master Swami, I call on your forces of darkness, your servants of the night . . .' She began to incant the words of her mother's chanting tapes, and rolled her eyes far back into her head as though she were in a trance.

'Bhutayan, Narayan . . . Jhoti Krishna Govinda, Hare Hare . . .'

All three of them stood stock still. The powers of serendipity were on her side, as the wind chose to shriek at that moment, high, like a widow's keen. They all jumped. Veronica pissed on the floor.

Kitty stopped chanting and gave them a thorough searching look.

'Goodnight. Sweet dreams.'

She swished out, pretending that she was wearing not a teddy bear nightdress, but robes of velvet, midnight blue.

She waited by the call box, willing the phone to ring. Her appointed phone time was seven-forty, and she was allowed to be on the phone for eight minutes. They set an egg timer.

'Is that my Magpie?' Her mother's voice was giggly, far away. 'I'm calling you from a car phone in a limousine; imagine that! So as you're standing in Wheaton, I'm zipping around Fifth Avenue. Isn't that funny?'

'Ish.' Kitty scowled at her reflection in the window.

'Darling, let's not waste our precious phone call being grumpy. Tell me about school. Are you having the best time? NO, take a right here please, that's it, 740.'

'Where are you going?'

'To meet a gallery owner for lunch. Can you believe I've already sold four paintings, and I've been offered a show too – I've never worked more in my life. You might even have a rich mummy soon. It's so inspiring and alive here. Until the new house is ready we're staying in a hotel. The Mark, it's called. Violet thinks she's Eloise, and she and Sam have pancakes and maple syrup for breakfast every day. What do you have?'

'Alpen,' Kitty said grudgingly.

'That's nice. I've made lots of friends; people keep throwing parties for me, it's very jolly. What parallel lives we're leading, you and I, both new girls at school.'

She couldn't remember anything she wanted to tell her mother, and though she had written a careful list of all those things, highlighted in order of importance, it was left on her locker in the dorm, and she knew if she ran to get it, three minutes would be gone. Kitty heard New York in the background, the sirens and traffic, a taunting steady whine.

'I can't think of anything to say,' she said.

'That's all right, I'll talk for both of us, and when you remember, you can write me a letter.'

'It's not the same.'

'I know, but what can we do? You could send me a psychic message, I'll get that. Have you seen Bestepapa and Bestemama?'

'Yes, they took me out for tea.'

'Well, would you mind not telling them anything about me, darling? I don't need them poking their noses into my life any more. Did they ask about me?'

'No,' Kitty said.

That night she made her mind white and blank until it was a page and her one thought the pen. 'Call me back, Mummy,' it wrote over and over again. If you call on Mrs Phelan's line you can say it was an emergency and I'll be allowed to take the call. She waited for Mrs Phelan's now familiar footfall, the soft catch of the door.

'Kitty,' she'd say, 'your mother's on the phone from New York, she HAS to speak to you, it's urgent.' She would get out of bed, and she could tell her mother everything that she'd forgotten, and they would laugh.

The page of thought became black with words, and Kitty struggled to keep her eyes open, but sleep came, the message returned to sender.

* * *

'Dear Mummy,' she wrote, 'I have three hairs under my left armpit and two under my right. I am on the reserves for netball. I have been meditating for half an hour every day. Mrs Phelan says I need more practical mufti clothes, in darker colours. Olivia has started her period. How are Violet and Sam? Please kiss Nora's ears for me. Could you send me some more writing paper, as I have run out. I am seventy-five per cent homesick, which is an improvement, down from ninety-eight.

'I love you with great alacrity; you are the best mother in the world.'

Mrs Phelan flicked her eyes over the letter dismissively. This was part of the Saturday night ritual at Dourfield. Letter home, shoes polished, then the tuck shop. Which wasn't a shop, just a shelf of sweets in Matron's office.

'Very good. Shoes?' Kitty showed her the loafers she had polished.

'Perfect. One pound for you, the tuck shop's open.'

Her mother didn't send letters by post. Kitty got letters from Federal Express in big white and purple envelopes. Marina's writing was very big, and four sentences took up one page. 'Please don't be homesick, there is no point. Be "home well". There is nothing to miss here, life is very boring, and everything keeps breaking; the central heating, the telephone, and my heart. That is a joke! I had a boyfriend who lives in California, and I went to stay. You would like it there. It is hot, and we had picnics on the beach. He is not my boyfriend any more because he still loves his old wife, who is not old, but ex. Isn't it good we have God, so we don't need men? Imagine what life would be like if we didn't have GOD? I love you, Mummy.'

Kitty wondered who 'we' was.

Nora was shy and formal on the phone, but she always was, so it was comforting.

'Hello, Kitty,' she said. 'How are you?'

'I'm fine, how are you?'

'I'm very well, thank you. How's school?'

'Good. How are Violet and Sam?'

'They're well, thank you. Naughty. I had to put hot sauce on Violet's tongue as she bit Sam. I don't think she'll be biting in a hurry.'

'My minutes are up.'

'It's worse than a prison. Well, I love you.'

'I love you too. Quickly, do they have Angel Delight in New York?'

'Actually, they do,' Nora said, a smile in her voice.

The train to London took four hours, the coach to the train station thirty-five minutes. By the time she reached Hay, it was dark and she couldn't make out anything familiar in the black.

Bestepapa stood at the train station, smoking his pipe. He wore a grey raincoat and green wellingtons.

'There's my girl,' he said. 'I thought we'd walk so you could get a feel for home. You don't get that in the car. Sweet?'

He handed Kitty a lemon barley, and took her small case from her, the one with her initials on it.

The smell was the thing that made it all feel real, a smoky woodsy smell, and Bestepapa next to her, with his smell of tobacco and India lime. They trudged up the lane, treacherous with frost, the only light a flickering ember from the bowl of Bestepapa's pipe. They spoke in hushed voices, as though they might disturb sleeping giants in the woods.

'It smells of home now,' Kitty said.

'What are you reading?'

'*The Great Gatsby*. I imagine that Daisy looks like Mummy.'

'Ha! No red dot though.' He laughed.

'Bestepapa, why do you think there has to be change?'

'I used to think there had to be but now I'm not sure. I think change is unnecessary. The old ways are the best ways.'

'Well, I liked it before, just so you know. I like the old ways too,' Kitty said.

'I think, my Kitty, that you and I were born in the wrong time then.'

The table was covered in candles, and it looked long without everyone at it. Bestepapa sat at the head, carving the lamb.

'Thought we'd go to the farm in the morning, get some eggs. Would you like that?'

'She probably wants to go to town, and buy records from Our Price.' Bestemama handed Kitty the spinach.

'No, I don't need to go to town,' she said.

'After supper,' Bestepapa said in a jovial voice that didn't sound like his real one, 'we'll have to take Ibsen up to the woods for his walk. He didn't have a long enough one today, so he's itching to go.'

Ibsen lay prostrate on the floor, sleeping.

Kitty wanted to stay awake, savouring every minute of being at Hay, lying in Ingrid's bed, surrounded by Ingrid's things, a poster of Adam Ant grinning down at her. This is what it feels like to go to sleep being Ingrid, she thought. An old copy of *Madame Bovary* was on her bedside table. Kitty rubbed the cocoa butter from the Body Shop on her elbows and knees like Ingrid did, and fell asleep.

It was raining, and the sky was moody. Kitty revelled in waking up on her own, of her own volition. She went downstairs in her nightdress. Bestemama was making lunch. She kissed her.

'You must have been tired, darling,' she said. 'I've never known you sleep so late. I thought you must need it, so I decided not to bother you.'

'What time is it?' Kitty felt a trickle of panic.

'It's twelve. We'll have lunch in half an hour, quick walk, and Bestepapa says he'll drive you back, so you don't have to do that miserable train journey again.'

'I've missed the morning!' Kitty said. 'Why didn't you wake me up? I've missed the morning, and the same one will never happen again.'

'That's all right; there'll be many mornings for you. Your body wanted to sleep.'

'It wanted the morning! It wanted to do normal things. Now I don't have time, now I'll be rushed. I've ruined the whole weekend! Now it's not the same. I had a list of everything I wanted to do, and now I can't do any of it!' Kitty started to cry.

'Darling, we'll do everything on your list in double the time, that's all. Please don't cry. Everything here will still be here the next time you come. Take a deep breath. Would you like a nice cup of tea?

*   *   *

She was in a cave, and it was empty. The whole world had ended and she was the only person left. She could hear the voices of Sam and Violet calling her urgently, but she could not find them. There was another voice too, one she did not recognise, smooth and male.

'Kitty! Kitty! Where are you? We can't find you. We're with someone who wants to meet you!'

They were ducking and weaving in the silence, like ghost children.

The male voice called through the rocks, 'Kitty, I can only stay for a bit. I have to go, I have an appointment. I want to see your face before I go.'

'I'm here!' she called back. 'Mr Fitzgerald, I'm here! Please don't go!'

She ran among the rocks pounding at them with her fists and arms, but they were immobile. The male voice left, and Sam and Violet's voices died with his, whispers that turned into thick black nothingness.

When she woke up, her arms looked like she had torn through a bramble patch.

'Vampire get you in the night?' said Evie, and she laughed.

'No, it was my master communicating with me.' Kitty glowered at her darkly.

'You are such a spas, Kitty,' Evie said.

On the phone her mother said she thought it would be fun to fly to California for the Christmas holidays.

'The sun always shines there,' she said. 'Can you imagine a place where it never rains?'

Palm trees swayed, and neon Father Christmases skied

with snowmen on lush green lawns, untouched by frost. It was warm enough to swim, even though her mother didn't.

On Christmas Day, Kitty played mermaids in the pool with Sam and Violet, in a new Adrienne Vittadini swimsuit she had bought from the gift shop in the lobby of the Beverly Hills Hotel. It was white, and in it her bosoms pointed high and men looked at her, which Kitty sort of liked.

Her mother said that Christmas in California was out of the ordinary, and that's why she chose it. They watched movies on the movie channel, and ate enormous strawberries and grapes that were so cold they made Kitty's mouth ache.

It was the opposite of Christmas at Hay. Kitty ate shrimps for lunch with lots of happy strangers.

'I like it traditional,' Nora said. 'What is Christmas without a turkey?'

Marina told Nora she was a creature of habit. They opened their stockings in her room which was pale pink with a huge marble fireplace that roared so they could make believe it was cold outside.

Her mother seemed to have friends wherever she went: tanned women with gold jewellery and houses that had belonged to Rudolph Valentino or Gloria Swanson. Kitty stole up to their bathrooms and tried on dusky scents with names like Giorgio and Poison.

Nora took them to Disneyland, and Kitty wanted to go on the Peter Pan ride again and again. She convinced Sam that it was his favourite ride, so they could keep going back. Flying up, out of the Darlings' window over London, swooping down on the island of Never Never Land, which was sunny with a soundtrack.

California orange juice was the best orange juice she'd ever tasted. Kitty thought maybe America was a decent place after all. At night the dry Santa Ana wind blew hotly over her as she slept, carrying away with it any thought of what they were doing at Hay on the first Christmas they were not a complete family.

Dear Kitty,
Your mother tells me that you are progressing well with your studies and that is good. I have just returned from Paris, which was unseasonably warm. If you need supplies ETC, please do not hesitate to call my secretary, Anna. She will assist you.

You seem to be proficient at sport; keep up with the netball. Sports are good for keeping the mind straight.
With all my best,
R. Fitzgerald.

'"Proficient at sport", that's a good one,' Rosaria said.

Mr Fitzgerald wrote her short informative letters every week, in neat, measured writing. Anna, the secretary, wrote cheery postscripts on his letters that made Kitty laugh. She noticed he never mentioned meeting her. When she wrote back she tried to impress him with her words, to create a technicolour version of herself that leapt off the page to meet him, but her letters felt pallid and bland like school rice pudding, and after writing them she felt like an imposter.

Kitty owned one photograph of Mr Fitzgerald in which he looked happy, rich and slightly baffled, with a beard. The beard was distracting because she couldn't find her face underneath it. She studied the picture obsessively looking for a clue. There was the merest suggestion of a dimple on his left cheek, and that was it as far as she could see. Rosaria told her she had his smile, but as it was obscured by the beard in the photograph, Kitty told her to shut up if she didn't have anything constructive to say.

Mr Fitzgerald lived with Mrs Fitzgerald in a huge white house in Eaton Square. Kitty knew this because she copied its address down from his letters, and one Saturday half-term afternoon on their way to Miss Selfridge she and Rosaria peered through its windows.

'Looks cold and miserable,' Rosaria said.

'Poor him. Shall we send him an anonymous dressing gown? Or break in, like in *The Little Princess* . . . His life should be less bare than this. Do you think she's foul to him?' Kitty sought out signs of a colourful internal life, a record, a bunch of flowers, an ashtray, but she saw nothing that revealed him, just the plush antiseptic of a show home.

'Pussy-whipped, most likely. Let's go.' Rosaria spun round on her small heel.

Her mother was fearful of the cold. She loved squashy overstuffed sofas and paintings, and the rooms to be filled to bursting with flowers, molten with fires roaring. She said she liked comfort. She understood better than anyone that school was cold, and she sent Kitty beautiful thermal pyjamas from New York, and a cashmere-covered hot water bottle with her initials on it.

Mr Fitzgerald never minded that men were after her mother, she said it herself. The part she didn't say out loud was that it was because he understood that she was beautiful and impetuous and men would always love her. Kitty didn't mind either because it meant she got bountiful presents from people she'd never met, who were just trying to get into her mother's good graces. One Christmas, she got £500-worth of vouchers from HMV. Inexplicably, the one after, lingerie from Janet Reger, which her mother deemed inappropriate and hid until Kitty was 'old enough'.

June proved triumphant, the Federal Express man was kind. Kitty received the ultimate benediction: a letter, Smythson writing paper covered in her mother's childish curly hand. With that same familiar hand her mother released her from purdah. Marina explained that Swami-ji had appeared to her in a vision and informed her that all of her children should be in the same country, and she had written him a letter to check it wasn't a spiritual crossed wire, and he had written back confirming that yes, it was a good thing, he had meditated upon it. Kitty should come to New York.

Swami-ji was temporarily Kitty's hero, and during prep she ran up to the empty dormitory and cradled his photograph, whispering, 'Thank you, thank you.' She took to sleeping with it under her pillow, like a charm.

Maybe her letters had made her mother miss her. Maybe her mother had noticed how brightly Kitty's shoes and hair shone when she saw her at half term. Evie had laughed when, on the rare Friday nights her mother was in England, Kitty wore face masks and rag curlers to bed like a spinster aunt with no one to take her out on a Saturday.

'Are you getting ready for your boyfriend?' she hooted as Kitty lay carefully on her pillow, head upright.

'No, my mother,' she wanted to say. But who could understand why she wanted to have curly hair and flawless skin for her own mother? Why she cared what knickers she wore to go home in and how she begged Imogen Holliday to lend her a pale-pink bra made by Sloggi? She knew it was strange, but she thought maybe a bit of Imogen Holliday would rub off on her, permeate through her white skin, all the way down to her bones, until they were shiny and new like a Christmas ten-pound note.

She smiled at everyone. Nothing could touch her. At suppertime when Veronica poured salt in her tea she didn't care.

'Why are you looking so pleased, you little whore? Did you get ten per cent in your maths instead of five?'

'I'm moving to New York. I'm going to live with my mother,' she answered dreamily.

'No you are not. You're a liar.' Veronica's face became an angry ham, red and pulsing with arterial veins.

'She is, actually,' said Rosaria, pouring sugar on her white bread and butter.

Veronica paused.

'I don't believe you. Everyone knows your mother doesn't want you. Why should she suddenly want you now? If she wanted you why did she take your brother and sister to New York and not you? I heard Ma'am Rachel say two illegits are enough to travel round the world with like suitcases. She says you'll be here for the duration, because you're difficult and your mother can't cope with you.'

Ma'am Rachel was their matron. She was a real bitch.

'My mother didn't want to disrupt my education,' Kitty said, parroting what she knew. 'And Sam and Violet are not illegitimate.'

'Perfectly sensible,' said Rosaria in a grown-up way. 'If I was your mother, Veronica, I would have sent YOU away at birth. To live with a Hottentot tribe. Perhaps they would have liked you. But probably not. They certainly would have wanted to eat you, you're so juicy and fat.' She took a measured bite of her bread and sugared butter.

Veronica was rendered speechless, and purple-faced she lurched off to torture the African toads in the science block.

'Oh Kitty,' Rosaria said, 'I can come and stay in the Christmas holidays and we can ice skate in Central Park where we'll bump into Johnny Depp and Luke Perry and they can take us to see *The Nutcracker*, after which we'll go to Studio 54 and dance all night.'

Kitty had a feeling Studio 54 was closed but she said nothing. She would love Rosaria for ever. Her haughtiness always made people stand down, even the foulest teachers. When Kitty had babies Rosaria would be their godmother, she decided, and Kitty's children could wear her shoes when they played dressing up.

The night before term ended, they played truth-or-dare. Kitty always chose truth, because she didn't have anything to lie about yet.

'What turns you on?' Laura Hill asked.

'Oh you know, the usual things,' Kitty said in the dark.

'No, we don't know; it's specific to you, which is the whole point of the game. Don't be a bad sport.'

'Fine, well, OK, the usual things like that bit in *Lady Chatterley*, uh girls on page three who wear stockings and suspender belts, Seal and Adamski, that feeling when you go over a bridge, and um . . . trains.'

The silence felt infinitely longer in the dark.

'Very strange, Kitty,' Imogen said. 'Very strange indeed.'

Kitty flushed.

'Well, what turns you on?'

'It's not my go, but, boys with blue eyes and dark hair, and Chris the Australian tennis instructor when he fingered me behind the music room.'

'Gross, Imo,' Olivia said.

She and Rosaria perched awkwardly on Kitty's bed.

'Do you think you'll meet Mr Fitzgerald when you move to New York?' Olivia whispered.

'Unlikely. Besides, it would spoil his mystery.'

Rosaria and she held hands and cried as if the world would soon end.

'Promise you'll write every week.'

'I will write to you every week,' Kitty said.

Bestemama and Bestepapa had gone to a wedding in Sweden, and the local taxi driver drove her to the airport, after promising Mrs Phelan he would see her to the door. The year's worth of belongings in her trunk felt insubstantial, as she pushed it to the check-in desk.

Kitty felt nothing as the plane took off. Swami-ji had deemed it so and that was proof. The living, breathing, spiritual proof that she had to come home. Perhaps he knew, in his infinite wisdom, that she would be a devoted devotee now, no longer mocking his chanting, or thinking sexy thoughts while she meditated. If it meant she got to stay at home, Kitty decided she might even shave her head, like his friends in the photographs.

She saw England beneath her, in miniature like a toy town.

Her mother would make up with Bestemama and Bestepapa, they would all have breakfast at Tiffany's. Rosaria could come for the holidays. She would love it. Kitty knew it would all be fine, though she wished she had had her split ends trimmed in the advent of seeing her mother. New York was magic, her mother had made this clear. New York, home of the English muffin, the Beastie Boys, Central Park muggers and Victoria's Secret, and now Kitty. She turned on her Walkman and smiled.

As they make their descent she sees green fields unfolding before her, the Thames curling its way through London, Windsor Castle peering up from the mist. She has always imagined, from this vantage point, the London of Shakespeare, with boats carrying people to where they are going, pickpockets and courtesans, streets screaming with mud and human traffic, the Rose Theatre filled to the eaves with a jostling rowdy throng. Until they get closer to the cars and motorways, superstores and redbrick houses spreading out as far as she can see, an industrious ant village beneath her, stamping on her fantasy.

Violet is pacing under the arrivals board. She is wearing a scarlet coat, and her thick black hair is pulled back in a ponytail. Kitty marvels at how beautiful Violet is, and how unalike they are. Violet looks as though she has skipped off the pages of *The Arabian Nights*, and Kitty feels, watching her, blonde, pale, pedestrian and very pregnant.

'Violet!' she calls quietly.

'Oh my God, Kitty! Here you are! And you're really truly pregnant!'

'I really am,' she says, and they hold one another.

* * *

Violet's car is a mess. Kitty squeezes herself in amidst Coke cans and magazines. Violet lights a cigarette, then she looks stricken.

'Oh Christ, I forgot,' she says, going to stub it out.

'No please, breathe it all over me, it's been so long, and I could really use a vicarious fag.' Kitty breathes in the air deeply, and fans the smoke towards her. 'See? I'm already treading the path of bad motherhood,' she says.

'You're going to be brilliant. You were born to be a mummy,' Violet answers, placing a placatory hand on her sister's belly.

Chapter Three

The limestone house was as anonymous as a hotel. Kitty expected men in tails to appear from behind every corner with a handful of Martinis or Earl Grey at teatime. It was just her mother and she though, swimming through the slippery heat of New York in July. Violet and Sam had gone home with Nora to County Kerry, where they were, no doubt, eating soda bread piled thick with Nora's mammy's gooseberry jam. Kitty discovered that in New York you could order food from a million different countries, and it would show up on the doorstep within fifteen minutes.

'Mum, what's eggplant parmigiana?'

Her mother lay on the sofa in a lavender slip, slick with heat.

'Uh. Don't speak to me of food. It's so hot the thought of it makes me feel sick. Eggplant parmigiana is something that will make you fat. It's deep-fried aubergines covered in cheese.'

Kitty thought it sounded delicious.

Her mother turned her head and looked at Kitty.

'I meant to tell you before, Kit-kat. You've grown a little chubby this past term. It would be good to lose it before school starts in September.' Her eyes wound around Kitty's body.

'I don't think I have,' Kitty said, her voice echoing in the furnitureless room. 'I didn't mean to. I think it's this dress.'

'No, it's not the dress, it's definitely you, Magpie. Don't worry, we can lose weight together. I need to lose seven pounds.' Marina poked at her washboard stomach critically.

In England they didn't have staff. They had Nora, who was family, and Mrs M from the village, who 'did' the cottage once a week after she'd 'done' Hay House. In New York Vladimir, the silent Russian trainer, came every morning to define her mother, as MTV blared in the background. Kitty put on a tracksuit and watched as he stretched and moved her mother like putty.

'You won't join?' he said, casting his melancholy black eyes at her.

'No, I'm going for a run actually,' Kitty said.

She hated running. She walked up and down Lexington Avenue, and bought Tasti D-Lite, the fat-free frozen yoghurt that was everywhere in Manhattan, and sat on a step savouring each creamy mouthful.

Fat was to be avoided. Anything fat-free was acceptable. She read it in *Mirabella*. She counted calories voraciously. Her mother, at Vladimir's insistence, had bought a treadmill, and it had a built-in calorie counter. As you ran, it told you how many calories you burned. Kitty loved to watch the numbers go up, so definite and sure. One hundred, that was the bagel she had for breakfast; fifty, the apple she had for lunch. When you finished, it gave the final calculation, with a red CONGRATULATIONS! that ran across the screen like a banner.

In the morning, Precious would come to clean the house, and bring her mother fruit on a tray. Precious was from Jamaica and she thought her mother was really funny.

Kitty asked her questions, just so she could hear her speak, her words spilling over each other like a poem on speed.

'Why are you called Precious?'

'Because mi mammy tink it a beautiful name.'

'Where did she get it?'

'Oh you got chat, Kitty! From a perfume bottle, dat's where. Now move you skinny bum girl, you in my way.'

'Have I really got a skinny bum?'

'Too skinny. No Jamaican man ever want you with a bum like that. Someone tell you you fat?'

'My mum.'

'Your mum CRAZY. You not fat.'

By the end of the summer she weighed one hundred and five pounds. Twenty-five pounds less than her mother, and she was only two inches taller. She was also fourteen pounds less than Jackie Kennedy when she lived in the White House, and Jackie, Kitty noted with satisfaction, was renowned for being a sylph.

Her summer job was to reorganise her mother's Filofax. This was an arduous task, because her mother knew so many people. Kitty had to ring them all to check that their phone numbers and addresses were current. This inevitably led to chat she did not welcome.

'Kitty! How is Marina? Are you having the most glamorous time in New York? Is Marina still seeing the funny Indian man with the turban? You must come and stay, darling, you're always welcome. Send Mummy our love.'

She simpered, 'Yes thank you, well, thank you, yes, it's great, really great.' Like a good child would, she thought, displeased with herself. She started to pretend to be a French secretary to eradicate the possibility of these timely exchanges.

'*Bonjour*, I mean, 'ullo, I am Francine the secretary of Marina, would you please verify your address, *s'il vous plaît*?'

As Francine she did not have to have the long annoying chats. As Francine, Kitty idled with honeyed voice, and spent her afternoons, and pocket money, on Third Avenue buying stripy tights from Hue.

On the top floor of the limestone mansion lived their landlord, Mr Frazi. Her mother told her that Mr Frazi was gay but she was not to allude to it. Mr Frazi's apartment was smooth and polished and it smelled like birch trees and vetiver. He had a butler named Philip who spoke no English, and they conversed through a tunnel of nods and smiles and sighs.

Mr Frazi usually spent his summers in the South of France or in Mykonos, but he had been hospitalised after a nasty asthma attack, and been instructed by his doctors to rest in his fragrant tomb of an apartment.

Kitty longed for him to ask her to read the classics to him, like an old-fashioned ill person. He never did, but they spent the close mornings together, drinking tea from bone china so thin it was almost see-through.

When her mother was locked away in her studio, Kitty called Hay House reverse charges, Bestepapa's voice billowing down the phone, like a proud sail.

'We accept the charges. Put her through.'

She told him about Vladimir and Precious, tea with Mr Frazi and Philip. When she said it out loud it became full and round, she could experience it again through the telling.

'Ibsen misses you,' Bestepapa said sadly. 'And Elsie's going out with a French pop singer with a moustache. Can you imagine? Disgusting.' Kitty heard Bestemama chiding him gently in the background.

In New York the buildings were so high that you could see nothing about them but patches of sky. If Kitty looked up too long it made her dizzy and anxious and she thought she would pass out.

'Don't look up then,' her mother laughed when Kitty told her.

'I have to. I have to know there's sky and grass beyond the buildings, otherwise I feel like a little ant.'

'My sweet country mouse, you'll get used to it. You just need to practise thinking that you're a New Yorker – they don't notice.'

Kitty's New York bedroom, up eighty-nine steps, was white as virgin's bones. Her bed was austere, dark-painted Victorian metal. She liked it: boarding school had made her orderly. Kitty craved order and neatness and made her bed every morning with hospital corners. Her mother found this inexplicably funny. Marina's bedroom was huge and paint-splattered. The bed looked like a confectioner's dream. Frothy laced curtains and a sea of soft pillows bobbed around her head. She was a mermaid sleeping in an oyster shell.

Kitty's room seemed naked and unformed somehow, so she bought a stencil from the hardware store and painted hearts in pink above the windows. The result, she thought savagely, looked like Heidi's room. She didn't finish it and five hearts floated, unmoored, in the glaring white. In England her bedroom had always been the creative domain of her mother. Now there were choices. She did not know what to do with such artistic freedom.

There was a huge rainstorm the night before Sam and Violet came back. The city was scorching all day, on the brink, like a bowl about to break. Kitty lay in bed, between the worlds of dream and wake, where everything had melted, and hovered in magic time.

'Kitty?' Her mother stood at the end of the bed. 'Do you want to come and see the rain? It's incredible. I've never seen anything like it.'

They were both barefoot, and the street was hot and empty. The rain fell in slanted sheets, and the air was smoky, filled with the smell of earth and pennies.

They spun around and around, water pouring down their faces, drenching them, an urban baptism.

'This is our life, can you believe it?' Faster and faster her mother spun, like a dervish. 'We're so lucky, and it's just the beginning, Kitty, it's just the beginning of our new wonderful life. Can you believe it?'

Sam and Violet returned with Irish accents and freckles.

'Violet, Violet, we live in a feckin' mansion like Daddy

Warbucks!' Sam flung his Teenage Mutant Ninja Turtles backpack on the marble floor. 'Howareya, Kitty?' he said.

'Cool house, right?' she said, shy of him.

Violet said, 'I'm only staying here if Sam and me have the same room.'

'Well that's a lucky thing, because you do. Have you said hello to your sister?' Her mother swooped down, scooped her up and nuzzled her.

'No. Hi.' Violet buried her face in her mother's T-shirt. 'I remember you, from when I was a little girl. But now I'm big, so I don't remember you as well.'

'Well, I do,' Sam said.

'That's good,' Kitty said, because she couldn't think of anything else to say.

'Come on, skinny bones.' Nora passed Kitty a plate of her macaroni cheese. 'Eat up.'

'No, thank you, I don't want it.' Kitty handed it to Violet.

'Kitty, will you just eat the macaroni, I made it especially for you.' A vein throbbed in Nora's temple.

'But I don't want it. I'm not hungry.'

'What do you want?'

'Nothing. I'm not hungry.'

'But it's suppertime.'

'Just because its suppertime doesn't mean I have to be hungry. My stomach doesn't have a clock that says "Oh suppertime, I must be hungry!"'

Sam found this hilarious.

'"Oh suppertime, I must be hungry! I'm so hungry I could eat all of you, attack of the supper stomach monster."'

'Please will you eat some macaroni?' Nora enunciated each word. 'Stop it, Sam!'

'No,' Kitty said. 'None of you understand me! Why can't you understand?' She threw her chair back from the table and ran upstairs.

'Kitty?' Violet stood awkwardly at Kitty's side, clutching her fairy wings. 'You can have my fairy wings if you like. Look, they're pink and very expensive, Mum said. I wore them at Halloween.'

'Are you sure?' Kitty said.

'Yes, positive.'

'Thank you. I think that's the loveliest present anyone's ever given me. I'll put them on my dressing table so I see them every morning when I wake up, and every night before I go to sleep.'

'Aren't you going to wear them?'

'I will on special occasions. Like Christmas and my birthday.'

Violet smiled.

'Can I tell you a secret?' She leaned in towards Kitty and her breath was like strawberry saucers.

'I don't like macaroni either; I think it's horrible, like feet on mush. And last night, I stuck my finger up Sam's bum and made him smell it.'

'I don't think you should do that any more,' Kitty said gravely.

'I know. It made him cry, and so I just gave him my witch's costume from the Halloween before I was a fairy.'

Violet lay down next to Kitty.

'Can I tell you something else? I do remember you from

before, I just said I didn't. You used to play with us in the bath, and you were really nice.' She flung her arms out and wriggled around like a sugary minnow. She threw her head down on Kitty's chest.

'Ow, Violet! My bosoms. You have to be careful, they're growing . . .'

'Like rabbits. Oh, everything in my life is soft,' Violet said happily.

Kitty's thirteenth birthday arrived charitably to claim her on a Saturday.

It rained, a damp pervasive rain, and she skulked around the empty house like a ghost glaring out of the windows on to a sodden New York, overcome with self-pity. In the kitchen she found Nora, who informed her that her mother was off doing 'birthday things' and would be back at one.

When she looked sulky at this, Nora said, 'Lord, for goodness sake, the fuss you lot make about your birthdays. In my family it was just a normal day.'

Her mother's surprises sometimes backfired. The year before, in child time a decade, on Sam and Violet's fifth birthday, she took them to Disney World. Marina's best friend, Katie, flew out from England with her four-year-old daughter Lily. They wrapped Lily up in a box festooned with ribbons and presented it to Sam. Her mother's sense of excitement mounted.

Sam had marched around the box like a little general, prodding at it with relish. As Lily burst out, 'the present' in a Cinderella costume, Sam looked at first bewildered, and then seriously cheated.

'Oh hi,' he said, and departed to play with his Lego in the walk-in wardrobe.

'But, darling, it's Lily,' Marina said sadly.

'I haven't seen her since I was a baby and she's wearing a Cinderella costume,' he answered as he shut the door.

Her mother arrived home at three.

'Fine birthday this is,' Kitty muttered as she jangled in, bracelets and curls and a cloud of scent.

'Oh don't be cross. Violet, Sam and I have bought you a surprise.'

''Lo, Kitty,' said Sam in his deep teddy-bear voice.

'Kitty, we got you a present,' Violet said. 'But we liked it so much, I got one too.'

'Actually, Violet, we are sharing it,' Sam said.

Marina led her to the sitting room and covered Kitty's eyes with her hands.

'Tada!' she said.

A fat white Persian cat sat on a pink cushion. The cat and Kitty looked at each other with distaste. She didn't quite trust cats, she realised. Dogs were much more straightforward.

'Mine is called Bruce,' Violet told her.

'Brutus,' corrected Sam.

'Bruce,' Violet said, dancing around him.

They flew off downstairs to the nursery like flames.

'What will you call her?' her mother asked.

Kitty felt dumb and uninspired.

'Splendour?'

'That's a marvellous name. Happy birthday, Magpie, are you in a better mood?'

'Mmm.'

'Fitzgerald sent you something. Here.'

She held out a tiny, beguiling blue Tiffany box. There was a card: 'To the birthday girl'. It was a gold heart. Precise, simple and perfect. She hung it from Kitty's neck. Kitty stroked Splendour uneasily and sat, the birthday gloom dissipating.

'Is Violet really calling her cat Bruce?' she asked.

'We've already got a Barry in the family, why not a Bruce?' Her mother grinned and Kitty laughed.

'I do love it when you laugh,' her mother said.

That night they had supper at the smartest restaurant on Madison Avenue. Kitty wore lip gloss and a dot of Chanel No. 5 behind her ears. She drank a glass of champagne, which made her feel hot and a bit deaf. Everyone who walked by the table said hello and happy birthday and that she looked like her mother, which made her feel like she was in one of the Aerosmith videos she watched on MTV. Kitty wished she had dangly earrings and a red Camaro.

She had stopped wearing her glasses when she landed in New York and nobody had seemed to notice or mind. Not even Nora, since her return. She had worn them since she was six. Life looked delicately blurred, a dream forgotten.

Tonight her mother was in a question-asking mood, and bathed in the wattage of her curiosity, Kitty chatted away like a mongoose, falling in love with her all over again.

When they got home Kitty climbed the eighty-nine steps to her bedroom and lay on her bed, fuzzy from champagne, warm and light. Her mother lay next to her and stroked her forehead.

'I'm glad you liked my surprise,' she whispered.

It was the first week of September, but it was still summer hot, endless heat that kissed their bones with content. The garden at 78th Street was wild and unkempt. In its dusty grass amongst plump bushes of hydrangeas, her mother and she lay, on stripy wooden deckchairs.

'I should really be painting,' her mother said drowsily, wearing a pair of polka-dot bikini bottoms, her breasts small and high. 'If not painting, at least sketching or something . . .'

Kitty shut her eyes.

'Mummy, tell me about when you met Andy Warhol.' It was her second favourite story.

'You must be bored of it by now . . . No? All right. I met Andy Warhol in the summer of 1975 at a party. I was wearing an Ozzie Clarke dress and I was dancing.'

'. . . to a Donna Summer song.'

'To a Donna Summer song. "Love To Love You Baby", I think, and he said in that silly, whispery little voice, "You are the most exquisite girl I've ever seen."'

Violet wandered into the garden in a sundress with cherries on it; on her feet she wore pink jelly sandals. She was brown and rosy.

'Hi. You've got much bigger bosoms than Mum, Kitty. What are you talking about?' she added suspiciously.

'A painter called Andy Warhol. Shush, Violet. So he said, "I'm going to sketch you." And he did. And on the bottom of the drawing he wrote "To Marina, the most beautiful girl in the world".'

Kitty covered her face with her hands.

'And what did you do with the sketch?' she asked, knowing the answer.

'I threw it away,' her mother said with a smile,' because I was so sure.'

'So sure of what?'

'I don't know. Just sure. I thought he was just another man that thought I was beautiful. Silly really.'

Swami-ji asked to meet them, all of them, including Nora. Her mother got a letter from his private secretary, a letter embossed with gold Sanskrit writing. Swami-ji's ashram was in Pennsylvania, and they were going to drive up for the weekend.

'But where will we sleep?' Kitty asked her.

'In a dormitory. Life there is very simple.'

In Kitty's experience dormitories were not fun places.

'It will be lovely, I promise,' her mother said. 'Now Nora, we need to get the little ones smart clothes for Satsang.'

'They have smart clothes, Marina.' Nora looked at her sharply. 'I'm not sure that your man's place is a good place for the children . . . what will they do there?'

'They will receive the Swami-ji's Shakti,' her mother said. 'There's lots of other children there they can play with too. It will be wonderful.'

'Well, I'm not going.' Nora said. 'It's against my religion.' She got up out of her chair and gave Marina a mutinous look. 'Hare Krishna rubbish,' she said quietly.

'What do you mean against your religion, Nora . . . you're an atheist! Swami-ji embraces many religions; you are not excluded by faith. He's like Jesus, he loves everyone.'

'Jesus? For goodness sake.' Nora stalked out of the room, her tiny figure erect like a sword.

'You shouldn't have said that,' Kitty said. 'She hates talking about religion.'

Her mother raised her eyes in appeal.

'Honestly, she's so narrow-minded,' she said peevishly. 'We'll all be happier without her and her judgement anyway. Her loss.'

Privately Kitty thought that this probably was not the case.

The limousine cruised, shark-like, through small towns where the houses looked like they had been transplanted from England. They made Kitty feel homesick.

In the car her mother was agitated and bossy. It was searing-hot outside, and the air conditioning came blasting out in icy spikes. They all wore white, and Sam and Violet, roused at 6 a.m., sat in silent starched protest, like grumpy cherubs. To Kitty's surprise her mother had actually let her wear make-up. 'Swami-ji likes everyone to look their best. It makes him happy.'

She felt nervous, like she was about to sit an exam that she hadn't revised for. The towns that they passed began to get smaller and more run-down and Kitty wondered whether the ashram had picked up and moved in the night like a circus. She looked at her mother questioningly.

'We'll be there soon,' Marina said.

They turned into a town with one main street in which

all of the windows were boarded up but one, where a huddle of men sat on the pavement, looking up with momentary interest as the car slid by. Kitty smiled at them from the open window, a smile to show them that they weren't rich people cruising by in a limo; they were on a benevolent spiritual quest. The men sneered, and she shrank back into her seat. She noticed an ominous sign that read 'Penn Gun Club' with an arrow.

Sam and Violet saw it too, and they immediately perked up.

'Is this a town of cowboys?' Sam said, his brown eyes wide.

'Sort of.' Her mother smiled weakly. She mouthed to Kitty, 'The town's people aren't very TOLERANT of us.'

The men on the street were not looking at the limo with admiration; they wanted to carjack it and kill. She wondered if they would kill her quickly or torture her a bit first. Perhaps they were rapists too.

'Can we lock the door?' she said.

'Don't be silly, Kitty. We're nearly there.'

They drove in silence for a few miles.

'Look!' her mother said, pointing. 'There it is!'

In the hazy shimmer of heat, placed improbably on a cornfield, was what looked like an ice-cream castle, with turrets and fountains, surrounded by a large razor-wire fence.

Swami-ji sat on a throne at the end of a very long room. People stood in a line to bow at his feet. Kitty had to take her shoes off. She wished she had painted toes like her mother. Her feet looked like they belonged to a defenceless piglet. A sitar wailed, alone in the echoing white. There must have been 500 people in the great domed room. Around her to the left and to the right, people sat cross-legged, swaying blissfully to the soft music. Incense curled around her like an embrace.

'Don't speak to Swami-ji unless he speaks to you first,' her mother warned.

'I won't,' Kitty said, giving her what was meant to be a chastising look.

'Good girl,' her mother said.

As they got further in the line, her heart beat faster and faster, until she could feel it in her mouth, pounding.

The throne was before her. She had an urge to laugh. Her mother got on her knees and bowed, her head touching the cool marble floor. Kitty followed what she did. She peered up at Swami-ji and saw his feet poking out of his long saffron robe. They were small, and his toenails were curved and wizened, but pink like the shells she collected on the beach when she was little.

They used to call them elephant's toenails.

Suddenly his foot shot out and tapped her lightly on the shoulder. Kitty sat bolt upright in surprise, and stared into his eyes, which were like blackcurrants, kind and tender. She felt when he looked at her that he knew everything there was to know about her. Every bad thought she'd ever had, who she fancied, what colour knickers she was wearing. Why it was that misty English mornings made her ache, and how she wanted to have dinner with Mr Fitzgerald every Saturday night religiously. She felt sorry for being angry with Swami-ji.

He spoke to her with his eyes; they said, 'I've known you

for a thousand years. You are infinite. You are precious, you are my child.'

She didn't know why, but she could feel tears bubbling up inside her. She felt very old and tired, like she had come home after being at sea for years. The world made sense. She held her breath, and her head back so the tears couldn't fall. Her mother stood up, gathering Sam and Violet, each in an arm. She stood too. She bowed her head to her hands.

'So serious!' Swami-ji pointed at Kitty, giggling like a little boy. His lips curved down when he smiled, his smile was so wide. 'So serious, Lakshmi, your eldest child!'

A strangled noise came out of Kitty's throat that was half sob half laugh. Tears coursed down her face and the hysteria that had threatened to engulf her poured forth. She quaked with laughter. The more she laughed, the more Swami-ji laughed. He shook and bellowed and hooted. He jiggled like jelly.

Sam and Violet began laughing.

'You're funny!' Sam said.

'So are you!' Swami-ji called back. 'But you, serious one, you are the funniest.'

'Thank you,' she said shyly, because he said it fondly.

He reached out and patted her hand with a hand that was strong and dry like the branch of a tree. He passed her something that glittered and shone.

'Wear this and think of your Swami-ji, little one. Imagine it as my hand touching yours.'

'Thank you,' she whispered, rubbing her eyes.

Afterwards, her mother was very pleased.

'Oh Kitty, what a blessing! I can't believe it. Let me look.'

It was a gold bangle coloured with semi-precious stones, and it was beautiful.

'Swami-ji sees how special you are; that's why he gave that to you.' Her mother seemed very proud. She started asking Kitty lots of questions. How did you feel, what were you thinking, why were you crying?

Kitty tried to answer but she didn't have the words to explain. She wanted to be alone.

'Do they have biscuits at this place, Mum?' asked Violet.

'Yes, they do.'

'Good. Do you think next time I'll get a present? Because it wasn't really fair that Kitty did and me and Sam didn't.'

'I'm sure, my darling, that you guys will get a present soon.' Marina winked at Kitty.

'All right, I think I like it here then.'

Violet skipped down the thickly carpeted hallway, her white dress billowing behind her.

They were assigned to do chores, which were meant to help you concentrate on your spiritual growth. Violet and Sam did a class for children about the lineage of the Hindu gods. They drew pictures in splashes of scarlet with peacock greens and velvet blues of Lakshmi the goddess of abundance and Hanuman the mischievous monkey god.

Her mother painted a mural in the temple. Kitty worked in the kitchen, making vats of fragrant chai tea, and tiny little coconut sweets.

Everyone seemed to know her mother and love her.

'Lakshmi!' they said. 'These are your kids? How beautiful they are. What grace for them to come to the Guru so young. It's the best gift you could give them.'

'I know,' her mother said, smiling. 'If only we had all been so lucky.'

'Before we had the Guru we had drugs, we had sex, we had negative patterns of behaviour; then we found God, and now we are free.'

'What does that mean?' Kitty said to her mother, her ears pricking up at the sex bit.

'It means that the Guru freed us from human bondage.'

'What do you mean us? Did you take drugs like them?'

'No. I was lost, though, and kept trying to find myself through other people. Now I know who I am. Gosh, you look so pretty in a sari.'

There were so many rituals to remember. It was disrespectful to let her feet point at Swami-ji, whether she was in his presence or bowing to a photograph of him. She had to curl them beneath her, or tuck them to the side. In the temple, she had to bow to the statue of the god in the middle of the room, then walk clockwise three times, bow again, touch her head to the silver feet of the god, put money in his box, then touch her hand to her head, then her heart.

Women sat on the left, men to the right. Sometimes in the meditation room people made funny animal noises in the dark, screeching like monkeys, or bellowing low like cattle. You weren't meant to laugh, her mother said, because it was recognised as a manifestation of being connected to the divine. Kitty thought it was spooky and embarrassing. She didn't like to be in the pitch black with a crowd of people sounding like they were auditioning for *The Jungle Book*. When one started, three followed, calling each other in strange animal voices. Her mother told her in a whisper that she thought they were showing off.

The thing she loved best was Satsang with Swami-ji, which happened at six every day before supper. You went and did your bowing which was called 'Pranam'. And then you took your seat and he gave a talk, which was always funny and wise without being tedious. After the talk the lights were dimmed, and the sitar called, the people answering in unison, chanting, calling on the gods, asking for their divine protection and benevolence. Then they had to meditate.

Kitty watched Swami-ji secretly during the meditation, while the eyes of the others were shut. He sat straight, cross-legged in his throne, his back perfectly erect, and light emanated out of him in waves, so that she could almost see it floating through the air like little darts.

She also watched Ram, who worked in the kitchen alongside her, who was fifteen and from New Canaan, Connecticut. He smelled like patchouli oil and had beads in his curly chin-length hair. He wore Birkenstock sandals, which Kitty found upsetting, because staring at his naked feet felt obscene to her. She concentrated on his face, which was strong and handsome, and imagined their wedding, in the temple, officiated over by Swami-ji, as Brahmins threw rice, stained yellow with turmeric, over her and Ram.

She tried not to think of being sexy with him, because she didn't think it was appropriate in the company of an enlightened being. So instead Kitty imagined riding through the streets of Jaipur on an elephant, chastely kissing him on the lips. In her fantasy he wore boots like a maharaja, and a turban with cabochon rubies dancing around it.

Whenever Ram tried to talk to her in the kitchen, she was mute and turned an unbecoming shade of purple. She wore her hair down, and managed to hide behind a curtain of it, until Ghoti, the kitchen manager, told her it was unsanitary and she had to tie it back. Ram had lived in the ashram since he was three, and he could meditate for seven hours without stopping.

Back in New York, Nora surveyed her bindi with distaste.

'I hope,' she said, as she quickly removed Sam and Violet for their bath, 'that you're not going to school like that. People will think you're very strange. Touched maybe.'

She now had something else in common with her mother, but Kitty wanted to surrender to it fully. She would be a monk when she grew up, and walk with Swami-ji under the banyan trees in India, speaking of God in a secret language no one else would understand.

Chapter Four

There was one day before school began. Kitty sat on the edge of her mother's bed; she was sleeping.

'Mummy,' Kitty whispered.

Marina liked to be woken gently and slowly. She stayed up late painting and singing. Kitty had been carried off to sleep by Bessie Smith and the clink of the Martini glass.

'Mummy, I need clothes for school. I don't really have any clothes except your old ones. I need jeans and things.'

'Christ, of course you do. You don't have a uniform.' Marina opened one eye. 'Could you please, please, please make me a sugary milky coffee the way I like it?'

Kitty marvelled at how her mother could look so lovely and unsquashed after sleep. She knew she looked like a spectre of her mother, whose bones were etched in fine; hers were yet to be formed, like a half-finished drawing.

'Can we go and play Spy Games?' Sam asked as Kitty carried the coffee upstairs.

'What's Spy Games?' Their games were still new to her.

'It's when we go around the streets pretending to be spies and Mum is the head spy. We bring our walkie-talkies.'

Kitty supposed her mother could be a spy, but a winsome French one, who wore Armani raincoats and suede Maud Frizon pumps.

'OK, but I need clothes for school, so can we do it on the way?'

'Right, I'll get Violet. It's a school-clothes cover mission.'

Her mother hid behind a corner.

'The subject has been spotted at twelve, carrying a large bag of M&Ms. How should we proceed, agent V?'

Violet radioed back from two feet away.

'Subject is carrying gold. Stop him with caution.'

Her mother sidled up to Sam.

'Excuse me, sir,' she said. 'I think you must come with me. You have what we need.'

'You must be mistaken, madam.' Sam made an innocent face. 'I am on my way to meet my wife for a coffee.'

'I know your game,' her mother said. 'I know you're single and work for no one but yourself.'

'No,' said Sam. 'Here's my wife right now.'

Kitty swept down upon him and kissed him on the eyebrow.

'Yuck,' he said. 'Hello, wife.'

At this moment an elderly man in mismatching shoes came running towards her mother with his arms outstretched. He looked like a crow, with straggling fabric flying around him like moth-eaten wings.

'Mummy!' Kitty said. 'Be careful. There's a mad person.'

'Hey, baby!' the mad man called to her mother. 'Hey, my favourite pretty lady! You got some sugar for me?'

But her mother didn't run away. She opened her arms and kissed him on his leathery cheek.

'Hello, Norm,' she said. 'How's the mansion rebuilding going?'

'Norm lived in a mansion but George Bush blew it up with a Scud missile and he's raising funds for a new one. Until it's built he lives in a box,' Sam said in a stage-whisper to Kitty.

'Five bucks, lady. Five bucks will pay for my satin sheets. The satin sheets that bastard Bush set on fire!'

'Five bucks?' her mother said. 'Norm, we should go shopping together, you clearly know where to find a bargain. Here, take fifty, and you can buy ten pairs.'

Norm jumped in the air, his arms punching up.

'Yes!' he said. 'That's right! We'll show Bush . . . Your man a lucky son of a bitch, I tell you.'

'Don't have a man,' her mother said, touching his cheek fondly, leading her children down the street like a gaggle of goslings.

On her first day of school Kitty dressed for battle. She wore blue mascara and ripped jeans and a crocheted and complicated sexy top.

'You can't wear that,' her mother and Nora sang in unison at breakfast.

'I can, I must, I'm trying to be sexy.'

'Clearly you're sexy,' said her mother. Kitty felt a thrill at this. 'But you don't need to advertise it.'

Kitty gave them a weary smile.

'I'll be fine,' she said.

She was. She was fine. She was no longer bespectacled,

with her chest jutting out in an empire-line uniform. She was slinky and five foot eight and to her astonishment everyone wanted to be friends with her.

At lunchtime Kitty saw her: her best friend to be. She was sitting at a table of girls from Kitty's class, but she didn't belong with them, in the gym cum cafeteria that smelled of boys and macaroni. She looked like a patrician Debbie Harry, the way she shimmered, heart-shaped and spotless, her long legs folded beneath her. She wore a cream cashmere sweater and a short kilt. She was reading *The Bell Jar* by Sylvia Plath. Kitty knew her mother would have called the girl a preppy; she thought Sylvia Plath was pretentious.

The other girls fired questions at Kitty about England and her parents.

'They're divorced,' she said. 'He lives in London with my stepmother. I don't get on with her, so I don't see him that much now.'

'What does your mom do?' asked an eager little brunette called Natalie. She reminded Kitty of a fox terrier.

'She paints,' Kitty said.

'Oh . . .' The girl seemed confused. 'That's nice.'

The Debbie Harry lookalike looked up finally.

'That's really cool,' she said. 'I'm Charlotte.'

Boys. Everywhere boys, laughing and looking her up and down, their jeans hanging below their boxer shorts, their smiles sly and foxy.

Charlotte sat on the steps looking bored, a swarm of eighth-grade boys buzzing around her. She read her book, swatting them away with it.

‘All right there, English,’ one of them said. His English accent was Dick Van Dyke. Kitty turned red. His name was Noah; she’d seen him at lunch throwing bagel chips at a fat girl.

Charlotte smirked.

‘Kitty, I waited for you.’

‘Thanks.’ Kitty ran her hand through her hair and smiled at Charlotte.

‘Where do you live?’

‘78th and Park Avenue.’

‘I’m on 75th. We can walk.’

Charlotte liked Adamski and Beats International. She didn’t like schoolboys. She was an only child and her parents were ‘narcissists’. Her mother was an actress. She was famous. Her father wrote ‘self-involved plays’. The narcissists went to the country every weekend and she stayed in the city on her own if she wanted. She had shaved her legs since she was ten. Kitty did not want Charlotte to see her bedroom. She thought she might think it childish.

‘You can come over on Saturday. If you want?’ Kitty said. She could make her room appealing.

‘Cool.’

Charlotte turned down 75th Street and blew her a kiss.

‘“This is jam hot. This is jam hot,”’ Kitty sang as she walked through the front door. ‘Mum?’ she called.

‘Is that my angel? I’m baking,’ said her mother from the kitchen.

Her mother baked when she was happy. Kitty jumped up the stairs.

‘Hi, lovely. How was school?’

The kitchen looked like a bomb had hit it. Violet and

Sam stood on tall chairs helping her mother at the pink marble counter.

'It was great.' Kitty dipped into the bowl and licked her fingers, then remembered that icing was fattening.

'I'm thrilled. Why was it great?'

'It just was. Everyone was really nice and what I wore was OK and French is really easy. They're masses behind me.'

'Do you have a best friend?' asked Violet, chocolate ringed round her raspberry mouth.

'I think so. She's called Charlotte.'

'I have a best friend. She's called Summer. But I have to pretend I don't like her because she's a girl,' Sam confided.

'Mum has a date, Kitty,' Violet said. 'With a very young boy named George.'

'Young being the operative word,' her mother said dryly. 'He's twenty-two.'

'Bloody hell! That's only nine years older than me!'

'Will you help me decide what to wear?'

This was their favourite pastime, one that had begun when she was little. Kitty loved her mother's wardrobe. At Hay she used to climb in amidst fur coats and taffeta dresses that slid against her with a sigh of history. She sat with a torch, reading for hours. The cupboards contained the essence of her mother. Overalls, paint-smattered, and T-shirts thin and soft with years of wear and washing. Dresses that swore fun and seduction, heels worn down with dancing and late nights in the rain.

They surveyed her mother's wares like hawk-eyed cloth buyers, dismissing scraps of silk, a heel too high, a sweater too mumsy.

'The rose,' Kitty declared finally. The rose was her

mother's standard date dress. It had a heady history of success.

'Aren't we a bit bored of it?' Marina asked fretfully.

'No, it's good. Honestly,' Kitty said.

She watched her mother's party ritual, the long bath with orange-blossom oil (a witch had told her it made men crazy), body cream swept on surely, the make-up applied with the fine strokes of a painter. She looked like a pert-lipped Matisse woman but thinner. Kitty told her this and Marina crossed her eyes and stuck out her tongue. She wasn't wearing any knickers.

The doorbell rang.

'Darling, give him a drink and tell him I'm on the phone to my gallery in England.'

'It's midnight in England,' Kitty said.

'Oh, my gallery here then. Please, and try to keep Violet out of the sitting room. She gets a little over frank with new people.'

Kitty answered the door.

'Hi,' she sing-songed. 'I'm Kitty. How do you do. Mummy's on the phone to her gallery in New York but do you want a drink . . .' She looked at him. He was unbelievably handsome. She fancied her mother's date.

'You look just like your mother,' he said. 'I'm George and I would love a Martini. Do you know how to make it or shall I help you?'

'I know how,' she said faintly.

'Good girl.'

They sat in the sitting room with the huge bay windows. It was still light. She wished she had put on her dot of Chanel No. 5.

'Kitty, you make a mean Martini. Have you started school yet?'

'No, I'm at university.' It fell from her mouth.

He raised an eyebrow.

'Seventh grade. I started today,' she said, blushing.

'Seventh grade, that's cool. How is it?'

'I liked it. The lessons weren't difficult, but that could have been because it was the first day. It's odd having boys, I'm not used to that.'

'Somewhat different from boarding school, I'd imagine?' he said, and his tone was sweet.

'Oh yes,' she said fervently.

They talked about books. His favourite was *Catch 22*. She told him about *Sense and Sensibility*, which he'd never read. He laughed quite a lot at the things she said, as though they delighted him, and she didn't mind, because he was not patronising or humoring her, she knew. She felt like they were on a date, that she was amusing him with her witty little stories. When she laughed, she touched Mr Fitzgerald's necklace at her throat as she had seen her mother do when she liked a man.

The reverie was broken when Marina burst in, vital and awash with colour, trailing orange blossom behind her.

George swallowed.

'God you're beautiful,' he said.

'Thank you,' she said smartly. 'I'm sorry I kept you waiting.'

'Kitty's been amusing me.'

'Yes, she's jolly good company, my big girl.'

Oh go away, Kitty thought.

'Do you want a drink, Mummy?' she said.

'No darling. I think we'll go now.'

George stood up. Kitty felt that he was being disloyal. He followed her mother out of the room like a hungry puppy.

On the stairs Violet greeted them, cherubic in her nightie. After a careful kiss goodnight, she bellowed down the stairs, 'Mum, Mum, why aren't you wearing any knickers?'

Through the sitting-room window Kitty watched them walk hand in hand down 78th Street. He leaned into her mother and whispered something and Kitty saw her laugh her low laugh. It was adult and secret and it gave her a pang of loneliness. She wanted to be a part of their Indian summer night, not just there for the dress rehearsal. She felt like an understudy. She wanted her own secrets.

She lay on the sofa with Violet and Sam and they watched *Mary Poppins*.

'I'm glad Mary Poppins isn't our nanny,' Violet said.

'Why? If she was, we could fly, and our room would tidy itself. It would be awesome!'

'No, Sam. If Mary Poppins was our nanny she'd think Mum was naughty, and she'd fly up the chimney and go away. I'd rather have Nora any day. I bet Mary Poppins made nasty rice pudding without the jam.'

'Mum isn't naughty, Violet,' Kitty said.

'Just a little bit.' Violet yawned. 'Knickerless girls shouldn't climb trees.'

Elsie and Ingrid were coming to stay. Her mother sent a limo to pick them up from JFK, while Precious made the guest rooms perfect. They'd ordered little bouquets of freesias from the florist, and the beds were piled high with linen sheets that had been ironed with rosewater.

'Why can't my room be like that?' Kitty said. 'I'm jealous.'

'Because you live here,' her mother said. 'You're not a guest; I want you to stop this woebegone nonsense.'

'Fine,' Kitty said.

'Oh my God, Marina, you are living in LUXURY,' Ingrid gasped as she was led through the door by the chauffeur, who carried her duffel bag like it was a Vuitton trunk.

'LUXURY,' Elsie echoed.

'I've sold a few paintings. Do you like it?' Her mother asked, beaming shyly.

'We want to move in! Holy fuck! Look at you, Kitty, you're so tall and skinny and sexy! I can't believe it! I have to have a nap, it's all too much.'

Kitty helped Elsie unpack. Her milk hair was cut short, like Jean Seberg's, and she looked elfin in black tights and a black jumper, her blue eyes ringed with smoky grey.

'Can you make my eyes look like that?' Kitty asked her.

'Yes, of course, oh, we've missed you so much . . . do you have a boyfriend?'

'No. But I could very soon. This boy in the eighth grade – that means form – he really likes me. His name is Noah. He plays the guitar and has a band called the Dirty Things. He told my friend Charlotte he fancies me. Did you like Paris?'

'Paris was amazing. I fell in love with a pop star who sang terrible songs, and he asked me whether I respected his talent, and I said no, frankly it was hard, because I like reggae and ska and French pop music is just awful. Then he cried, and I told him it wasn't going to work. Ingrid and

I lived above a bakery and every morning the smell of *brioches* would waft up through our bedroom window, and we would run down in our nighties and get a big bag and dip them in coffee. We got so fat! You would adore it there. Can I smoke in here?'

Her mother decided to have a dinner party in honour of Ingrid and Elsie's arrival. She invited Mr Frazi, and George, and a frightening writer who didn't like children, so Sam and Violet were hidden in the nursery.

'Now, I've invited lots of groovy people for you,' she said. 'There's Nell who has a nightclub, a famous one downtown, and Nick, who is an incredibly handsome actor, and a dancer, who's straight, and one who isn't . . . and lots of people. You'll like them.'

Kitty was excited because she was allowed to go to the dinner party. Elsie made Kitty's eyes smoky like her own, and Ingrid lent her a cashmere sweater from Chanel, with big pearl buttons.

'Lamb dressed as mutton,' her mother said laughing when Kitty walked into her bathroom. 'You look glorious. But not for every day, OK?' A whip of concern passed over her brow.

'I know, I know,' Kitty said, rolling her eyes. 'Do you want me to scrub your back?'

'Yes please.'

'What do you want to be when you grow up?' the frightening writer boomed at Kitty.

'I'd like to be a writer, or a lady of leisure like Mummy,' Kitty said.

The table laughed. She was embarrassed.

'Your mother is not a lady of leisure,' the writer said. 'She is a very important artist.'

'I know,' Kitty said slowly. 'I should have said that because that's what I was thinking. It's just that she does lovely leisurely things, and she makes people laugh, and she's beautiful. That's what I meant by a lady of leisure.'

'You should think before you speak,' the writer said. She had dirty fingernails.

'Oh relax, Josephina . . . She's being sweet. I know what you meant, Kit, it was a darling thing to say.'

Kitty smiled in relief. Her mother came over and touched the top of her head with a soft palm.

Ingrid and Kitty were happily eating Nora's French toast at the dining-room table when Elsie came down in her linen pyjamas.

'Tell me,' Elsie said immediately, giving Ingrid a beady stare.

'Tell you what? There's nothing to tell.'

'I know there is. I know you snogged him. I tell you everything, and I normally have much more to tell. You're being unfair.'

'Who? Who did she snog? Nick the actor?' Kitty clamoured.

'I'm trying to read the paper. Be quiet.' Ingrid winked at her.

Her mother walked in, clutching her silk dressing gown around her. She had chopsticks in her hair to hold it back.

'Ingrid kissed that man, and she won't tell me,' Elsie said to her mother.

'Oh leave her alone, darling. Now I need my coffee, and then I'm going to meditate.' Marina seemed distracted.

Elsie looked around the dining room, which was painted a Georgian blue, with high white corniced ceilings, and she said, 'You're no fun any more, Marina, do you know that? I can't believe you won't get it out of her, you can get secrets from a stone, and stop pretending you're not interested in sex; it's very clear you and that boy George are doing it, which is really pervy of you.'

'He sees me as a mother figure. Kitty, have you seen my prayer mat?' her mother said, as though she were having a different conversation entirely. Kitty thought it was clever.

'You've become all boring and SPIRITUAL,' Elsie said sadly.

'You really have, Marina.' Ingrid looked up from her paper. 'Sort of . . . rich and spiritual,' she added.

'I haven't! I'm not rich! I'm fun! I'm very fun, ask anyone!' Her mother sounded like a little girl protesting. Ingrid and Elsie looked at her dubiously. She lit up one of Ingrid's Gauloises, and took a long voluptuous puff.

'Fine. I'll take a meditation sabbatical for the length of your visit. You spiritual saboteurs! I am not boring. I am having an affair with George, if you must know, not that it's any of your business. I have been for some time, he's sweet. Now, Ingrid, did you kiss Nick the actor?' She was breathless and giddy.

'Yes. I did,' Ingrid said.

'Kitty, do you want the day off school so you can spend time with your wicked wanton aunts?' her mother said, ruffling her hair.

'Definitely,' Kitty said. She lived in a house of carnal intrigue, this much was clear.

* * *

'Don't leave,' she said to Elsie, who was packing. 'If you stay then it will be like it was before. All of us together.'

'We have to go. We've got jobs now. I had such a lovely time with you though, and we'll come again. Everyone will make up, and we can bring Mama and Dad.'

'What would they DO here? It's too noisy, they wouldn't like it.' Kitty stared out of the window morosely.

'Dad would build some shelves, and Mama would hide the paper. They'd see you and the littlies.'

'Well maybe it would be all right. I could take them to the park and the museum. But I'd have to know in advance, so that I could prepare.'

The car was waiting on the kerb, and Ingrid and Elsie's voices echoed down the marble stairs. In five minutes they would be just a memory trapped in the bones of the house. It made Kitty feel sick.

'Ingrid! Come here!' she hissed in the hall.

'What is it Kit-kat?'

'I have an ache in my womb. A warm, dull ache. It's my period, I know it.'

Ingrid gave her a huge hug.

'When it does come, truly, I want you to send me a postcard and let me know. We'll have to throw it a coming out party.'

Kitty had always dreamed of slumber parties; they existed in her Judy Blume fantasies of teenage American life, along with diners and malted milkshakes.

'You have to keep Sam and Violet away,' she told Nora bossily.

'It's their house too.'

'Nora!'

'Fine. Now what will you have for supper? Shall I make a shepherd's pie?'

'No. You can't have shepherd's pie at a slumber party. We'll have pizza. And Doritos and popcorn, and Coca-Cola. And we don't have a bedtime. That's the rule. We stay up and we watch films and we talk and we fall asleep when we want.'

'You can sleep in my room if you want; I'm not going to be here.' Her mother walked in wearing exercise clothes.

Kitty felt a rush of disappointment. She wanted to show her mother off.

'Where are you going?' she said.

'Away. You're allowed your sleepovers and I'm allowed mine.'

'That's not fair.'

'Life's not fair.' This was Nora's favourite saying.

'Oh my God! Your mother is so pretty.' Natalie looked at the black-and-white photograph of Marina by Irving Penn hanging on the stairs.

'Was she a model?'

'No. Lots of people asked her to be, but she had me when she was really young, so she started painting instead.'

Now she had all of the girls from school in her house, Kitty was not sure what to do with them.

They went into raptures over her mother's bed, the dressing table crowded with paint and make-up, the paint-stained floors.

'I feel so bohemian,' Stephanie said dreamily. 'Charlotte, don't you wish your house was like this?'

'My house isn't unlike this,' Charlotte said.

'I love your house,' Kitty said to her. 'And I love your dad, he's so nice.'

'Charlotte's dad is so cute. I want to marry him. Charlotte, I wish my dad was like yours.' Natalie held her tanned little hands against her tan sweater. She was a symphony of beige.

'Why can't all of you just be happy with what you have? Really, it's so pathetic.' Charlotte lay on the floor, with one leg up like a Varga girl. 'Can we DO something? Kitty, do you English people even have televisions?'

Kitty laughed nervously, and felt as though she were wearing glasses again.

'Yes. We do. You know we do, we watched *Twin Peaks* last weekend.'

She looked at Charlotte questioningly. In her head a voice said, And I told you all my secrets and that I have a crush on Noah Redner, and you told me that when you can't sleep you touch yourself, and I've never heard anyone admit that out loud, and we decided that maybe we were separated at birth, because we think lots of the same things, but I'm not like you really which I know you know. I'm pretending to be pretty, but you're a proper beauty like my mother is a proper beauty, and I'm not really cool, everyone just thinks I'm cool because I'm new and I'm from England.

Charlotte gave her a lopsided smile.

'I'm only kidding. God, you're so neurotic. Let's watch a movie.'

Charlotte rested her blonde head against Kitty's while they watched a film called *The Serpent and the Rainbow*.

'You're my best friend,' she whispered. 'Everyone else here is a dork.'

Her mother came home at midday the next day, just before everyone left, and she did her proud. She was wearing a dress that could have belonged to Daisy Buchanan, and her lips slid with gloss. She looked tired but it suited her; there were violet shadows under her eyes.

'I'm so glad I got here before you all left!' she said. 'I'm Marina.' She snuggled up next to Kitty on the floor.

'I would have had much more fun with you guys,' she said winningly. She began telling a funny story about the nightclub called Nell's and a stolen fur coat.

Charlotte nudged Kitty.

'Somebody's had quite a hold on your mom,' she whispered. 'I don't think she's telling the truth.' She gave a knowing smile, and indicated with her eyes Kitty's mother's wrist, which had a faint bracelet of bruises around it.

'Yes, she is.' Kitty put her hand over her mother's wrist and held it there as she talked, tracing her fingers over her mother's arm as if she could read her like Braille.

'Happy Birthday to you! Happy Birthday to you!' Sam and Violet wobbled in with the cake, and Kitty carried a tray with flowers and coffee.

'My babies,' her mother said. 'Is it a lovely day for my birthday?'

Kitty pulled back the curtains, and the sky was a clear uninterrupted stripe of blue.

'OK, because it's my birthday, you get the day off school and I get to do whatever I want, and I want to spend it with you three.

'First we get to go and buy me a present from Barneys and Kitty too; then we go to FAO Schwarz and Violet and Sam get whatever they want. Then we have appointments to keep and things to do. George is throwing a lunch for me at La Grenouille, which you're invited to, and an Indian feast is happening at Ranjit's house in the evening. There are two more days of parties but I don't think Nora will have it if I keep you off school for that long, after all, we all know she's just not that big on birthdays. But my real true birthday present is you lot, do you know that?'

At lunch the table was piled high with presents, and her mother sat at the head like a queen. She wore her birthday present to herself, earrings of opals and aquamarines that swung down until they grazed her collarbone, which was bare in a strapless pale-cream dress. George, who sat next to her, wore a dazzled face, in slow motion, and each time she smiled at him, or brushed his hair from his eyes, he looked around the table as if to say, She chose me?

'Were you sick yesterday? Why didn't you come to school?' Charlotte's arms were crossed, and she looked angry.

'It was my mother's birthday; she let us do things with her.' Kitty shrugged.

'What? Your mom's birthday is a national holiday or something?' Charlotte made a face.

'Sort of. It's silly . . .' Kitty said quickly, 'Did I miss anything important?'

Her mother left for London in a rush of secrecy. She packed her globetrotter suitcase with tweed suits and court shoes. No jeans or sailor's T-shirts. She gave Kitty a distracted kiss goodbye. When she left, the house felt empty. Violet and Sam were sleeping; Nora was in her armchair by the television puffing away.

Kitty went into her mother's bathroom and ran a long bath filled with her Penhaligon's bath oil. She didn't turn the light on, just the heat light so the room was red and dreamlike. Naked, she stared at herself in the mirror. In the red light she didn't look like herself. Her face was still and blown out like a Victorian photograph. She pretended she was a courtesan preparing for an evening's soliciting, smoothing lotion along her collarbone down over her ribs. She sprayed scent behind her knees, stuck her bottom out coquettishly and turned her head to the side, smiling.

'What on earth are you doing?' asked Nora.

'Nothing.' She scrambled for a towel, mortified.

'You're not meant to be in your mother's bathroom and it's bedtime.'

'Fine. What's your problem?'

She stomped off to her bedroom and stayed up all night reading Nancy Spungen's mother's biography of her daughter, her new favourite book.

It was Wednesday when everything changed. She got an A in her English homework and chipped her tooth on a hard bagel at lunchtime. The boys watched her attempts to play volleyball, laughing as she dropped the ball every time. She walked home from school smiling at the doormen on Park Avenue. When she got home she talked to Noah Redner for an hour and he played his guitar down the phone to her. He asked her to the eighth-grade dance and when Kitty rang Charlotte to tell her, she said in a throaty way, 'You sexy bitch.'

Thanksgiving was coming, her first real American Thanksgiving, and she was going to make a pumpkin pie for her mother. Rosaria was coming to stay at Christmas and Kitty had bought a dress for the parties they might go to that was tight as seal skin, midnight blue and highly inappropriate.

She was sitting on the sofa in Nora's sitting room watching *21 Jump Street* when her mother called. Violet wouldn't go to bed and clung on to Kitty's ankle like a koala bear.

Nora picked up the phone.

'Och,' she said. 'Oh Jaysus, Marina.' She looked sorry for Kitty. 'It's your mummy.' She passed her the phone.

'Kitty, I have some bad news.' Her mother sounded high and oceans away. 'Your daddy Fitzgerald died this afternoon.'

'Oh,' Kitty said, picking at her pink nail polish.

'I think you should fly over for the funeral.'

Her mother talked a little bit more, told her she loved her, and that she must be strong, and then she asked to speak to Sam. Sam, who was still confused by telephone etiquette, repeated everything she said to Violet, his captive audience.

'Mummy has good news and bad news, Violet.' He let the phone dangle as he told her.

'Pick up the phone, Sam,' Nora said. 'Mummy's still talking.'

'Oh,' he said. 'What? Mr Fitzgerald has died. Mummy, what's the good news? Violet, Mr Fitzgerald has died but we're going to get a tortoise!' He hung up.

Violet began to cry, fierce, fat tears running down her cheeks.

'Can I sleep in your bed?' she wobbled to Nora. 'And can I have hot chocolate?'

Nora went upstairs, clucking.

'I'm going to call the tortoise Torty,' Sam said.

'Why are you crying, Violet? He was my father and you didn't even know him,' Kitty asked her, curious.

'Neither did you know him. And besides, I didn't want to sleep in my bed. And I got hot chocolate. I'd rather have a lizard than a tortoise, though.'

Violet was so triumphant it made Kitty laugh, hard, out loud.

'You are a very funny girl,' she said.

Kitty climbed the stairs to her room and shut the door. The wind continued like wolves' song and the tree outside her bedroom slapped the window furiously. She told her picture of Swami-ji, 'My father died today,' because saying it out loud made it true. She heard the comforting slip of Nora's shoes outside.

Nora sat next to her as she howled like a small animal, patting her back rhythmically like an old nursery rhyme.

'My poor Kitty. I'm so sorry.'

'It's all right; I didn't know him any better than Violet,' she cried.

'You'll need a hat,' Nora said softly. 'We can go to Bloomingdale's tomorrow and buy you a hat.'

* * *

Outside the terminal her head throbbed. Everything was magnified and raw. Kitty felt unprepared. The fields looked too green, and everyone that walked by seemed to be shouting not talking.

A driver picked her up from the airport. He was listening to Capital FM and she didn't know any of the songs. He drove her to a hotel on Sloane Street. Her mother was on the phone in her nightie, smoking a cigarette when Kitty walked in.

'Hello, darling,' she mouthed.

Kitty sat in the corner and flipped through *Vogue*. After dusty hours her mother hung up the phone.

'We're going to have lunch with Peter,' she said.

Kitty liked Peter. He was her mother's boyfriend before she moved to New York, before Kitty went away to school. Even Bestepapa liked him. He had discovered her mother's G-spot. She knew this because her mother told her best friend Katie on the car phone driving her back to school. Kitty tried to look for hers with a mirror and a copy of *Our Bodies, Ourselves* but she couldn't find it.

Peter had taken her to Battersea Park on Sunday afternoons and when the cottage had an infestation of wasps, he killed them. Her mother was allergic to wasps. Peter also wrote her the sort of letters she thought a father should write when she was at school, even after he split up with her mother. He came to see her on sports day and she came third in the high jump competition. Even though Kitty knew this wasn't really very good, he kept saying, 'That was brilliant. Legs like your mummy.' Afterwards they went for lunch in Wheaton and he took her to W.H. Smith to buy her mother a Mother's Day card. The tiniest things made him cheerful.

'Look at this glorious day,' he'd said. And it was, she remembered. Except that she had to go back to school and he could drive back to London in his Mercedes listening to the Beatles singing their happy songs.

'Hello, Kit-kat,' he said when she and her mother walked into Da Mario's. Peter gave her mother a huge bear-like hug. She shook away like a dragonfly.

They all sat down and her mother began to talk as though they weren't really there. Kitty studied her. She smoked and talked simultaneously, taking great, gasping breaths, shooing away the waiter who removed her untouched food with a mournful sigh. She asked Kitty to go and sit at the bar so she could have a 'grown-up talk with Peter'.

Kitty rolled her eyes and Peter winked at her. She pretended to be deeply involved in Nancy Spungen but cast surreptitious glances their way. After a time they came over. She was drinking a cappuccino and pretending to be a beat poet. Peter kissed her goodbye. He smelled like cigarettes and Eau Sauvage. Kitty didn't want him to let go.

'She'll be all right, Kit-kat,' he whispered in her ear.

'I know,' she said. But she knew that this was a half-truth.

Mr Fitzgerald's funeral was at the Catholic Church on Cheyne Walk. She and her mother waited till everyone had gone in. Kitty felt nervous.

'Are we definitely invited?' she asked her mother anxiously.

'People don't get invited to funerals. You can just go,' her mother said.

Marina wore a black Chanel suit and her curly hair was fighting to get out of its ponytail. Kitty was wearing a navy-blue suit from Benetton and woolly tights that made her knees itch. Her hat had caused a fight. It was bottle-green felt and she thought elegant and befitting her own father's funeral.

'No,' her mother said.

'Why not?'

'It's too sophisticated.' Her mother stubbed her cigarette out in her untouched porridge. 'Oh wear it. I don't care any more.'

Mr Fitzgerald had a lot of friends. Perhaps they were business associates, colleagues. Kitty didn't know anyone who had the sort of job where you had colleagues. The word made her mother laugh, like 'partner'. They sat at the back.

Her mother was composed until they took the coffin away. Then she made a noise like a kitten being strangled and gripped Kitty's arm so tightly with her nails that she thought she would be branded.

Mrs Fitzgerald came out after the coffin. She was blonde and fat and if she was an animal she would have been Splendour the cat. Her hair looked hard, like it would crackle if you touched it.

They waited for everyone to walk out. Kitty wondered who she was related to. Nobody really looked like her. They zigzagged round the people condoling with Mrs Fitzgerald and walked on to the street. A milkman wolf-whistled at her mother and Kitty scowled at him. Her mother lit a cigarette and crossed the street to look for a cab.

Kitty felt a soft, doughy hand on her arm.

'You look so familiar,' said Mrs Fitzgerald.

'I don't think so. I don't think we've ever met,' Kitty stuttered.

She looked for her mother on the other side of the street. She was not paying attention. It was like a scene from a film, Kitty thought. In the world there is just Mrs Fitzgerald and me.

Mrs Fitzgerald was very tall. Bestepapa would have called her an AMAZON. Kitty could see up her nostrils. They were hairy. Kitty felt her lips curling upwards, and willed them down, into a comic twisted frown.

'You have his smile,' Mrs Fitzgerald said.

Kitty realised she knew, and her heart beat fast, with adrenalin and something like excitement.

'Thank you,' Kitty said in a small voice.

She wanted Mrs Fitzgerald to like her. She looked at her mother puffing across the street; she looked little and defenceless and Kitty felt disloyal. Mrs Fitzgerald and she observed each other for about forty-five seconds.

'Actually I have my mother's smile,' Kitty said coldly and ran across the street. She took her mother by the arm. 'Mum, we'll find a taxi on the King's Road,' she said, and dragged her down Justice Walk.

'What did she look like, Mrs Fitzgerald?' Rosaria said.

She and Kitty were sitting at the Garage on the King's Road, sharing a hot chocolate. Marina had a headache and was lying in the darkened hotel room, napping.

'I don't know, hard and untouchable, somehow,' Kitty said. 'Not like I imagined.'

'Your father clearly had very diverse taste in women. Do you want to come and stay this weekend? Mummy said she'll call your mother. My brothers saw a picture of you from the yearbook you sent me, and suddenly they fancy you. It's really repulsive.'

'I can't,' Kitty said. 'I've had a week off school. We have to fly back tomorrow; I'm going to have so much work. But I'll see you at Christmas.'

Rosaria touched her arm and her eyes filled with tears.

'I'm so sorry, Kit,' she said. 'It's not fair.'

'Life's not fair,' Kitty said, and she laughed. 'Come on, let's go and buy something, my mother's given me fifty pounds. Do you want anything?'

'We could share those silver hot pants,' Rosaria said thoughtfully. 'They could be transatlantic.'

Chapter Five

Noah Redner called her and asked if he could come over. She felt sick with excitement. Her mother was out, so she couldn't ask her what she should wear, but she knew she wouldn't mind if she borrowed something because it was a special occasion. Kitty put on her black leggings and a long pink striped cardigan of her mother's that came down to her knees. In her mother's bathroom she covered herself with scent, and she put blusher on the apples of her cheeks like her mother did.

She asked Nora to get the door when it rang and Nora said, 'Why can't you get it yourself like a normal person?'

'Because it's a DATE. Please? I'll give you anything you want.'

'I don't want anything.'

'But will you do it?'

'Oh, all right, I suppose so. But you're not to go up to your bedroom, OK?'

'I don't want to be in my bedroom, we'll be in the sitting room.'

She put Carly Simon on the CD player, and decided 'Let the River Run', would be playing as he walked in the door. She reclined on the sofa, but decided that this was too casual, so she stood against the window with her back to the door, so that when he walked in she would look as though she was deep in thought.

As she heard them coming up the stairs Kitty hit play. The music resounded throughout the sitting room. She concentrated on looking lost in thought.

'Kitty!' Nora shouted. 'Your guest is here.'

Kitty turned slowly and smiled beatifically at her.

'Thank you so much, Nora. Hello, Noah.'

She walked slowly over and kissed him on both cheeks.

'What's up?' He looked uncomfortable.

'Could you turn that music down and leave the door OPEN.' Nora gave her a look of warning.

'Certainly.' Kitty smiled again.

'Would you like a cup of tea, Noah?' she asked.

'Can I have a Coke?'

'Oh yes. Of course.'

She ran into the kitchen.

'How's it going?' Precious smiled.

'Really well, I think.'

'Who was that weird woman?' Noah said.

'She's not weird, that's Nora, my brother and sister's nanny. What do you want to do?' They were sitting on the squashy sofa, two feet apart.

'I don't know, what do you want to do?'

'I don't know. We could play Scrabble?' Kitty put the cushions on her lap, like a barricade.

He was silent.

'Why don't we go up to your room and listen to some music?' He moved closer. 'I'd like to see your room.'

She inched away.

'No, let's stay here. It's better. I can change the music if you like.'

'Yeah, this sucks. Do you have Guns N' Roses?'

'No. I've got Stevie Wonder.'

'That's really funny. Why don't you shut the door?'

'I've got to go and get something from the kitchen. I'll be back in a minute.'

'Precious, help! He keeps telling me to shut the door . . . don't tell Nora, what should I do?'

'You want me to t'row him out?' Precious looked excited.

'No! Just tell me what to do!'

'Aks him to go for a walk.'

'All right, I'm going back in, wish me luck.'

'Sorry about that. Noah, do you want to go for a walk? We could go and get coffee, I know a really good place on Lex.' She perched far away from him, on the edge of the sofa.

'I'm kind of tired.' Noah Redner yawned expansively, and stretched out like a lion, till his fingers were resting on her thigh.

She jumped up.

'Come on, I really think you should see this place, it's really cool.' Her mother had taken her there one Saturday morning for breakfast, but she couldn't remember where it was.

'Fine. Then can we go to your room?'

'Yes.' By the time they came back her mother would be home and Kitty was sure she would know what to do.

'Make him leave,' Kitty hissed to her mother as she made a pot of rose tea. 'You have to make him leave in a subtle way.'

'Noah darling,' her mother said. 'I'm so sorry to drag

you away, but Kitty's godmother Katie has flown in from London for a surprise and we have to go and meet her for a drink. I do hope you come again.'

'But Mum, I'm busy!' Kitty said. 'That is so unfair. God!'

Her mother was perfect. 'I'm sorry to put a spanner in the works, darling, but I promised we'd be there at five.'

'Can I see your room next time?' Noah breathed in her ear on the way out.

'That was so awful,' Kitty said to her mother. 'When we were on our own I realised I didn't like him at all.'

'Sometimes it's much better in your head. You're very mature; maybe you'd like someone slightly older. Do you want to go and see a movie? My head hurts; I'd like the quiet of a cinema.'

They saw *Cyrano de Bergerac* and sobbed throughout the film. Her mother cried so much at the end that Kitty thought she might explode.

'Love should be like that. As real and strong as that,' Kitty said afterwards, blowing her nose, as they walked on to Lexington Avenue.

'I completely agree, though without the unrequited bit,' her mother said, tears still pouring down her face.

'I can't come for Christmas.' Rosaria's voice was strained, and she sounded like she had a cold.

'Why? What's wrong?'

'We have to sell the house. Daddy wants a last Christmas here, all of us together. He's lost all of his money, because of Lloyd's.'

Kitty imagined a smart-suited banker throwing a safe stuffed with Mr Nivolla's money into the Thames.

'Lloyds Bank?' she said.

'No, Lloyd's of London. Please can we do it again though, maybe next year? I wanted to come and see everything you describe in your letters.'

'The door is always open.' Kitty thought this sounded appropriately sober.

'Luke Perry and Johnny Depp will just have to wait for us for one more year. The transatlantic hot pants send their love.'

'Noah Redner said you gave him a blow job on Saturday,' Charlotte said flatly outside school on Monday morning.

'No, I didn't! He came over and we went for a walk and then he went home. I don't even like him.'

'Well, he said you did. And he said your house is really weird, and you were wearing weird clothes, and listening to weird music.'

'I promise you that's not true. Do you believe me?' Kitty thought she might laugh, or cry, she couldn't tell which.

'No, I don't. You can tell me, I won't tell anyone.' Charlotte looked bored. 'I won't think you're a slut or anything. I know you like him.'

'I didn't. I swear. What shall I do?' Kitty took her hand.

'I think we both know that you're lying.' Charlotte snatched away her hand. 'I have to go, Natalie's waiting for me. And by the way, you know that Monica's having a pool party? Well, we decided at Gwen's sleepover that you're so skinny you'd look like Nancy Reagan in a bathing suit. No offence.'

* * *

'Hey, Kitty!' Justin waved. 'Do you want to hang out this weekend? We could, you know, listen to MUSIC.'

'No,' she croaked. 'I'm very busy. I have plans.'

When she walked into homeroom everyone stopped talking, and stared through her, like she was made of paper.

She went to see the school nurse.

'Could I please call my mother? I feel like I'm going to faint.'

The nurse was so kind it made Kitty cry.

'Hush, hush,' she said, stroking her forehead. 'Didn't you just have a death in your family?'

'My father died,' Kitty said.

She couldn't be bothered to explain that she didn't know him. Mr Fitzgerald would have to be her excuse. Kitty was sure that, under the circumstances, he wouldn't mind, unless he was heartless.

'Well, sweetie, you must be under a lot of stress. I'll call your mom now.'

Kitty lay on the thin cot, with her eyes closed tightly, pretending to be a baby till her mother mercifully walked in the door, clucking concern, swaddling Kitty in her pale-pink shawl that smelled of love and home.

Kitty knelt down at the altar she had made for Swami-ji.

'I'll try not to think about boys,' she whispered. 'Because it just seems to get me in trouble, but if you could help me I would be very grateful.'

His eyes shined from the photograph, full of compassion.

'I'll be good from now on, and please bless everyone in

this house, Mummy, Nora, Sam and Violet, OM, Amen.' She bowed her head.

In the loo of the Three Guys Diner on Madison Avenue Kitty pulled down her knickers and her heart leapt. A red stripe, a definite red stripe: the heralding of womanhood.

Her mother was drinking a banana milkshake outside. Since Mr Fitzgerald's funeral she had existed upon cigarettes and the occasional sweet thing, like treacle sponge or milkshakes.

'Everything tastes bitter,' she explained. 'I just need sweet.'

Kitty walked outside like she had a secret. They sat and drank their milkshakes, paid the bill and left.

'I need to go to Clyde's,' Kitty said conversationally.

'OK,' her mother said. 'How happy are you that you never need to see those dreadful people again?' It was the last day of school, before the summer began.

'Happy,' Kitty said. 'I need to go to Clyde's though.'

'You said that.'

'I know but I really need to go to Clyde's, now, because I need to buy some sanitary towels.'

'Oh my God! My baby! My baby's become a woman!' Her mother's eyes filled with tears.

'Shhh. You're embarrassing me! You can't tell anyone, OK?'

'No, I won't. I promise. Oh my Lord! This is a red-letter day – a literal red-letter day. We shall have to go out and celebrate. Tonight, where do you want to go?' She looked at Kitty as though she were different somehow.

'Mum. Stop it. It's a perfectly normal occurrence.'

'Now who do you want for your celebratory dinner? Anyone from school? Sorry, silly question. What about George? He'll be fun. He loves women, it comes from having so many sisters.'

'Only if you do NOT tell him.'

'I won't, I won't.'

'Congratulations!' George stood on the doorstep and handed Kitty a bunch of peonies. 'I hear you became a woman today – that's very exciting.'

'Not really,' she said, blushing, and decided to kill her mother later. 'You know . . .'

'I don't really,' he said, leaning in to kiss her cheek. 'You look different. Grown-up.'

She was wearing a dress from Betsey Johnson, which her mother had bought her specially, a dress that was pale yellow and filled with grace. It was the best dress she'd ever had.

'No, I don't.' Kitty looked down at her feet.

'You do, I swear it. The most beautiful you've ever looked. I'm a lucky man taking you and your momma out tonight.'

Her mother had met another man, a man who lived in Canada, and she knew she was going to marry him. She told him, the night they met, an Indian fable about a pearl that held the world's light, and the next day she took Kitty around every antique shop in Manhattan to find a box, the sort of box that could house a pearl that belonged in an epic.

'I don't understand what you're doing,' Kitty said. She felt churlish and hot, and disloyal to George.

'Stop whining. We're on a romantic quest. I'm going to send him a pearl. In a box. But I'm not just going to send it; no, that would be far too pedestrian. I'm going to dispatch Precious on a plane to Canada, and while he's out at lunch have her slip the box into his office, on to his desk, so when he comes back from his boring business lunch there will be the pearl, just sitting there, as though an enchantress stole through the window.' She looked distracted.

'Hardly. Precious will be scuttling down his driveway. How do you know the timing will be right?'

'Kitty, you're being really mean. Don't spoil my fun. Life has been so very un-fun since the love of my life died. Thank God I have God. Anyway, I thought you were Miss Romantic. You should find this exciting. Now do you have something like this but a bit smaller?' Marina asked the harassed-looking salesman.

Precious and the pearl were dispatched to Canada, but the businessman did not respond as he was meant to. Kitty found her mother crying on the floor of the armoire in her bedroom.

'What's the matter?' she said, climbing in next to her.

'He didn't get it. He thought it was odd. That's what he said, that it was the oddest thing anyone's ever done, and then he got off the phone, and it's just so unfair because I thought I was going to marry him, and we could all live in Canada and eat maple syrup.' Her mother threw a shoe against the wall.

'Well,' Kitty said. 'If he thought it was odd then clearly he's not the man for you. It was the most romantic thing in the world, and if he can't appreciate that then he's a boring old sod and he's not fit to lick your boots. Not that you wear boots.'

'Do you really think that?'

'Yes, I do. I can tell you that we most certainly don't want to live in Canada either. It would be really boring. Lose his number.' Kitty put her arm around her mother's thin shoulders in the dark.

After about five minutes Marina said in a small voice, 'You're absolutely right. I'd hate Canada. All those trees and lakes. I don't know what I was thinking. I wish I'd never sent him that pearl. I want it back.'

'Send Precious to reclaim it, like an enchantress.'

Her mother started giggling.

'I wish I'd been there,' she said.

George did not get a pearl for his birthday brunch. George didn't get much of anything because his birthday was on a Sunday.

'You have to get him a present,' Sam said in the taxi. Sam was keen on birthdays, and all they entailed, even if they belonged to another.

'Yeah, Mum, he spent so much money on you for your birthday.' Violet was adamant.

'It's fine,' her mother said. 'We'll just go to the hardware store. That's open on Sunday.'

'You can't buy him a present from the hardware store, and we're already an hour late for lunch,' Kitty said.

'He'll wait,' her mother replied firmly.

'What is it?' George asked, surveying the rather battered cardboard box in his hand. He looked hungry.

'It's a clapper, darling. It's so clever. I wish I had one.' Her mother ordered a Bloody Mary.

'What does it do?'

'You plug it into the wall and when you want to watch television or turn out the lights it does it for you, if you clap.'

Sam looked pained when she said this.

'Oh. Great.' George looked like he might burst into tears. Kitty sincerely hoped he wouldn't.

'Great,' he carried on, 'a birthday break-up clapper. I'm so sorry, guys, I can't stay for lunch, I'll see you soon, I hope.' He ran into the street.

Marina rolled her eyes at them and followed him slowly; the children watched them fight on the street.

'That was a worse present than Lily in the box,' Sam said, and Violet and Kitty agreed that indeed it was.

In the car they fall into the shorthand of family.

'Is Sambo OK?' Kitty asks. 'What did he say when you told him?'

'He says that if he doesn't get a first he can blame Mum, so she's provided the perfect excuse; he's been given some sort of special academic dispensation. Has he told you about his girlfriend? She's really sweet, I met her last weekend.'

'Yes. She quotes Yeats to him as he rows. It's all very *Brideshead*, lucky old Sam. I spoke to him for an hour on Sunday.' Kitty turns the radio up. 'Do you remember this song from when we were little?' she asks Violet.

'No. You forget you're much more ancient than me. Why does Sam get to talk to you for an hour at the weekends? You never speak to me for that long.'

'Violet, I constantly leave you messages and you're either out or you never call me back. Sam is much more routine than you,' Kitty says lightly. 'He also calls me. You never do.'

'Oh well. I've been busy. I'm having an affair with a deeply unsuitable man. He's old with three children. He directed me in *Onegin*. Sometimes I take them to the park.' She looks at Kitty for a reaction.

'As long as he's kind to you I don't care how old he is,' Kitty says.

'What if I told you he was sixty?' Violet asks, taking her eyes off the road.

'Please concentrate, Violet – you're scaring the shit out of me. Even if he's sixty I don't care as long as he's kind to you. He isn't, is he – sixty, I mean?' she adds with a frown, knowing she's taken the bait.

'No, he's not. He's thirty-seven. I think I may even be in love. Can you believe it?'

'Yes. I can,' Kitty says. 'I really have to pee, is there somewhere we can stop?'

Violet is sweet and quick.

'Of course. I'm so sorry, why didn't you say before? Your bladder must be like a peanut with lots of baby pushing down on it.'

Chapter Six

Mr Fitzgerald, in life so capable and providing, was in death fatally unprepared. He had left the cupboard bare, and they were living on its crumbs. His legacy seemed to be Kitty's smile, and a hole inside of her mother that began slowly eating her inside out like a parasite.

Marina bought a small house, sight unseen, on the recommendation of an elder at the ashram. 'We're going to live a peaceful life,' she said. 'Fitzgerald's death has made me realise I can't just sit around, doing what I think everyone else wants me to do. I now have to fully embrace my spiritual life, because that is what I truly want. Do you understand?'

'Yes,' Kitty said. She agreed. She too wanted to lead a spiritual life, one free of cruel girls and unwanted deaths. It sounded lovely. She could concentrate on God and her future Swami-ji sanctioned engagement to Ram.

'Mummy doesn't want to live here any more,' Kitty told Bestemama on the phone. 'She says it will be better for everyone if we're in the country. I agree. New York is too fast.'

'Do you want to come back here and live with us?' Bestemama asked.

'I would love it, but I think I should stay here. Mummy needs me.'

'But what will you do about school, darling?'

'I'm going to go to school by correspondence.'

'What does that mean, my love?' Bestemama sounded concerned.

'The school sends me work in the post and I send it back. It'll be good – no distractions.'

'Can I talk to her, please?' Bestemama sounded angry.

'No, she's out buying a carpet.'

'All this money being spent and wasted. How is she affording all of this?' Bestemama sounded despairing.

'Don't worry, she's on a budget, I heard her say so. She's got a gallery, and people want to buy her paintings all the time – they wrote about it in the *New York Times*.'

With the furniture in storage, the house on 78th Street was more like a marble mausoleum than ever in the swampy heat. As quickly as it had come, the furniture had gone, and the house looked as though a family had never lived there, save for a naked portrait of Sam that Violet had scrawled in fuchsia on the nursery wall. Kitty found an enormous paddling pool in the basement, still in its box.

Mr Frazi had charitably offered his house in Southampton for Nora, Sam and Violet during the state of flux. Kitty had her mother to herself for a whole month, and as Marina was without love or distraction, she was starkly present, and apt for fun. Kitty was overwhelmed by the sheer magnitude of her attention, and went to bed exhausted every night, and like a child from *Opportunity Knocks*, her mouth ached from smiling and laughing.

Her mother's bedroom became a sort of designer Bedouin camp. The paddling pool lay, an oasis, in the middle of the flagstone desert. They piled all of the duvets on top of each other and at night lay side by side eating Turkish delight. They played the alphabet game, because the televisions were gone. The alphabet game was a game of insult designed for undesirable men who had betrayed them in some way. The goal of it was to artfully employ each letter of the alphabet creating suitably horrible names for the offender.

'Let's start with George,' her mother said, trailing a long foot in the paddling pool.

'No, not nasty enough. Unfair. Noah Redner. Go.'

'Anus.' Her mother said it slowly, savouring it.

'Bounder,' Kitty said quickly.

'Crawling cunt.'

'Dung fly on a dickhead.'

'Very good, darling! Egomaniacal extraspecially extraneous egg brain.'

'Fuckwit.'

'Shall we check into the Mark tomorrow? I want room service.' Her mother looked at her longingly.

'Stop cheating. If you win then we can,' Kitty answered.

'Grinching gonad. Ha.'

'Kitty, Kitty – our house has legs!' Sam was impressed. 'Legs and woods, woods and legs. I'm going to build a fort, right now. Will you help?'

She looked at Precious, who was staggering under a mountain of fur coats in the driveway, clearly regretting her offer to help over the weekend.

'I'll help you build a fort tomorrow, Sambo, OK?'

The house was at the end of a dirt track, and as well as legs it had a hot tub, and a wet bar. Her mother howled with laughter when she repeated these fixtures to her friends.

'Mum, the house has "UNIQUE features". That's what the man said. It means the house is worth more money than a normal house. I don't know why you're laughing.' Violet gave Marina a look of chagrin.

'I know, you're right, my dearest poundbuster. I just never imagined I'd live in a house with a wet bar of all things.'

'We're having the house blessed by Brahmins and Swami-ji might come.' Her mother was excited, and her hair was an unruly halo. 'Come on, we've got to start cleaning. Precious, Nora, Kitty, we have to make the house like a shrine. We need to clear the sitting room of clutter, because they're going to put a bonfire there, and we'll put lanterns down the drive . . .'

'What do you mean a bonfire in the sitting room?'

Nora gave Kitty a look of silent thanks.

'Not a bonfire in the floor, Kitty. They'll bring a pit with them.'

Nora looked relieved.

'I'll make sandwiches,' she said.

Nora spread tofu butter on spelt bread as Kitty watched. Her mother was now keeping a strict vegan household. The tofu butter didn't want to spread, and Nora stabbed holes that went through the bread on to the kitchen counter.

'Bloody vegans,' she muttered.

Kitty went up behind her and wrapped her arms around Nora's waist.

'When Mummy goes away on Sunday, we can have BLTs for breakfast. I can be vegan during the week, and have a rest on the weekends.'

Nora looked pleased.

The house with legs was filled with scarlet and orange, thick with incense and bonfire smoke. All of the female devotees were there, jammed into the sitting room, in special-occasion saris her mother had ordered from the ashram shop. Her mother told Kitty it was to encourage extra blessings, the purchase of material goods for people with less than them, to show that she wasn't attached to her money. Attached or not, she still smiled bashfully when they flocked to Kitty, to tell her what an abundant mother she had.

Marina braided jasmine in Kitty's hair, and they sat side by side, as the Brahmins threw rice and saffron on the floor in circles around them. Faces taut with kindness, their skin seemed to glow from within.

She was meant to pray to the gods with her intentions, but she could only pray to one god, because otherwise she thought her prayers would be diluted, and her god had a beard and a white dress, and he sat on a cloud, smoking a pipe like Bestepapa.

What were her intentions? She wanted to be pure and good. She wanted to be so filled with the spirit that she could not think about food or boys or being tired when she got up at four-thirty to clean the temple. She wanted to be so consumed by God that she was no longer human and did not suffer from human desires. In the lectures, the elders talked about ego. The ego was binding us to the earth, they said, and in order to attain enlightenment, they had to break free from the chains of it. Kitty imagined her ego, a long green horrid viscous thing, rooting her feet down to the hard earth, binding her from flying up to the state of nirvana, weightless and free.

On a silent retreat, where they could utter no word but this ubiquitous 'OM', she had sat at Swami-ji's feet in the dark of a small round room called the cave for three days. She thought she might go mad in the dark, looking at all of those bowed pious heads, her mother's among them. She looked up at Swami-ji, whose eyes were slits of bliss, and she listened to his 'OM', which was the loudest of all. Its bass resonance hour after hour became another heartbeat, a thought that was chopped in mid fancy flight, until there was nothing but space, and her head was finally still and quiet.

The Brahmin made them jump over the fire, as the final part of the blessing, and Kitty leapt, feeling the flames whispering at her feet. Everyone clapped and then they had tea.

Kitty still wasn't sure whether Ram fitted in to being good, even though he was a devotee. People were married in the ashram, but they didn't want to be monks. If only she could banish the thought of his smile, crooked and wide. Or the sweet hay smell of him next to her in the kitchen. He asked her whether he could walk her home, and he took her hand as they walked down the dirt path to her house. Her mother said he could stay and watch a video, and they watched *Dirty Dancing*, which was the first film she'd watched in months. When Baby lost her virginity to

Johnny, Kitty stared straight ahead and said 'OM' in her head a hundred times.

'Mum, do you think Swami-ji would mind if I had a boyfriend?' she said after she'd waved Ram a chaste goodbye.

'I don't know. You could ask him. He would probably think you're too young. I certainly have no time for boyfriends at the moment; I'm trying to work on myself. It's so funny, before we moved here, I tried so many things to feel complete, and I felt so lost and confused, and the entire time, without me knowing it, God was inside me waiting to be woken up. Just by being here physically I feel like I'm working out the dharma between Bestemama and Bestepapa. I pray for them, I pray they see God's grace like I have. I do feel loss at Fitzgerald's passing but I don't feel bereft, because I know that we will meet again, and God has a reason for everything. Fitzgerald would be so proud of you, my sweet girl.' Marina drew her close. 'You're a good girl; you know the right thing to do. Trust your instincts.'

Kitty stopped getting her period, but that was OK because enlightened beings didn't menstruate, that's what they told her mother. Shortly afterwards Marina stopped getting hers too. Kitty was happy. She felt proud of her body's ability to translate the spiritual transformation that was occurring within it.

'Don't tell Nora,' her mother said. 'She wouldn't understand, she'd be worried.'

Kitty lived on delicious sugary chai, it made her feel awake, and warm. She couldn't really be bothered to eat much of anything else, because it interfered with the lovely weightless feeling of spirituality. Sam and Violet ate ras malai and coconut sweets to their hearts' content, and soon mango lassis took the place of Mars Bars for Marina's frequent bribes.

The lake was close to the house, and by August it was warm from a summer's worth of sun. Her mother woke them before dawn, and they walked along the forest path, which Marina had paid to have landscaped, in their pyjamas, their swimsuits underneath.

'Listen, the woods are waking up. Can you hear the trees talking to each other?'

Sam and Violet, holding towels, listened intently.

'Yes I hear them! They're talking to the birds.' Sam beamed.

'That one is old and grumpy; he doesn't want to wake up,' Violet said, cocking her head to the sky.

'Do you see the spider webs? They're not really spider webs; they're hammocks that the fairies sleep in.' Her mother pointed, holding a finger to her lips.

'Where are the fairies?'

'They've gone to have their morning bath in the lake. If we're quiet we might see them.'

They slipped into the water, like thieves of the morning. Her mother lay on her back floating.

'I'm going to take my swimsuit off,' she said. 'The water feels too blissful not to.'

'What if someone sees you?' Kitty asked, shocked.

'No one's going to see me. Why don't you all do it too?'

Kitty wriggled awkwardly out of hers, and swam it to the bank so she didn't drop it.

* * *

Mornings bled into nights. The mantra, for she had finally been entrusted with her own, played like a record on repeat in her head. Was it dawn or dusk that met her as she walked down the dirt track in her sari, on her way to give the statue of Krishna his daily ablutions?

She did not see Sam and Violet; she did not see her mother. Each of them was entrusted with their own lone spiritual practice, and that was the path with which they trod the summer. Kitty floated on air, garlanded, fully made-up and bejewelled at all times, knowing that this was what she had been born for.

'Swami-ji asked me whether we were all right financially during Satsang,' her mother said. 'His concern was so loving. I said we didn't have much money left, because of my donations and buying the house, but it didn't matter, now we have the house, and our own expenses here are so low. I said that we were rich with spirituality and for the first time in my life I didn't care about material possessions. He smiled and he touched my hand. He told me that God would provide for us.'

Kitty heard her mother cry sometimes, and she did not know whether it was for grief, devotion, or both. She knew that whatever the reason, God would take care of her mother, and all of them. They were his children, and that was what he was meant to do.

Ram's arm brushed against hers, as they mixed the batter for the dosas.

Warm and solid, he whispered in her ear, 'Come and meet me in the woods later.'

'OK,' she said.

It gave her a pain, this proximity. She felt like her nerves were on fire. What if he wanted to kiss her? Did she have time to go home and brush her teeth first, and rub orange blossom behind her ears? The last time she had done this, it seemed to work. He had told her she smelled like heaven, and asked what scent she was wearing.

'None,' she had answered. She thought it should be a secret.

'That's because you're an angel. You smell like that naturally.'

The woods sang of earth and mystery, and Kitty wondered if she would come upon the ghost of an American Indian. She felt like an interloper, and walked carefully, quietly, so she did not disturb whatever ancient magic went on there at nightfall.

Ram leaned up against a tree; he held a guitar. A cigarette dangled from his lips.

'Hey.'

'Hi.'

Kitty sat carefully down next to him, arranging her legs. She had a scab on her knee, and she draped her hand casually over it so he wouldn't see it.

'You want some of this?' he said.

'I don't smoke.' Her voice sounded prim in the dark.

'It's a joint.'

God was testing her. He had put a snake in the body of a handsome boy and he was testing her to see if she was good.

'I don't do pot either.' Kitty shook her head firmly.

He laughed.

'You don't DO pot. You smoke it. That's OK, it's all good.'

He smoked with pleasure, and the musky smell fitted in, somehow, with pine and earth. He ran his finger up and down her spine.

'Such tiny bones,' he said, 'like a little bird.'

She did not feel tiny. She felt clumsy and awkward. He bent his head towards her. All right, God, I'll make you a deal, she thought. If I let him kiss me on the lips, but with no tongue, then technically I'm not doing anything that wrong. I didn't smoke the pot, so I am still pure.

He kissed her.

'No tongue,' she said frantically.

'Shush,' he said.

Their lips met, and it didn't feel wrong, it felt like peace. Her eyes were open and Kitty watched his face to see how he did it.

They kissed like this for a long time, with their mouths shut, and he kissed her face, her eyes, and her temples as if she was a marvel, or some uncharted foreign land.

'I have to go home,' she whispered. 'My mother will get worried.'

'Don't go,' he said.

'I have to. I'll see you tomorrow?'

'Tomorrow. I'm going to sit here for a while and pretend you're still with me.'

The shower rained frigid water down on her, cold enough to freeze all of her hot thoughts in their tracks, and she chanted, soap cascading in foamy mountains all over her body.

I am cleansing away all impure thoughts; they are washing down the drain. I know you tested me, God, but I am still made of flesh, it won't happen again, I will perform any duty you ask of me, to erase spiritual dues incurred by my act of passion. Did you not wrestle with the same mortal desires? Help me, show me the way. Swami-ji, I'm sorry I have betrayed you; forgive me, I'm only a girl . . .

'Kitty!' her mother called from the door.

'I'm in the shower.' Did her mother not realise she was in no place to have banal conversations? Kitty was having an epic worthy awakening with a bar of rose Castile soap.

'What?!' Kitty said.

'Hurry up. I have to talk to you. Something has happened.'

Her mother's eyes were dull and red.

'We're going back to England,' she said. 'Swami-ji has seen some bad karma coming up for us here. We will only be safe from it in England. I asked him what I should do about the house because I bought it with the last bit of big money I had, but he said it didn't matter, that it was more important just to go, he would look after it. I can't work out what I did wrong. I tried so hard. He said that I'll take him with me wherever I go, but it won't be the same. What could I have done? Am I that bad?'

Kitty looked down at her arms. They were red from scrubbing. It was me, she thought. He knew I couldn't control myself. He was saving me. He is the all-seeing; he knows what everyone is doing all of the time.

'What time did this happen?' Kitty said in a small voice.

'I had an audience with him two hours ago. We were looking for you. We're leaving tomorrow morning.' Her mother's forehead looked clammy, her hands shook.

'Can I say goodbye?' Kitty asked.

'No. He thought it would be best if we left quietly without a fuss. I'm sorry.'

They packed throughout the night, silently, taking just their clothes. Her mother said it was best to let Nora sleep and tell her in the morning. Everything else could come later, her mother said, by ship.

They are waiting for the train to come in, the heating covering them in smoky bursts of air.

'When do you think it all fucked up, Kit?' Violet says. 'Was it when we left Hay? Everything seemed fine before then, happy even. Did it all get mad when we left for New York? Do you think we were too much for Mum to cope with?'

'I think there were problems before we left Hay, but I think that they were contained because of Bestemama and Bestepapa. I think we just remember halcyon days; I don't know that it was ever perfect. It seemed like Mummy always needed a father figure to moor her, whether it was Bestepapa, my father, a Swami-ji, God . . . so she could run off and do her thing, knowing that they were in the background to pick up the pieces. I think when Mr Fitzgerald – I can't believe I still call him that in my head! – my father died . . . I don't know, maybe then she realised that she was truly on her own. Maybe that's why we moved to the ashram – she was too proud to go back to Hay. And then, when that didn't work, because she wasn't as rich as they thought, that was when it all really went to shit, because she felt like she had nowhere else to go.'

'I used to think it was my fault,' Violet says. 'I thought we got in the way. Do you remember when we used to sing to her? We were tiny and we used to sing to her to make her laugh? It's so surreal . . . I thought that if I was quiet and good then somehow she wouldn't be so sad.'

'I think we all felt that. I felt that way until pretty recently. But it wasn't our fault, not really hers either. She was so young and ill equipped, and they didn't really know about depression. She was younger than you when she had me.' Kitty stares at Violet through the dark.

'We're OK though, that has to be a testament to something, doesn't it?'

'Look, there's Sam!'

Sam lopes down the platform, in a navy pea coat. He looks like a man, Kitty thinks.

'All right, sexy!' Violet shouts.

Kitty begins to giggle.

'Shut up, Violet. Kitty, how was your flight?'

'Good, thank you, darling. How was the train?'

'It was all right. I sat next to an old man who kept touching my leg and calling me "my boy", so I had to move. How's the Yank?'

'Sorry he couldn't see you both; he can't miss work. They're brutal with how much time they give him off; he's a slave to the man now. I always thought I'd marry a poet, but no, I'm literally sleeping with corporate America.'

Violet lights a cigarette and says, 'All right. We're all here now. We're allowed to go there late, irrespective of visiting hours, because I said you were flying all the way from America. Are you starving? Do you want to go home first for supper or shall we just get it over and done with and go straight to the mental ward?'

Kitty begins to laugh hysterically at the absurd banality of the question, and Violet and Sam follow.

They sit in the car park, rendered immobile, lapsing into calm until Sam mutters, 'Mental ward!' and they are all beset by hysteria again.

Somewhere Violet's laughter turns into sobs.

'It's not funny,' she says. 'I was there.'

'I know, sweetheart,' Kitty says, rubbing her cold hands. 'I know.'

Violet buries her face in Kitty's neck and cries.

Chapter Seven

'We are on an adventure. We don't need things to weigh us down,' Marina told Sam and Violet, who asked her why they had to leave their toys behind. They sat in disbelieving silence, looking at her red eyes dubiously. Marina held close a small leather bag which contained her one and only wedding dress.

They flew back to England first class because, her mother said, they were first-class people.

'But I thought we didn't have any money,' Kitty whispered to her in the British Airways lounge.

'I bought the tickets with air miles,' Marina said sharply. 'Please be quiet. I can't hear myself think, I've got such a headache.' She took a pill from her bag and sat back with her eyes shut. Nora sat with Torty on her lap, grim-faced. She hated flying and upset.

It was a long day. From the airport Violet and Sam were dropped off with Nora at Peter's, whilst Kitty and her mother went straight to the accountant's office. Kitty wasn't allowed in. She sat on the squeaky leather sofa and read about sex in *Cosmopolitan*. Her mother's lips wobbled threateningly when she emerged, four hours later, rigid-backed. Kitty heard the accountant say, 'Well, you're just going to have to get painting.'

In the taxi Marina whispered as she looked out of the window, 'Doesn't anyone understand? I have to be relaxed to paint. It's not a reflex.'

She had begun to wring her hands like Lady Macbeth. Kitty didn't know whether she was meant to answer.

A friend of her mother's, Sarah, had lent them her house in Clapham. She was in Poona, finding herself. It was on a street with row after row of redbrick houses that had a uniformly mean look about them.

'I don't like this house,' Sam said.

Her mother's lip resumed its alarming wobble.

'Come on, Sambo,' Kitty said. 'It's a nice friendly house, like in *The Family from One End Street.*'

Her mother turned the key. The house smelled of old parties. They all stood there.

'Well, come on, gypsies, let's set up camp!' Elegantly stepping over mountains of bills her mother beckoned them in like Grace Kelly.

'It's lovely,' Kitty said. 'I bet there's a secret passage . . .' She held out her hand. Violet took it gingerly.

Sam remained on the doorstep in the damp darkness.

'I'm sorry,' he said. 'I can't come in because a sorcerer, an evil one, put a spell on this doormat and I'm stuck, glued here for eternity.'

'Bad luck,' said her mother. 'We'll be having tea, if the spell should break.'

'God,' she whispered to Kitty, surveying the decrepit hall. 'She could have found a bloody cleaner before she went to find herself.'

Kitty spent a month taking the bus to a flat in Fulham where she was tutored by a Rubenesque redhead surrounded by enormous knickers that hissed as they hung from the radiators to dry. Finally, she was deemed scholarship material.

They had two choices, her mother told her, an all-girls Catholic school in Chelsea, or a 'progressive' school in North London that had boys. Her mother felt she would learn more about the world at the boy school. 'I think it will be more diverse,' she said. 'And they have a fantastic arts programme.'

The term had already begun. Kitty didn't know anyone her age in London, and Rosaria was tucked away at Dourfield, lands away in the country, eating sugar sandwiches. Marina gave Kitty £200 and told her to get some sensible clothes that were suitable for school.

'But where should I go?' Kitty asked her.

'I don't know. The King's Road?'

She decided to get some Levi 501s, white ones. The girl in the shop had great big arched eyebrows like Elizabeth Taylor. Kitty asked her what size she thought she was, because she didn't know.

'Twenty-four waist,' the girl said, as she cocked the eyebrow and carried on reading her magazine.

Kitty got so nervous in the changing room that she bit her thumbnail to the quick and she realised when she put the jeans on that they were speckled with her blood like rust. The jeans were too short.

'I'll take these,' Kitty said, handing her the jeans, which she'd folded up.

The woman unfolded them. She took in the red smearing their snowy perfection.

'How disgusting,' she said. 'Forty pounds.'

Kitty decided good underwear and hair were more important than clothes anyway. She took a taxi to Beauchamp Place and bought a silk bra and knickers for £97.50. The bra, a 32B, was a good investment for her future life of romance, she felt.

She walked into a hairdresser's called Bardots. An Irish man with sparkling eyes called Callum asked her what she wanted.

'Highlights?' Kitty said, confused.

'Wicked,' he said. 'You'd make a great blonde, really bring out your eyes. The mousy look is not for you.'

Two hours later, with a stinging scalp, she emerged with swinging hair the colour of treacle. A man getting out of a cab gave her a searing grown-up look. Kitty looked away, and turned to look back. He was still looking.

'Hi,' he called.

'Hello,' she said.

'Would you like to join me for a drink? In that pub?' He was flushed like a boy.

'I'm sorry but I can't. I have to go home,' she said.

'Can I have your phone number?'

She didn't want to be rude to him. He looked fragile somehow. She gave him the number and ran off into the dark, smoky afternoon to catch her bus, back to the safety of Clapham Junction.

Nora and her mother were in the kitchen drinking tea and looking secretive when she walked in.

'Good afternoon, fair gentlewomen of the south,' Kitty said, afraid that her mother might be angry with her wanton purchasing.

'My darling heart,' she said. 'Please tell me that there are lots of nice sensible jumpers hidden artfully in that Janet Reger bag.'

'No, there aren't. Sorry.' Kitty tried to look winning beneath waves of treacle. 'The woman in the shop was mean to me, and I bled on the jeans, so I had to buy them, and I didn't feel like shopping after that.'

Her mother smiled a bit sadly.

'Oh Kitten. You look like jailbait.'

'Thank you,' Kitty said. 'Also, I did a stupid thing. I gave a man my phone number on the street because I was embarrassed, and I didn't know what to do, so if he rings could you tell him I don't live here?'

Nora gave Kitty her doom look, and said gloomily, 'Oh, you're not your mother's daughter for nothing.'

And at this her mother laughed for the first time in weeks.

Kitty wore her new too-short white jeans to school, with a Vivienne Westwood cardigan that she took from Sarah-in-Poona's wardrobe.

Nora caught her, as usual.

'That doesn't belong to you,' she said.

'Well, she left it. I mean she's not going to need it, she wears saris now.' Kitty buttoned it around her tightly, and crossed her arms.

Violet screeched from upstairs.

'Nora, I don't want this uniform, it's disgusting. Where are my pink leggings?'

'See what you've done? Jaysus help me. I give up.' She spun out of the room like an angry wasp.

Kitty found some pale-pink suede boots with a vicious

stiletto heel and put them on. She wobbled down the stairs before her mother saw her and fettered the outfit entirely.

'Goodbye, Mummy,' she sang up the stairs.

'I'll pick you up, OK? We can have tea at the Savoy for a treat,' her mother called drowsily from her bedroom. 'I love you,' she added.

Her school was perched at the top of a hill in Islington, its Gothic spires twisting up to the sky, as though it were waving to God.

At this school if you were a girl you were either a beck or a hippy, or you were just hard. If you weren't hard, a beck or a hippy, you were a loser and that's all there was to it, she realised. The becks wore jeans, much longer than hers, with tight bodysuits and bomber jackets from French Connection. They had poker-straight hair and Tiffany necklaces. They shopped on Hampstead High Street. They smelled sweet and powdery, like Narcisse by Chloé or Trésor. The hippies wore vintage faded cords and rainbow sweaters and Doc Martens boots. Every Saturday they went to Camden Market and bought bootleg Dylan tapes. They were in love with Alex James from Blur, with his long swinging hair and downcast eyes.

The becks didn't go to clubs, they 'went round people's houses' and watched the boys get stoned. The hippies went to gigs and stage-dived, they were long and pale and vegan, the object of derision for the raggamuffin boys who moved down the halls, Walkmans on, bouncing to the beat of their drum and base music. Kitty didn't understand most of the things the raggas said. Every sentence was followed by 'innit'. Like a question. 'Your jeans are too short, innit?'

Kitty was neither a beck nor a hippy. Her hoop earrings were too small to be hard, and she didn't have a Stüssy jacket. She was too tall and blonde to be a loser. The boys decided Kitty was a substitute teacher.

'Oi, Miss! You're really tall, innit? Where do you live? Miss, have you got a boyfriend? Who are you dealing with?'

Honor Freeman was the exception. She was neither a beck nor a hippy, and she became Kitty's best friend. She had skin that was white like the moon, and eyebrows like a silent-movie star's that just grew that way. She had the cleanest fingernails Kitty had ever seen. Honor was friends with everyone.

Kitty wanted Honor's family to adopt her. They were all so nice and sensible. They lived in a mock Tudor house in Highbury, and they couldn't understand why her mother had sent her to school so far away from where she lived. They thought it wasn't responsible.

'Oh Kitty, you must get so TIRED, you poor lamb. That awful journey from Clapham . . . You can come and stay the night with us whenever you like.' Honor's mum Ruth gave her a look of sorrow. Kitty smiled bravely at her, trying her best to look tired and woebegone.

'We'll get some meat on your scrawny goy bones,' Honor's dad, Roy, said, passing her a huge slab of challah bread dripping with plum jam from their garden. Kitty was happy to be called scrawny.

Everything about Honor was lovely. She sang in the school music group and her voice was sweet and otherworldly. The girls at Kitty's other schools had always hero-worshipped Kitty's mother and couldn't wait to spend the night at her house, but her mother's swearing and eccentric friends made Honor nervous, and she always had piano lessons or Amnesty International when Kitty asked her to stay for the weekend.

'Why can't Honor come here?' her mother said crossly, as Kitty set off to the tube station with her backpack yet another Saturday morning.

'She can't. It's Ruth and Roy's twenty-fifth wedding anniversary. They're having a drinks party and we're going to be the waitresses.' She shrugged.

'Well, bully for Ruth and Roy.' Marina gave Kitty a black look. 'We're your family, and SOME people would feel very lucky to have such a fun young mother.'

'It's got nothing to do with that,' Kitty said. 'I just do different things there.'

'What sort of different things?' Her mother looked miserable, and she felt guilty.

'Nothing really. They're so nice. You'd like them.' Kitty knew this was probably untrue. She imagined her mother in Ruth's pristine kitchen and knew that they would hate each other.

'Well, have fun in suburbia.' Her mother waved, and Kitty left bolstered by a blithe creeping power from her upset.

'Can I use the phone?' Kitty asked Ruth.

'Yes dear, do you need to call your mum?'

'My grandmother. I won't be long. I need to tell her something.'

'Bestemama? Guess who?'

'Kitty? Darling! Ingrid told me you were back – she

spoke to Mummy briefly. I'm so happy that you're in England. Are you all right?'

'Yes. I'm fine, thank you. I'm in the school play, and I have a friend called Honor Freeman whose house I'm ringing you from and she's in the school play too.'

'That's marvellous news. How is everyone? Are you going to come and stay? I've forgotten what you like. You can bring your new friend.'

'I can't because of my play rehearsals; but I promise I will soon. I'm a 32B bra size.'

'Golly. Well, we have news, or Elsie does. Would you like to talk to her?'

'Where's your mad mother?' Elsie said, coming on the line.

'She's at home. She's not mad. What's your news?' Kitty felt wrong talking about her mother.

'I'm moving to New York! I'm going to work as an assistant at *Vogue*.'

'That's so unfair!' Kitty said. 'Now I'm back and you're leaving.'

'You can't get rid of me. I'm your family,' Elsie said. 'You're stuck with me for ever.'

Kitty told her about school and the new house.

'Well, it sounds moderately more sensible,' Elsie said. 'Come and stay with me in New York. Bestemama wants to say goodbye.'

'Bestemama, in the school play a boy named Dylan O'Sullivan has to pinch my bum after my dance, because Matthew the drama teacher says it creates sexual tension.'

'My goodness,' Bestemama said. 'What sort of play is this?'

* * *

'Why can't Dylan pinch Selena's arse?' Kitty complained to Honor, after rehearsal. 'She'd like it.'

'Matthew thought it should be you, because you look innocent and like you mind.'

'I do mind.'

'It's only acting.' Honor could say that; she had a soaring solo and didn't have to wear a cheap fringed flapper dress.

'I'm sorry about having to pinch your arse, yeah?' Dylan O'Sullivan stood by the bus stop, engulfed by his Chipie puffa jacket, the Dream Warriors pounding out from his Walkman.

'It's OK. Well, it's not, but you know what I mean.' Kitty tried to scurry past.

'Nah. I said to Matthew, it's DEMEANING to Kitty, yeah? But he won't listen, says it's method acting, innit? Poof. My mum thinks it's a disgrace.'

'Does she?' Kitty couldn't imagine Dylan's mum.

'Yeah. Cause she's an original feminist, innit? She was gonna complain to Richard.'

Richard was their bearded headmaster, a peaceful man. He blushed when her mother came to parent-teacher evening and clutched his hand to emphasise her point.

'Oh no. That would be really embarrassing. Let's not make a fuss.'

She noticed in the gathering dusk that Dylan had really green eyes. Suddenly the thought of him not pinching her arse was sad.

'It's only acting,' she said. 'Don't worry.'

'You going to the tube?' Kitty nodded. 'I'll walk you there. By the way, I'm sorry I took the piss out of your jeans before.'

'That's all right. They're longer now. I didn't know.' She smiled at him.

They ran down the hill, and at some point their arms linked, and they talked so much he got on the tube with her all the way back to Clapham, and her mother sent him home to Kilburn in a radio taxi on the only account of Mr Fitzgerald's still active.

'He seems like a nice Irish boy,' Nora said. 'With a lovely colour to him.'

'He is, he makes supper for his granny every night. He said she's his feminine inspiration,' Kitty said. 'His dad is a lawyer from Tobago.'

Kitty noticed her mother spending a lot of time on the phone and waiting anxiously by the fax machine. She thought more bills needed to be paid. But then the flowers started to arrive. Moyses Steven's vans double-parked outside the house as delivery men staggered in, orange trees dripping sweetly before them. The lovebirds came next, in an antique wicker cage, christened with obscure names from T. S. Eliot. Her mother was clearly bubbling to tell, but she pruned her orange trees and chattered to her lovebirds, murmuring into the phone long through the night, in a secret shorthand that was incomprehensible and flagrantly annoying.

'Have you noticed anything about Mummy?' Kitty said to Nora.

'No.' Crossing her arms, Nora shook her head.

Kitty pressed her, but she was tight-lipped and unyielding.

A telegram came. Her mother tore it open, greedy-fingered, the envelope turning to confetti in her white hands.

'What does it say?' Kitty said. She decided that being proud was no way to get information.

'The Magician's in town,' her mother incanted, stroking the paper.

'What does it mean?'

'It means he's here.'

'Who's he? Barry?'

'God no!' her mother said. 'Jenkins. Jenkins is here.'

'Who's Jenkins and why is he a magician?' Kitty asked.

Her mother smirked.

'Because he can do magic,' she said.

'God, you're so disgusting. I don't want to know about your sex life. Yuck.'

'No, he does proper magic. Tricks and things. That's not what he does for a living though. He's a composer.' She said this rather grandly.

'Mum, have you noticed a theme in your choice of men?'

'I happen to like sparky people, that's all. Magic has nothing to do with anything.'

'Well, when did you meet him, and why don't I know about him?' Kitty felt affronted.

'I haven't seen him since I was a teenager; he was the first man I kissed,' Marina said.

'No, he wasn't. The first man you kissed was the doctor's son.'

'He was a boy. Do you want to hear or not?'

The story of Jenkins was long and complicated and seemed to involve a lot of wives and children. Kitty pointed this out.

'That's all incidental,' her mother said airily. Jenkins kissed her when she was fifteen, at a party where Princess

Margaret wore red shoes, and danced (quite well) with Omar Sharif to a song by the Kinks.

'Get to the point,' Kitty said.

'I'm setting the scene, Kitty. The details are important.'

As she spoke her mother's face was lit with colour and memory. Kitty saw the party, the long curved mahogany staircase, the dress like a cobweb, Jenkins asking her mother to dance, and kissing her long and hard, until she was dizzy with kissing and felt as though she were a complicated coat, whose buttons he had mastered, and hung up finally with great care.

'Yes and then we went and sat down and he introduced me to his wife.'

'Oh no he didn't!' Kitty said, like the pantomime child she longed to be.

'Oh yes he did,' her mother replied.

Jenkins was staying at the Athenaeum on Piccadilly. They were going to have lunch.

'Why don't you run in and get him?'

Her mother double-parked her Beetle outside and was putting on lip gloss, oblivious to the furious honking that she was incurring.

'I'm not going to know him,' Kitty said.

'Yes, you will. He'll be the most ravishing man in the lobby. Anyway he'll know you. Go on.'

She couldn't see anyone remotely ravishing in the lobby. It was full of overfed tourists. She wondered what to do. A tiny, wild-haired man came up to her and clapped her on the back causing Kitty to scream in terror.

She glared at him.

'Yes?' she said imperiously, thinking he might assume she was a lady of the night hanging around in the lobby.

'You're a bit of a chip off the old block, my darling!' he boomed, kissing her firmly on both cheeks.

'Jenkins?' she said, incredulous.

'Indeed, indeed. Sorry to startle you, Magpie. You look so like your mummy.'

No one but her mother called her Magpie, yet she didn't mind. She loved him immediately. He wore a shell suit, and the pouches under his eyes would have housed a baby wallaby, but he reeked of fun.

He grabbed her arm.

'Let's get some nosh,' he said.

Within five minutes Jenkins had possessed the hearts of everyone in the car. Sam, Violet and Kitty sat, sardines in the back, hanging on his every word.

'Is that old man your father?' Sam whispered.

'No, he's Mummy's boyfriend. My father's dead, remember?'

'Oh yeah. We got Torty when he died.'

As he talked, the hands of Jenkins danced. They foxtrotted across the table, one moment reaching up to stroke her mother's ear, tenderly, the next wandering off on a tangent about his politics, stabbing at the air like a pickpocket's knife.

With his hands, Jenkins conjured up the faces and sizes of his four sons, who lived with their mother on a horse farm in Montana. Each boy was a different inflection, a story untold, until, crafted through his father's fingers, he was real, as real as if he were sitting right there with them in the steamy womb of the Italian restaurant.

The oldest, Tex, could tame and ride a wild horse bareback, and every animal he met was putty in his hands. Kitty immediately wanted to meet this Tex and have his babies.

The little one, Otis, was a small tender gesture, painted as shy, with glasses and a love of books.

Her mother looked over at Jenkins proudly, like he was something amazing she had found, and brought to the classroom for show and tell.

Jenkins didn't talk about the mother of his boys, but alluded to the fact she had American Indian blood. This made her supremely glamorous in Kitty's head, a tough, fearless Bukowski beauty, presiding over her pride-of-lionheart boys.

Jenkins wanted to know what each of them wanted to be when they were older.

'Bus driver,' Sam said.

'A sensei.' Violet had recently discovered a passion for karate.

'Admirable strong professions, both.' Jenkins gave them a nod of approval, under which they glowed.

'And you, Miss Kitty, what will you be?'

'A writer and perhaps a contessa.'

Jenkins looked grave.

'Where will you live in your titled splendour?'

'Oh I should think in Venice, in a decaying palazzo with a melancholic count.'

'Why is the count melancholic?' her mother asked.

'He just would be. Family curse, dark past, I don't know.'

'What about Count Dracula?' said Sam. 'Then Kitty would be a vampire, which would be quite interesting.'

'I'm in love with your children and I'm in love with you,' she heard Jenkins say to her mother.

'When will you come back?'

'I just need to sort a few things out. I will be back as soon as it is humanly possible. I don't think I could survive without your face for many weeks.'

'You managed to before.' Her mother looked down sadly.

'Jenkins, can we come and see you in Montana?' Violet pulled at his hand.

'Princess Violetta, I shall bring Montana to you.'

'How can you do that?' Sam gave him a doubtful look.

'My dear boy, I am a magician. I can do anything.'

They all believed him.

The flow of faxes was a gushing river, the flowers coming three times a week, like clockwork. Nora became very tight with the Moyses Steven delivery men, and often returning from school Kitty found them having a cup of tea and a chocolate digestive, telling Nora dirty jokes.

In these months her mother painted her best work. Bleak landscapes that went on and on, with glimmers of light if you looked hard enough. In her self-portraits she could have been three different women at the same time. There was a soft ripeness that replaced her girlish lines.

When Jenkins rang, he always spoke to Kitty after her. They had inside jokes, words, nicknames. It was as though he had been ready-made for them.

Kitty told Honor about him, and his sons, and the thick of passion that swam through the house, causing each of them to be dizzy and restless.

'You speak like it's a story. Something from a novel.' Honor folded wax paper carefully around what was left of her brown bread and avocado sandwich.

'It is though. It's the most romantic thing I've ever heard. They found one another again, after years of being with the wrong people. They are each other's one.'

Honor and Kitty spent many hours talking about the ONE.

Dylan O'Sullivan could be the one in a few years; he has potential,' Kitty said.

Honor shook her head sagely.

'Dylan O'Sullivan needs to grow. He's too short to be the one. The one has to be at least four inches taller than you.'

'Jenkins is moving in with us!' Sam opened the front door before Kitty got her key in; his face was a huge smile. 'Mum's gone to pick him up from the airport. He's moving in with all his clothes and everything! A truck will come and bring it all after he gets here.'

She kissed Sam with smacking noises all over his little neck.

'It's going to be so brilliant. Get off me, disgusting, it's going to be so brilliant. He'll teach me magic and we'll go to the park and the fair and he can pick us up from school . . .'

'. . . and what about his work? When will he work?'

Sam gave her an indignant look.

'He's going to have a something beginning with S which means a holiday. I heard Mummy tell Nora.'

Jenkins directed a group of baffled removal men, wearing her mother's pink towelling dressing gown and no slippers on the street, to the astonishment of Sarah-in-

Poona's neighbours, whose curtains twitched with excitement. In his hand he held a large Bloody Mary. He had thin bandy legs like a malnourished child.

Kitty had been given the day off school to help unpack. Nora was not happy. Jenkins tried to dance down the street with her whilst she was clutching a bust of Mozart's head.

'"Fly me to the moon, and let me play among the stars . . ."' Jenkins sang.

'Are you moving in or not, Mr Jenkins?' Nora said icily.

'I'm just trying to have fun whilst I move,' said Jenkins, chastened, and he sang with less volume for a bit.

Her mother whistled and shone, and embraced Jenkins every ten minutes.

'Where's the pub?' Jenkins asked after supper.

'What, my darling?'

'Where's the nearest pub? I need my drink.'

Her mother made her worried face.

'I don't know; I've never been. Do you know, Kitty?'

'Why would I know where the pub is? We can go and find one.'

'Yes, of course we can, we'll find one, I'm sure. Isn't there one on Lavender Hill?'

'Yes, I think so,' Kitty said.

They set off in the dark, and they passed by many pubs.

'Not old-fashioned enough,' Jenkins said. 'Not good enough to be my local.'

'What about this one?' Her mother pointed. 'This one looks nice and jolly.'

'No.' Jenkins shook his white head darkly. 'No it doesn't.'

After two hours the mood in the car had shifted. Every pub within a two-mile radius had been deemed unsuitable.

Her mother's hands tensed on the wheel of the car, and she bit her lip.

'There's one!' Kitty called, her voice sounding shrill. 'Look, that one is exactly as you described, Jenkins, exactly.'

'Fine.' He looked straight ahead, and it was difficult to work out what he was thinking, which frightened her.

'A pint of Guinness, my good man, with a chaser of brandy.' Jenkins was jovial again, and he looked as though he was born to drink in the pub Kitty had found.

She ordered a Diet Coke, and her mother had a gin and tonic. Now he was happily ensconced in the pub, things went back to how they were supposed to be. Kitty breathed out. Jenkins became expansive and rubbed the small of her mother's back with the hand that did not have a drink in it. Her mother began to unfurl. Affection and jokes puffed her up, until her eyes were half moons of pleasure.

Jenkins drank five pints of Guinness that needed seven shots of brandy to chase it on its way. The bell rang for closing time, and Jenkins looked sad.

'The loneliest sound in the world, that is.'

As they left, her mother gently leading him like a stubborn sheep, he sang a raspy rendition of 'Eleanor Rigby', which made Kitty's bones ache with a hopeful sort of sadness.

The hands did not dance with life in the morning. They did a jerky puppet dance, like Baron Samadhi come to commune with the dead. Quiver and shake. His coffee cup rattled, a little typhoon contained in ceramic.

Kitty saw her mother get a miniature bottle of whisky from the fridge, and pour it neatly and without words into his coffee. The skin under her eyes looked like a child had squashed a lilac crayon there.

He reached up and kissed her mother's nose.

'Thanks, Fred,' he said.

Kitty studiously ignored the moment, Jenkins reading the paper, her mother stirring porridge. She picked up her backpack.

'I'm going to be late for school,' she said.

'Bye, darling! Have a lovely day!' her mother called.

'Knock 'em dead, tiger,' Jenkins growled, saluting her.

The first phone call Kitty got on her own phone line was from Dylan O'Sullivan. The phone was an old-fashioned one, where you dialled the numbers with your fingers. Her phone number ended 0070. Sam called it her Bond line.

'Kitty, you're so posh, innit? One phone not enough in your house?'

'My mum said that teenagers use the phone all the time and she didn't want to vie for the phone with me. Which is a bunch of crap because I'm not on the phone that much. Did you ring me to insult me?' Kitty pursed her lips, but inside she was happy.

'Nah, I just rang you to say all right.'

'All right, Dylan?'

'Yeah, I'm all right,' he said.

Sam and Violet built sandcastles, the sky overhead close and grey with rain unshed. Their fingers were blue, but they worked tirelessly under Nora's supervision. They were building a citadel, with pebble walls.

Her mother and Jenkins were sitting on the beach, deep in conversation.

'Do you think they ever get bored of each other?'

Rosaria said, watching them closely from the bench she and Kitty had chosen.

'They don't seem to. They find each other really amusing.'

It was Easter. Her mother decided that they should get the sea air. She and Jenkins said Torquay would be a 'jaunt'. Kitty wanted to go to Cap Ferrat, and wear a dress of broderie anglaise, whatever that was. Violet and Sam didn't care as long as there was sand and buckets and spades. Kitty insisted that Rosaria come, because sometimes her mother and Jenkins left her out.

They were staying at the Imperial Hotel, whose long corridors were empty like *The Shining*, and her mother stayed in bed till noon, joining them for lunch, sleepy and bad-tempered.

Jenkins loved Torquay in its off-season squalor. He made the children accompany him to the funfair every morning, where they were the lone riders on a rollercoaster whose rickety skeleton caused Kitty to well with panic. His appearance was more eccentric than ever due to the haircut she had given him. Her mother told him that he desperately needed a trim and Kitty volunteered, saying that all of her friends let her cut their hair she was so good, which was a big lie.

She liked the idea of someone putting their head in her hands and trusting her; it made her feel warm and important.

They gathered in the Imperial Suite. A round room, where her mother and Jenkins slept, with heavy velvet curtains and a piano, which faced out to the impassive sea.

She borrowed scissors from the front desk. She draped Jenkins in a towel, and rubbed his white head thoughtfully, examining him from all angles.

'OK,' Kitty said. 'We shall begin. You need layers.'

Sam and Violet sat on the bed, eating jelly babies as they awaited the transformation of Jenkins.

At one moment Kitty's haircut had potential, but it was brief, and she realised with each final snip that cutting hair was not her forte.

'Perfect. Finished.' She rumpled the limp strands.

Violet and Sam started giggling.

'Great!' Jenkins smoothed it down. Hair sprang up in wild tufts.

'I look like my hero Ken Dodd. You are clever, Kitty.'

There was a pause. Her mother, from the bed, began to quake with laughter.

'That is the ugliest haircut I've ever seen in my life. Jenkins, you're lucky I love you so much, because you could now PLAY Ken Dodd in a film biography. Good thing no one's making one.'

'Kitty, my lamb,' Jenkins said. 'You are good at a plethora of things, but I don't think hairdressing is among them. We must immediately go out and get rosettes for a prize-giving. I win as the recipient of the ugliest haircut ever given in the world, and you as the bestower of said haircut. We will have a celebration tonight, following the prize-giving. Fred, you will give out the prizes. Sam and Violet will perform a re-enactment of the tragedy; Rosaria will be the barmaid, and Nora the director. Fred in bed is also the audience.'

Fred became Fred-in-bed-a-lot, because Jenkins kept her up all night. Back at home he shouted and raged like the devil himself, after which there was dark silence and she heard her mother cry, ragged, like a piece of barbed wire.

Kitty heard them through the floor. So did Sam and Violet. They crawled into her bed.

'Can you turn the television up there off, Kitty?' Sam said. 'I don't like the programme that's on.'

'Let's pretend that we're on a boat, Violet is the captain, Sam is the oarsman. I'll be first mate,' Kitty whispered, pulling them close. 'We're escaping the old country, and we're going to an island where they eat nothing but rice pudding and drink coconut milk, and they dance on the shore, and toys grow from trees. Before you go to sleep there there's a royal arm tickler, whose only job is to tickle your arms. The king of the island is a big jolly man who looks like Father Christmas in a skirt, and the queen is the tooth fairy. Shall we row?'

'Yes,' the twins said in unison, their small starfish hands pressing against her.

After the crying, there was the making up, which she couldn't give a form to, because she had nothing to relate it to. Murmurs, soft molasses sentences that culminated in gasps, and breaths and the bed creaking. Her mother's pleasure sounded like surprise.

The house was still then, and her mother and Jenkins slept, oblivious to dawn, or the milkman.

Sometimes the phone rang, late in the night, but there was never a voice, just a crackle that sounded like it came from seas away. When her mother answered, and was greeted with silence, she hung up crisply, but if Jenkins and she were out, at dinner, or drinking with one of his many friends at the Chelsea Arts Club, Kitty hung on for minutes, repeating 'Hello, Hello?' deep into a space that did not answer her.

Marina wanted to show off Jenkins to her friends. She took him like a prize to many dinners and Sunday lunches and his charm spread infectiously throughout her mother's circle of friends.

They drove down to the country to have lunch with Katie, who had a title and a new husband. Lily in the box was with the old one for the weekend. Nora loved going there because they always got good food, and after lunch she could take Sam and Violet to the estate farm to see the sheep and collect eggs from the bantams who nested in the barn.

When Kitty was little she thought that she must have lived at Slip Hall in another life because being called for dinner by a bell and having someone turn down your bed and warm it before you got in it seemed so utterly natural to her.

Jenkins made Katie's wizened deaf Aunt Tory, who sat in state permanently affixed to her chair by the fire, blush and twitch like a schoolgirl. She was usually allowed one watery sherry before lunch, but Jenkins slipped her sly tumblers when no one except Kitty was looking. She drank them as though she had been in a drought, her rheumy eyes sparkling with gratitude.

At lunch Jenkins sat between Katie and Kitty, and he did magic tricks with the napkin ring, and whispered jokes that made Katie clutch the pearls at her neck and giggle.

Oliver, Katie's new husband, looked over in disdain.

'Where is it you live – Jenkins, is it?'

'I'm living with Fred and the brood in Clapham,' Jenkins replied, kicking Kitty under the table.

She swallowed a laugh.

'Yes, but where are you FROM?' Oliver curled his lip.

'Bromley by Bow,' Jenkins answered him, his gaze unwavering and clear.

'Oh. Quite. How novel.'

Katie rolled her eyes. Kitty saw her mother talking to the bishop next to her in an animated way; he looked slightly dazed and was nodding vigorously.

After lunch, Kitty went with Nora, Violet and Sam to the farm. Kitty felt the same thrill as her seven-year-old self had when she pulled an egg brown and warm from a hole in the hay. They walked down the lane and watched the lambs, gawky and unsteady, teetering away from them to the safety of their mothers.

Jenkins appeared, equally lamblike in his gait, yet there was nothing soft about his face, which was stretched into an unfamiliar mask.

'We're leaving.'

'What about tea?' Sam looked disappointed. He loved tea.

'No. No tea. We're going. Your mother's saying goodbye to Katie. I'll be in the car.'

Kitty looked at Nora, who shrugged her shoulders.

In the car everyone was quiet. Jenkins drove, very fast, his mouth a thin slash.

'Is something the matter?' Kitty said.

Nora gave her a warning look.

'Yes. Something is very much the matter,' Jenkins said. 'That man, that filthy unspeakable man . . .'

'Not in front of the children, please,' her mother said dully.

'No, fuck it. Kitty should know. That filthy little man

insinuated that I had some sort of disgusting interest in you.' Jenkins' voice trembled like reeds.

She didn't understand.

'What do you mean?' She felt like things were shattering in her head.

'I mean that he thought I was interested in going to bed with you.'

'Jenkins, please!' Her mother turned to him beseechingly.

'But that's not true! You're like my father . . .' Kitty shouted. 'That's bloody disgusting!'

Her brain couldn't connect this information to the rest of her. She thought she might be sick. All the way back to London she sat with her forehead pressed against the window, not looking at anyone, suffused with shame.

'If I told you something, could you keep it secret? Kitty asked.

Jenkins was playing old Rodgers and Hammerstein songs on the piano her mother had bought him.

'Yes. I'm good at secrets.' He took a swig of his Martini.

'I think, although she wouldn't admit it, that Mummy really misses her parents, even though she seems angry with them, and I think that the reason she's still not talking to them is because she's stubborn, not because she's truly angry . . . They didn't really do anything – they were just worried. I think that if you and I went to see them, and they met you, and saw how well everything's going, how happy you make her, that they might all make up. You're very persuasive, and I know they'd like you. We could surprise her. I've thought about it, and we could go on Saturday when Mummy goes to see Charleston. We could go on the train. If that happened, then everything would be perfect, more perfect then it is now even. What do you think?'

Jenkins rubbed his stubble. He paused.

'I think it is kind and dear and it absolutely has to work. I love a mission. Saturday it is.'

Jenkins bought first-class tickets, and they sat in the smoking car. He wore a fraying grey tie, and a white linen jacket, whose creases matched his own.

He sat down and ordered a bull shot. He opened a game of Travel Scrabble.

'Could my wife have a drink?' he said to the attendant.

'Jenkins!' Kitty said. 'He's not really my husband.' She felt herself turning red. 'He's just making a joke.'

'Don't be bashful, darling. I picked her up in Mississippi. Lovely, isn't she?' Jenkins wouldn't stop the game.

'What do you want to drink?' the attendant said as if Kitty was stupid.

'Orange juice, please.' She kicked Jenkins under the table.

'Ha! That'll give them all something to talk about,' Jenkins said after the attendant went away.

'Look at the fields! Look at the sheep! Look, the station's coming – that's the bridge that I had to walk under to get to school. We're here!'

Jenkins took a deep breath.

'It's beautiful,' he said, putting an extra-strong mint in his mouth.

Bestemama was wearing her big straw hat, and knelt over the lavender bush, her eyes narrowed in concentration.

Kitty called out, uncontained, running towards her. 'Bestemama, my Bestemama!'

Bestemama dropped her pruning shears.

'Kitty! Oh my Lord! Kitty, what are you doing here? You're so tall! Harald, Harald, look! Kitty's come home!' Kitty threw herself upon Bestemama, who held her tightly, laughing as she murmured Scandinavian terms of endearment, which rolled over each other, breaking gently.

'I decided to surprise you,' Kitty said.

'What a wonderful surprise. How did you get here . . .?'

Bestepapa came out of the front door slowly, resting on his stick.

'What's this noise for, woman?' he said. 'Can a fellow not have his forty winks in peace any more?'

He stopped abruptly when he saw Kitty.

'Is that my little one? Standing in my garden?'

'It's me,' she said.

He yelled out, dropping his stick, and tears bigger than normal tears fell from his eyes, coming a cropper in the craggy obstacle course of his face. He wiped them away with his huge hand.

'I knew you'd come back,' he said. 'Where's everyone else? Where's Marina? Where's my favourite Irish harpy?'

Kitty remembered Jenkins then, who when she turned to look, was teetering on the edge of the drive, as if he were afraid to commit to the lawn.

'This is Jenkins,' she said.

'Would you like a drink, Mr Jenkins?' Bestemama asked.

'I'd love a Bloody Mary. Don't worry, I can make it.' Jenkins poured himself a tumbler three-quarters of the way full with vodka, and the tomato juice that followed made a thin pink cloud on top.

'Jenkins is a composer,' Kitty said. 'And a brilliant musician. You should hear him play,' she added proudly.

Jenkins held up a shaking hand, as if to halt her, and put it quickly back on his lap.

'My agent here.' He smiled at Kitty. 'I'm on a sabbatical. I'm researching a book on Mahler.'

After lunch, Bestepapa took them to see his greenhouse, and Kitty knew that he liked Jenkins, and was glad.

Her mother was wrapped thinly against her chair, her arms crossed, when they came in through the door. Her collarbone protruded from her dress and she looked tired.

'My love!' Jenkins ran to her. 'How was Charleston? Was it magical? Do you want to get rid of me and run off with a Bloomsbury painter? We've been to market, Kitty and me.'

'I know where you've been,' her mother said, ignoring him. It was the first time. She looked up at Kitty. Her eyes were scornful.

Her voice was quiet but the quietness roared like the loudest shouting.

'If you ever, ever, do something like that again, behind my back, without my permission, I will send you back to boarding school, and you will stay there until you are eighteen years old, do you hear me? I've just had Bestemama on the phone for an hour, trying to interfere, talking about the company I keep, worried about you and Sam and Violet. I am your family, not them. I am your mother. If you ever try to undermine my authority again, I will punish you and you will live to regret it. How dare you?! How dare you do this to me, to us?!'

'She was trying to help, Marina, she was doing something pure. Besides, it made them so happy. They liked me too.' Jenkins put his hand on Kitty's arm, like a barrier.

'No, they did not. They did not like you. They said you were a common charming drunk. An old drunk.'

'They did like me,' Jenkins said. 'I know they did, I'm likeable. Your father showed me his greenhouse. Kitty says he doesn't show it to just anyone.'

'They appreciated you like people appreciate vaudeville,' her mother hissed.

'People like me,' he said. This last statement was delivered to an empty chair.

Kitty nodded mutely, as if to say yes, you are likeable.

'Kitty, wake up!' Her mother shook her. 'You have to help me, I can't find Jenkins, he's gone.'

'What? What do you mean he's gone?' She sat up. 'Is it the middle of the night?'

'No. It's two. Come with me. I'm going to find him.' How young her mother sounded in the dark, she thought.

'Can I get dressed?'

'No, there's no time for that. Just put a coat over your nightie.'

The street hung with whips of fog. A black cat ambled in their path and made them both jump.

'Is it good luck or bad?' her mother said desperately.

'What?' Kitty pulled her coat around her and hoped the neighbours weren't watching.

'The cat. I can never remember whether it's good luck or bad if a black cat crosses your path.'

'I think it's good.' Kitty squeezed her mother's hand.

Three streets down, they caught sight of him. He was weaving in and out of the road, his hair white against the black backdrop of night. He looked cinematic.

'Follow him,' her mother whispered.

'What's he doing?' Kitty asked.

'He's dancing.'

They watched Jenkins waltz by himself, taking sips from a brown bottle. He clung to a lamp-post lovingly, as if it were a lifebuoy and he were being washed out to sea.

Her mother stood in front of him with her arms crossed.

'Hello, Fred,' Jenkins said politely. 'Hello, Kitty. Nice night for it. My funny valentine . . .' he sang.

'Come home, Jenkins,' her mother said. 'It's late. Kitty was worried about you. Look, she's in her nightdress.'

'Oh why oh why does everyone always spoil my fun?' Jenkins said like a little boy.

'Come on, darling, please?' her mother pleaded.

'My funny valentine, I had a valentine in Montana. I have to go back there, my favourite suit's there. I have to go and get it; it will be lonely without me.'

'We'll get your suit, darling. We can have it sent tomorrow, all right?'

'No it's not all right. It's all very wrong indeed, Fred. The ladies come and go, they speak of Michelangelo. I will come back if you dance with me, both of you.'

He took their hands and they began an awkward ghost waltz home.

* * *

'I can't believe I'm at a children's party. I must really like you, Kitty.' Dylan watched Jenkins pull a coin from behind a bespectacled child's ear. The other children cheered.

Jenkins wore tails and a tall satin top hat. Sam wore a white rabbit's costume and Violet was, inexplicably to Kitty, Puss in Wellington Boots.

'Sam and Violet will now take you on a magical mystery tour, the likes of which you have never seen, through the tunnel of Zadora . . . Quick, follow them . . .'

Her mother had spent all night painting wooden packing boxes with snowy landscapes, and fairies dancing through pine trees.

'He's pretty good. I'd have him at my party . . . your mother looks foxy!' Dylan nearly dropped his Ribena.

Her mother came out in a black swimsuit over fishnet tights, black suede pixie boots.

'Ah ha, my magical assistant, recently exiled from the wilds of Slovenia. Please welcome the lovely Marina!' Jenkins spun her around the garden.

'Good afternoon,' her mother said in a throaty Baltic drawl. 'Ze forest can be perilous; each of you will need an invisible crown of safety.' Solemnly she placed a pretend crown on each child's head.

'I feel like such an ass.' Marina came over to where Kitty and Dylan stood, and sneaked a puff of Dylan's cigarette. She held hands with a tall boy, who had a big gap-toothed smile.

'Kitty, I want you to re-meet Tommy. You used to play together when you were little, do you remember? He's Natalie's son, he went to St Paul's till GCSEs. Aren't you at a tutorial now? I thought you should meet because he lives three streets away. It might be nice for you to have a friend who lives close by; and is slightly older . . .'

'How do you do?' Tommy said politely.

'St Paul's, eh?' Dylan said in his best rude-boy effort. 'That's a posh school, innit?'

'Oh Dylan,' Marina said. 'Isn't your mother in advertising?'

Tommy blushed.

'Hi,' Kitty said. 'Ignore him, he can't help it.'

'I'm so glad we've discovered Tommy again; it's perfect with him only down the road. All of her other friends live so far away; I mean where is NW8? What is Jenkins doing?'

Marina looked over at him lovingly; he was pretending to be frozen in the forest, as Violet waved a wand around his knees.

'Three cheers for Sam and Violet! Three cheers for you all! And three resounding cheers for my divine assistant, Mrs Marina Jenkins!'

Her mother looked stunned.

'Do you mean it?' she said quietly.

'I mean it more than I've ever meant anything. You, this, Violet wellington boots, you're all my life. We're a family now. But do let's buy a new house; Sarah-in-Poona's really won't do for all the babies I'm going to give you, the menagerie we'll have.'

'Oh Jenkins,' her mother said, melting into him.

Violet was waiting for Kitty by the garden gate.

'Jenkins has gone home to get his suit,' she said, 'and Mum won't stop crying. She says he won't come back but I know he will, because he loves us. I said don't worry, Mum, Jenkins will come back tomorrow, but that made her cry more. Do you think you can make her stop? I said she could have my pocket money, but that made her cry more as well. She's being very difficult.'

'She'll be all right,' Kitty said automatically. 'I'm sure she will. It's probably a joke or something. It was nice of you to offer her your pocket money though.'

'I thought so too.' Violet remained by the gate, like a cat waiting watchfully for its owner.

Kitty walked into the house. Her mother lay in the sitting room on the huge lily-pond rug, Thumbelina dissolving. She barely looked up when Kitty walked in.

'He's gone,' she said to the wall. She scratched at her arms, and made a noise that was so dark and deep Kitty shivered.

'What do you mean "gone"? He hasn't gone far . . . he's a wanderer. He'll come back in a few days, like always. Shsh, Mum, you're going to frighten the little ones.' She sat down on the floor next to her mother and stroked her back.

'I don't give a fuck about anything except for Jenkins, don't you understand? Nothing. Without him there's no point.'

'Well, what did he say? How do you know he's gone?'

Her mother looked through her.

'He said nothing. He said he was going back to get his fucking suit. Then he left. I just know in my heart that he's not coming back. I just know.' She made the animal noise again.

Nora opened the door and looked at Marina with a mixture of sorrow and disdain.

'I'm taking the children to the park, Marina,' she said.

Kitty put her mother in bed. She made a facecloth cool and laid it on her brow, and brought her a tray with a boiled egg and soldiers.

'I don't want it,' her mother said. 'I just want Jenkins. Please turn out the light and make it really dark in here, my head hurts so much. Can you call the doctor and get him to come; my head feels like it's going to explode.'

'Dr Cartwright?'

'No, the other doctor, his name is in my Filofax, under doctor. Call him now, please.'

The other doctor was smooth and handsome, and he came as quickly as a snake in the night. He carried a leather bag that rattled.

'Would you like a cup of tea?' Kitty said.

'No, I'll just pop up.'

They went into the darkness together.

'Is that the doctor?' her mother said in a small voice.

'Hello, Marina. What's the problem? A migraine again?'

'A terrible one. I can't bear the light.'

'I'm going to have to turn it on so I can give you an injection, OK?'

'Kitty, can you leave me with the doctor now, please?' Her mother pulled herself up and squinted at her.

Kitty didn't want to go, and she hovered by the door.

'I can take over now.' The handsome other doctor smiled at Kitty.

'What's wrong with her?' she asked him twenty minutes later as she showed him out.

'Just a migraine. Your mother suffers from them periodically. She'll be fine tomorrow.'

'Good,' Kitty said. 'Thank you.'

Kitty watched him get into a clean navy-blue Renault as he prepared to zip off to wherever he came from. She saw him look in the mirror before he drove off, and adjust his tie, and she wondered if he had a date.

They are gathered in her mother's house at Strand on the Green. Kitty looks in the fridge trying to find something to make for supper. It is empty save for four half-opened bags of rocket, and a chunk of Parmesan cheese. She feels that she has stumbled into something intimate and private; the barrenness of the fridge intimating something more than the lack of a visit to the supermarket.

'There's some risotto rice,' Sam says hopefully.

'That's ambitious,' she says. But she takes it, and opens the cupboard to find a pan.

Violet sits on the Aga as Kitty stirs. She remembers a childhood story, 'Stone Soup', in which a group of people come together and make a feast out of nothing. There is a bottle of Pernod on a shelf, and she pours it into the pan, filling the kitchen with a definite aniseed life.

'Will you ring Nora?' she asks Violet.

Violet dials Nora on speakerphone.

'Hello?' Nora says.

Kitty imagines her walking to the phone in her navy-blue cardigan, faintly annoyed at someone with the gall to ring in the middle of *Question Time*.

'It's us!' Violet says. 'All calling you from Mum's kitchen.'

'What are you doing there? Who's us?'

'All of your babies, me, Sam and Kit.'

'Hi, Nora!' Kitty and Sam clamour in the background.

'Are you on that bloody speakerphone thing? I can't hear you; you sound like you're in an aquarium.'

'We're cooking,' Kitty shouts. 'Nora, Mark is so excited that you're coming in January; he thinks we'll have a tidy house and an immaculate, well-mannered Anglo-Irish baby.'

'More fool him,' Nora laughs. 'New York again, after all this time. Who would have thought?'

'Don't you want to know why we're all here?' Violet says.

'I suppose so,' Nora says guardedly. 'I know you shouldn't all be there.'

'Mum had a black dog day,' Violet says.

As they lay the table Kitty sees one of her mother's yellow legal pads on which is written in black ink 'Do I dare disturb the universe, in a minute there is time, for decisions and revisions which a minute will reverse . . .'

They sit in their mother's kitchen, surrounded by her things. Her pug Little Dorritt sits on Violet's lap.

'Does she need clothes?' Kitty asks Violet.

'Yeah, she was taken away in a negligée. The ambulance men were thrilled.'

Upstairs Violet does pliés in her mother's bathroom as Kitty opens the wardrobe.

Chapter Eight

'We need an infusion of fun, Magpie,' Marina said. She and Kitty were lying on the sofa watching *Camelot*. 'I think you should have a birthday party, a belated one. Christ knows, you and I could use a party.'

'But, Mum, I don't know anyone that well yet, just Dylan and Honor . . . what if no one comes, and where will everyone fit?'

'Those are just petty logistics – we'll make everyone fit. It'll be cosy and intimate. We must make the best of the space we have. It's called imagination, and I know you have lots of it. Maybe I should dye my hair the same colour as Guinevere's, what do you think?'

'No,' Kitty said. 'It's really far for everyone to get here, and what if they trash the house?'

'Of course they'll come; that's how you get to know people, you throw parties. No one will trash the house, I'll be here. We'll have a disco, and all your girlfriends can stay the night.'

Tommy from three streets away was invited with his friends Ollie and Naim so the boy-girl ratio was equal.

'Tommy has lovely manners,' Marina said. 'It's good for you girls to meet boys with good manners. He wrote me a thank-you letter after Sam and Violet's birthday.'

Kitty didn't care about Tommy's manners. She was in love with Nicky, the sexiest boy in her year, who didn't have any.

Nicky didn't talk to her exactly; he placed her in a headlock in biology and watched as she froze under his touch, like a lab rat hypnotised by fear.

'You're having a party, innit?' he asked, his pale arm right next to her mouth. Kitty wanted to lick it.

'Yeah,' she muttered, sweat stinging her eyes. He had a gold tooth, and she wondered whether the dentist put it in, how it got there, into his wide smiling mouth.

'Am I invited?'

'Yes. Of course.'

'Wicked. See you there.' He bobbed off leaving her so weak she had to go and see Ruby, the progressive school nurse, for some Rescue Remedy.

Kitty wore a Lycra wasp dress to her party, with her mother's Donna Karan tummy-control tights. The DJ played songs that she had heard on *Top of the Pops* and the girls swayed like wildflowers in a field, while the boys stared mutinously from a dark corner. Bryan Adams's summer hit song from *Robin Hood* was playing. The girls looked desperately over to the boys, but no one moved. Except Nicky. Nicky swaggered over to her as the hired smoke machine belched out a plume of dry ice.

'Kitty do you want to go for a walk?' he asked, his voice curiously normal.

'All right.' Kitty smiled up at him, on fire.

Outside it was cold. She heard the buses rumbling towards Clapham Junction. They walked halfway down the street, silently. Nicky guided her by the elbow into a neighbouring driveway. He pushed her up against a black Saab and kissed her, his tongue darting in and out of her mouth. He smelt of vodka, horniness and pizza. My first French kiss, Kitty thought, concentrating on what exactly to do with her tongue.

With moist hands he grabbed the straps of her dress and pulled them down, swiftly exposing her breasts to the street.

'Please?' Kitty said in weak protest.

'Sorry,' he said. 'It's just you've got really beautiful tits.'

'Do you want to go back inside?' she said covering her nipples.

'Yeah. We can be private.' He looked excited.

In the house he propelled her towards the cellar.

The darkness was black and thin like Indian ink.

'Hello,' Kitty said, wanting to be like a romantic heroine.

'Stop talking. Just kiss me,' he said, his hand burrowing insistently up her dress.

The Donna Karan tummy-control tights caused a thankful passion intervention. They were impenetrable.

'Can you just take those off?' he asked.

'I think I have to go back upstairs, I can hear the doorbell. People will be leaving. I have to say goodbye.'

'Fuck's sake.' He sounded disgusted.

Kitty bolted through the blackness upstairs to see her mother dancing alone, her eyes shut dreamily, like nothing else mattered.

'Mum, the pizza man needs to be paid,' Kitty said.

'Jenkins was an incredible dancer,' Marina said.

As all the girls lay on Kitty's bedroom floor, Camilla said to her, 'Did you get off with Nicky?'

'Yes,' she said.

'Well, you're a really bad friend – I've liked him since the first year.'

'She didn't know that,' said Honor. 'It's not her fault if he fancies her and not you. Don't be such a drama queen.'

Camilla lay in silence and refused to speak to anyone.

'He took my top off on the street. I was so embarrassed,' Kitty whispered to Honor.

'I hate it when they do that,' she answered wearily.

Kitty walked into the kitchen after everyone had left and found her mother staring at the lovebirds with tears in her eyes. Kitty put her arms around her.

'Thank you for my party, Mummy,' she said. 'Everyone had fun; they said it was the best party all year, much better than Greta's and she's got a swimming pool.' She searched her mother's face for a clue, but it was closed.

'I told you no one would trash the house. They're not very wild for a bunch of teenagers.' Marina sounded disappointed.

A week after the disco Kitty woke to strains of fun coming from her mother's room. It sounded like somewhere she wanted to be. Along the hallway drifted the ghost of her mother's scented candles and Marlboro reds. She got out of bed and padded down the hallway, knocking at the door, excited.

'Enter!' her mother said.

She was in bed, VH 1 blaring, and she had a pleased look about her.

Lying next to her, prone, was a ravishing woman, fast

asleep, a tangle of baby blonde hair and whistling snores. Kitty gazed at her in fascination. She began to grind her teeth so ferociously Kitty jumped.

'Stop that!' her mother commanded. Kitty held her breath. The jaw quieted. Her mother looked smug.

'Poor darling, it's a wonder she has any teeth at all . . . Morning, Magpie.'

'Morning,' Kitty said faintly.

There was a bellow down the hall.

'Marina! I do hope you're not decent,' followed by Violet imploring, 'Billy, have you bought me a chocolate croissant?'

Her mother's friend Billy swaggered in clutching a paper bag, shadowed by Violet and Sam whose eyes were round with longing like hungry orphan children's.

'Mum, why is there a lady in your bed?' asked Violet.

'That's no lady,' said Billy.

'Woman. Not lady, Violet,' corrected her mother.

'It's my friend Candy. We went to a party and she came to stay the night afterwards, because we were far away from her house. Isn't she pretty?'

'Suppose,' said Sam.

Billy rocked with laughter, and muttered, 'You are the end. The end. I know who that is, she's a deal . . .'

'*Tais-toi*, Billy . . . *les enfants*,' her mother said, looking at him innocently.

'*Je comprends, Maman*,' Kitty said, because she didn't want to be left out.

Candy slept on, resolute as a soldier after battle won. Violet and Sam sat at Billy's booted feet, pretending to be dogs as he threw them scraps of chocolate croissant. They played Pictionary until four, when Marina decided it was time to get dressed.

At four-fifteen Candy rose like Lazarus, rolling one brown eye lazily around the room. She didn't seem alarmed.

'Mornin',' she said cheerfully. She had teeth sharp and pointed like a little vampire's. 'OHHH, I could murder a cup of coffee.'

'Darling, you're SUCH a sleeper,' Marina told her admiringly.

Kitty smiled at her.

'I'll make you a cup of coffee,' she said.

'Would you? You're an ANGEL. You must be Kitty, your Mum's told me all about you. I must say you really are sweet, look at your little face.'

Kitty decided in the kitchen that Candy would be her new best friend, after Honor.

At the end of the road there was an Italian restaurant called La Dolce Vita. Kitty was dispatched to get pizza for Sam and Violet. Candy came with her.

'I love pizza when I'm hungover,' she said. 'That and a Coke with loads of ice for breakfast.'

The pizza boys were in raptures at the sight of Candy.

'Is that your sister, *bella*?' they asked Kitty, making hot eyes at Candy.

'No, she's my friend.'

Candy giggled.

'My sister and I want a big pizza,' she said. 'A very big one, with lots of cheese, and a bit burnt, if you don't mind.'

They set them up at a table while they waited, and

brought Candy a Malibu and Coke on the house. Kitty ordered a Coke, but she didn't drink it.

'What do you do?' Kitty asked her. 'Are you an actress?'

Candy smiled.

'I'm in between jobs. I used to be a dancer. I've just had my heart broken by this guy I was going to marry. So I'm taking some time off, discovering myself. I've been reading lots of good books . . . Have you read *Women Who Love Too Much?'*

Kitty shook her head.

'Epic, it's like it was written for me. I try and fix people. I keep attracting bastards, though . . . Oh well . . . I'm trying to concentrate on going out and letting life happen.'

'How did you meet Mummy?' Kitty said.

'Oh I met her last night at this mad warehouse party. She's brilliant – it must be really fun to have a mum like yours,' Candy said. 'My parents are really boring and middle-aged. You're so lucky; your mother's very bohemian, being an artist and all that. She's a bit tragic, in a good way.'

'What do you mean tragic in a good way?' Kitty said, trying to imagine her mother at a warehouse party.

'Like Judy Garland was tragic, or Virginia Woolf. Really creative people are sometimes; they just carry it with them. You can see it in their eyes. It helps if they're beautiful.'

'Do I have tragic eyes?' Kitty asked her.

'No, sweetheart. Clear happy eyes, with a bit of mystery to keep things interesting. I'm an only child. I bet you never feel lonely, being surrounded by so many people. What's it like?'

'Not very private,' Kitty said.

'Oh darling, privacy's really overrated, trust me. One day you'll realise, you and your brother and sister, you'll link each other together. Explain things to each other. It's like the archaeology of family; you'll be each other's pasts. The only link to my past is a blind Labrador called Dolly. Oh, that is so sweet!' The pizza boys presented her with an enormous pizza in the shape of an oozing burnt heart.

On a frowsy day, from the phone box by her school, she rang the number Candy had given her. She was put through to the switchboard of a hotel. 'She's sleeping,' the northern voice on the other end of the phone said, thick with cigarettes and warmth. 'She's a bit poorly.' Kitty decided she would bring Candy some chicken noodle soup.

The Admiral Crichton Hotel was a crooked Georgian house off Camden High Street. The hallway was the colour of a miner's lungs, and behind a Perspex window sat a birdlike woman painting her nails electric blue.

'I've come to visit Candy,' Kitty said.

'Well, let's see if we can rouse the dead.'

The woman got up and led her through a maze of corridors. They arrived at room 109 and the woman thumped loudly on the door.

Kitty heard a shuffling from within followed by a sulky, 'What?'

'You've a visitor, darling.'

'Who is it?' Candy sounded angry. 'I'm not expecting anyone. If it's Stu tell him to bugger off. I told him not to come till eight.'

'It's Kitty,' Kitty said apologetically. 'I bought you some soup.'

'Who? Marina's Kitty?'

She nodded enthusiastically, and then remembered Candy couldn't see her.

'Yes. Marina's Kitty,' she said.

'Can you open the door with the master, Moira? I don't think I can move.'

Moira the bird woman opened the door.

In the dark, close room, incense smoke hung in the air like a memory.

'Hello, babe.' A voice sounded from what Kitty thought was the corner of the room.

The bedside light was turned on, and there was Candy, six feet of curves and angles sitting up in bed, wearing a pair of cream silk pyjamas that were exactly the same colour as her hair. She stretched out a long silky leg. Kitty stood in the middle of an ocean of mess, clothes and half-eaten bars of chocolate, magazines, lipsticks and twenty-pound notes.

'Sorry about the state in here, I had another late one,' Candy said.

'Did you want something for your mum?' She gave a lusty cough.

'No. I bought you chicken soup because I thought you were ill.' Kitty held out the warm container and felt stupid.

'Thank you, that's really sweet.'

Candy lit a cigarette. Kitty tried to think of another reason she might be there, in this virtual stranger's bedroom.

'I'm going to this club on Friday night and I don't know what to wear,' she said.

'Which club?'

'Hanover Grand, it's called. There's this boy . . .'

'And you fancy him?' Candy said.

'Yes, and I think he's forgotten I exist. I got off with him a few months ago and he told everyone at school I was frigid, and he hasn't spoken to me since.' Kitty looked apologetic.

'Men,' Candy said. 'Well, we better find you something to wear, so he remembers that you very much do exist. How do you feel about satin?' She beamed at Kitty, and she didn't feel stupid any more.

In Candy's satin trousers, she felt nearly sexy.

Honor had two friends she'd known since nursery school who were models. They were called Lola and Miriam. Lola had honeyed skin with gooseberry-green secret eyes, and Miriam was pale and wan with the tautest stomach she'd ever seen. Of the two, Lola was the official beauty. She carried her sexiness like a queen wears a crown, as though it were her birthright to walk into a room and cause pandemonium. Kitty wondered how it felt to wake up and be Lola.

She knew that Honor did as well, because when they went out on their own, and boys asked their names, Honor was automatically Lola and she Miriam. With new alter egos they were different creatures, the sort of girls who broke boys' hearts and never waited for a phone call. As Lola and Miriam their jeans didn't give them stretch marks, they hung confidently from protruding hipbones. Their large breasts were suddenly not cumbersome and matronly, they were pert and tiny, little question marks of sexuality.

Honor's mum did not like Lola. She thought she was common.

Marina loved her. They smoked cigarettes together, wearily, each puff easing the burden of being so beautiful, so wanted. Lola told them of her boyfriend Benny, who loved her so much he sat outside her house in his Golf convertible, just to be sure she wasn't out with anyone else.

'Sometimes,' she said to Marina, 'sometimes when we do it, he cries.'

Her mother roared with laughter.

'God, how sweet,' she said.

Kitty thought it was, but didn't say anything.

'I think it's really gay.' Lola gave a hard laugh.

Poor Benny, Kitty thought. If it were me, I would have cried back and asked him to marry me.

Lola called Hanover Grand 'Hand-over-a-gram'. She and Kitty went on models' night. Entrance was free if you were a model. The bouncer tried to charge Kitty twenty pounds but Lola told him strictly that she was with Elite New Faces.

He looked her over, sighed and said, 'Oh all right then.'

Honor and Miriam were already there sitting by the bar in the VIP room.

'Did they think you were a model?' Honor whispered.

'Yeah,' Kitty said.

'Me too. So is Nicky coming?'

'I don't know – I heard him tell Dylan he was.'

'He's a wanker. I can't believe he never rang you after you snogged him,' Honor said.

A boy with long hair, who looked like a girl, walked over and said to them, 'I'm James. Nice to meet you.'

'Angela.' Honor flicked her hair.

'Amber,' Kitty said.

They smiled at each other guiltily.

Lola had some ecstasy that weeping Benny had given her.

'They're doves,' she said. 'Really pure.'

Kitty's heart started to beat faster than the drum and bass that was playing. Swami-ji had told her she was really pure, that she should never be a follower, and that moral corruption was everywhere. But Swami-ji was not in Hanover Grand, she thought, and Swami-ji had grown up in a village in India, not in urban London. She was sure people didn't offer him grade A narcotics when he was a teenager. Kitty was tired of being GOOD all of the time.

She shifted her Wonderbra, so her cleavage had more of a V.

'I'll do it with you,' she said.

Honor scowled at her.

'You need to keep drinking water, yeah?' Lola said maternally.

'OK.'

Kitty put the pill in her mouth with a swig of Bacardi and Coke. She could never swallow pills dry. Down it went. She immediately had the urge to go and throw up. What if she died? Dying whilst pretending to be a model at Hanover Grand would be a truly sad end.

In the bathroom she put her fingers far down her

throat. She retched but nothing else happened. She did it again and again. She did it until her throat felt raw. 'Fine fucking bulimic you'd make,' she said out loud to herself.

'Kitty?' She heard Lola outside. 'Kitty, can I come in?'

'I'm coming,' she said.

She noticed outlines of cocaine all over the cistern. Smeared like snail tracks, marching down the porcelain, the ghost of so many strangers' fun.

'I wanted to be with you when you came up,' Lola said. 'Let's go and be by the music.'

Kitty had never been able to dance properly to hardcore before. She felt awkward and chalk white. The electronic opening of Candi Staton's 'You Got the Love' pumped into the room and filled it like smoke. Tendrils of feeling went shooting up her arms and down her legs. Her veins coursed with her very aliveness, the crown of her head felt like it had been opened and was suddenly a direct conduit to everything that was divine and perfect in the world. She felt seamless and liquid and sexy.

Kitty grinned at Lola like a maniac.

'Your eyes are enormous. You look like a gorgeous alien!' Lola said, laughing.

James the boy who looked like a girl whirled over and danced next to Kitty.

'Are you all loved up, babe?' he shouted.

'Yes,' she mouthed back at him. 'I think so.'

She thought she saw Nicky among the crowd, but she didn't care. She didn't want to find him; she wanted to keep dancing this strange dance, just her arms weaving in the air, leaving trails of phosphorescence in their wake.

She was inside the song inside herself and she never wanted to leave. Kitty wanted to ring her mother and tell her that religion didn't need to be so complicated. You could find it in a nightclub, in a seething snaking damp mass of strangers, people who for that moment loved each other with the ferocity of the world.

'Are you out of your fucking mind?' her mother said. 'You could have died! I'm taking you to see Dr Cartwright. You've probably got brain damage.' She was shaking with anger, her already white skin blanched with rage.

Kitty started to cry again.

'Can you keep you voice down? I know you're angry but I've got such a headache.'

'Yes!' her mother said. 'That's what's left of your brain melting!'

'I'm just having a comedown,' Kitty said. 'It's textbook.'

'Textbook?! Why can't you lot take coke? Why do you have to take mind-altering drugs that could kill you?'

Kitty put her head on the table, which was cool and steady.

'How do you feel?' her mother said, wringing her hands. 'What are your symptoms?'

'Mummy, I don't have an illness. I did something really stupid, which I really, really regret, and I'm tired and I just need to go to bed.'

It was the evening. They had been having this discussion since her return home, where she had blissfully thrown up on the doorstep, and confessed everything. She had not yet slept.

'Fine. Not fine. But – you will sleep in my bed, and we're calling Lola to see where she got these bloody pills.'

'Please don't,' Kitty said weakly.

'No. I will. I think she's clearly a VERY BAD INFLUENCE. You should spend more time with Honor. I never liked Lola . . .'

Kitty banged her throbbing head against the table.

'Are you having a flashback?' Marina asked anxiously.

'Mum, please!'

'Day off school tomorrow. You can help me do my book-keeping – we're besieged by bills. And – you're grounded for six months.'

'OK.' She was in no mood to argue. She never wanted to go out again.

Her mother woke her in the middle of the night.

'Kitty?' she said.

'Yes, Mummy?' Kitty sat up. She heard the familiar old inhale of a cigarette.

'Nothing, I just wanted to be sure of you.'

'I'm fine, Piglet,' Kitty answered as when she was little. They had always played this game from *Winnie the Pooh*.

After her cigarette was extinguished, and she was sure, her mother fell asleep in the crook of her arm like a child.

In her dream there was an alarm, a fire alarm, and she had to get everyone out of a rickety tenement building, but she couldn't see because there were wooden chairs blocking the way, which she had to throw over her shoulders like a lumberjack. When the alarm was at its most persistent, Kitty woke and realised it was the phone, ringing next to her bed. The clock told her it was four o'clock in the morning.

'Hello?'

There was a crackling silence. Then a voice, a husky old sad voice.

'Kit-kat?'

Her heart speeded up.

'Jenkins, is that you?'

'Yes. I'm in Hawaii. You'd like it here.'

She didn't tell him what time it was because she didn't want him to hang up.

'How are you?' Kitty whispered.

'Not good. Very bad in fact. I miss you all, I miss your mummy.'

'We miss you too.'

'How's school? Does Nora still hate me?'

'She doesn't hate you. School's fine, boring.'

'I miss you all,' he said again.

'Jenkins, why don't you ring Mummy? It would make her so happy.'

'You have to come to Hawaii with me one day, you'll love it. Sam and Violet could learn to surf. Your mummy could drink from a coconut and sit under a big umbrella so she doesn't burn her lovely skin. We'll go, I promise . . .'

'I'd like that. Jenkins, please call Mummy, she's so sad now. She cries a lot.' Kitty felt disloyal as she said this.

'I can't, you won't understand but I can't, but I do love her more than anything in the world, I need you to know that. I need you to believe me.'

'I believe you.'

She heard a woman's voice, playful in the background: 'Who are you talking to, baby?'

'I have to go. Don't tell your mother I called.'

'Jenkins? Jenkins?'

Then there was nothing but a smug-sounding voice telling her to please replace the handset and try again.

Her mother's migraines worsened, and she didn't seem to notice that Kitty was leaving for school late and coming home early.

Nora did.

'Are you skiving school?' she said to her. 'You seem to spend very little time there.'

'No. It's GCSEs – they let us do our coursework at home, they trust us, they know we're mature.' Kitty smiled at her, and buttered her toast.

'More fool them,' Nora said.

She liked to go to the Portobello Road and delve into the antique clothes shops, buying dresses, black lace sheaths and little Edwardian jackets. She bought records from Gaz, compilations of ska and roots, that sang of nights interrupted, jelly rolls and cocaine running around the brain.

'You look lovely, babe. I wish I had the guts to wear stuff like that.'

Candy lay on her pink sheets, wearing a man's shirt and marabou slippers. Kitty wondered whether the other residents of the Admiral Crichton knew of the splendour in which she lived.

'I'm so pleased you're here,' Candy said. 'I'm exhausted. I just had to kick this guy out. I came back with him after my friend Luca's party and he stayed for FOUR days. He seemed great for the first two; I even thought it could be love. After day three I couldn't get rid of him, I found him in the bathroom putting on my make-up, and that was it . . . I told him to piss off. I'm not THAT modern. He was very attractive for a homeless man though.'

'How do you know he was homeless?' Kitty took a long drag on one of Candy's Cartiers.

'He must have been to want to stay in this shit-hole for four days, darling; and he was carrying a large plastic bag. A bin bag actually. Never mind; soon I'll buy a big house. It works for now, and they take my messages.'

'Maybe he really liked you,' Kitty said. 'Maybe he was incognito rich.'

'Nah,' Candy said, but she smiled. She handed Kitty an envelope. 'Can you give this to your mum?' she asked.

'What is it? Is it drugs?' Kitty stared into Candy's spiky brown eyes. She was shocked by her question; she didn't know where it had come from.

Candy looked injured.

'No, it's a card. God, what do you think I am? A dealer? Why would you even say that? I thought you were my friend.'

'Sorry,' Kitty said, feeling ashamed. 'I was joking.'

She heard someone in the hall calling, 'Candy . . .' There was a faint shuffling of fingers rubbing against the wood. It sounded like a secret knock.

'That's Johnny,' Candy said.

'Can you give him this through the door? I can't be bothered to see him, and I'm not wearing any make-up.'

Kitty opened the door, and saw someone she'd seen on *Top of the Pops* the night before. He was wearing the same leather trousers.

'Hello, darling,' he said.

Kitty handed over the envelope and jumped when his fingers brushed against hers.

This time Kitty was allowed to watch the doctor. He pulled a glass ampoule from his bag, and tapped it with his fingers. He took her mother's thin white arm in his hand and she moaned.

'There, there,' he said, as if he was talking to a child.

'It hurts so much,' her mother said.

'I know. This will make it all go away, and you're going to have a sleep.'

As he stuck the needle in, Kitty wondered if he was poisoning her. Her mother gasped, and Kitty thought it was with pain, so she held her breath, but then she looked at her mother's face, which had dissolved, and was calm and peaceful.

'She'll sleep for a long time,' he warned, whispering.

'All right,' Kitty said.

When he left Kitty climbed into bed next to her, but not under the covers, because her mother didn't like clothes that had been in the street touching her sheets. The darkened room flickered with candles like a church. Her mother was still and waxy like a novelty Madonna. Kitty rested her head on her mother's breast to hear her heart; but somehow it felt wrong, this position, she felt big and awkward, like she might crush her, so she slid up, and cradled her mother's head in her hands, stroking her hair rhythmically until it was almost like a prayer, soothing in its repetition.

Dylan O'Sullivan invited Honor and Kitty to stay at his mother's cottage in Wales for half-term. He was bringing his friend Shone from school. Everyone said his father was an arms dealer.

When they asked Shone what his father did, he shrugged and said, 'Business, I think.'

On the train they ordered gin and tonics and watched England rush by. Dylan's mum was meeting them at the station. She had been in Wales for a week already with her boyfriend, Lester. Dylan told them that Lester was twenty-five to his mum's forty-five, and he was a DJ.

'They're massive puffheads,' he said. 'They keep it in a box in their bedroom.'

Honor looked scared.

'This is the problem of going to a progressive school,' she whispered to Kitty. 'It's always the parents you have to worry about.'

'It'll be fine,' Kitty said. 'Don't worry.'

She was excited. She had never met true hippy parents before.

On the platform she searched for someone in a woolly cardigan with rainbow stripes, and she was stunned when a tiny immaculate woman came rushing forward, dressed head to toe in Issey Miyake.

'Is that my little boy?' she cried in a throaty rich voice.

Dylan looked pained.

'All right, Mum?' he said.

'Oh cut the crap, you little state-school wannabe, and give your mother a kiss.'

The cottage was whitewashed with flagstone floors, lit by a fire that emitted great lurching flames. Everything fabric was cashmere or velvet. At a long wooden table a banquet was set, with deep silver goblets for wine.

'I love your house, Mrs O'Sullivan,' Kitty said as they sat down.

'Call me Lulu, and if you marry Dylan you can have it.'

'Just shut up, Lulu, all right!' Dylan shouted, apoplectic, but his voice had lost its North London twang somewhere between the train station and the muddy track to the house.

Lester came in with logs for the fire. He was tall and gangling, with bright electric green eyes and a nose ring.

'Hello, fairy,' he said, gathering up Mrs O'Sullivan in his arms, kissing her full on the mouth.

Honor kicked Kitty under the table.

'See!' she said very quietly.

They slept in a huge attic under the eaves, all of them on the floor. The lulled voices of the grown-ups wafted up the stairs, and in the effort of trying to catch their words Kitty fell into a heavy sleep, feeling that it would be strange to wake up next to a boy.

In the morning she regarded the milk suspiciously. It was golden; a fat cloud of cream gathered on the top.

'Do you have any skimmed milk?' Kitty was starving.

'No, sweetheart, I don't,' Lulu said. 'There are chocolate croissants if you don't want cereal.'

Kitty computed in her head which was the lesser of the evils.

'No. I'll have cereal, please. But I'll have it with apple juice.'

She poured the apple juice on to her Alpen, and took a bite. They were all watching her, she realised.

'Delicious,' she said.

In the next village over there was a rave. She had never been to a rave. Dylan went to raves all the time, he told them about Raindance, Vicks inhalers and glow sticks. Kitty put on her Lycra black dress and tights with a pair of platforms. She thought it was a suitable costume for a rave.

'You might get a bit cold like that, Kitty.' Dylan was wearing jeans, trainers, and a duffer-hooded sweatshirt.

'Oh, I never get cold, don't worry, I'm hot-blooded,' she said.

They walked the seven miles back, because Lulu and Lester had gone to see friends, and they weren't coming to get them until midnight. Kitty thought the rave was probably not a rave at all, because it was a crowd of teenagers in a church hall drinking cider and dancing to the Prodigy, who you could hear on *Top of the Pops*. She felt cheated, but also a bit relieved. Dylan was disgusted.

'My fucking cousin,' he said morosely. 'That's what comes from living in Wales. Cloud thinks a tea party in a church hall is a rave, cause he's never been to Spiral Tribe. Hippy Loser.'

'Dylan, I'm freezing! My feet are killing me.' Her teeth chattered.

'I did TELL you,' he said to Kitty. 'Give me your hands.' He rubbed them hard.

Honor and she were both barefoot. Their shoes from

Office were not equipped for rambling in the mountains. There were no cars on the roads, just nothingness, and air so rich and full it took Kitty's city breath away and made her chest sting. It was thicker than the air at Hay, but she felt at home, the sheep watching with placid eyes, and greenish black as far as the eye could see. Honor and Shone, children of London, were nervous, every animal noise making them jump, cowpats an assault course. They held hands, and looked miserable. Kitty was in her element. She skipped and jumped and ran and sang at the top of her lungs, her voice echoing back to her like a friend. Dylan joined in, and he knew all the words to James Taylor.

'God. You two are so gay.' Shone and Honor glowered at them.

She forgot about Jenkins and her mother, and she didn't worry about what her mother was doing without her. I don't need to think about her all of the time, she thought. Joy welled up in her. She had the same feeling she'd experienced daily in the ashram, which was one of inexplicable love for everything in the world.

Honor and Shone were fast asleep, Shone snoring like an old Morris Minor starting. Kitty's eyes were shut, but she was awake and buoyant with living. Dylan's hand lightly stroked her arm. She was still, her face turned away from him. Slowly the hand moved higher and higher, till it rested on her shoulder, then her collarbone. She ached for him to move it further, across her rib cage and her breasts, further still, but she didn't want to be complicit in those light torturous butterfly strokes, she wanted to be willing as if in a dream.

His fingers fell about three inches above her nipple. There they stayed, stroking the same spot, until she felt raw as sandpaper. She stretched out, murmuring a little, pretending to be asleep, until his hand actually connected with her nipple. She didn't know what should happen next. His hand ceased moving, as if it was surprised, and she fell asleep with it rooted to her.

When the sun's rays were hot on the floorboards, she opened her eyes and saw he was looking at her. She didn't want him to know she remembered, so she said, yawning, 'I slept so WELL last night. It must have been that walk, I felt exhausted.'

'Yeah, so did I,' he said quickly. 'I was knackered. I went straight to sleep, nothing like the country air.'

During the day, she kept looking at his hands, and every time she did, a shock went through her like a mini electrocution. It seemed magical to her that the mere glimpse of his hand could cause her cells to leap in such pleasurable recognition.

'You're being very weird,' Honor said.

'I know. I can't explain it. I think I feel very happy,' Kitty said truthfully.

She wanted to stay in the cottage, bathing in the river, knitting big scarves for Dylan to wear in the winter.

Back at home they had roast chicken for supper. Sam and Violet had been to Alton Towers. They fought over who could define the rollercoaster with the best aplomb; her mother smiled affectionately. She seemed happier.

'Did you have a nice time?' She put her hands on Kitty's

shoulders as they did the washing up. They were dry and thin, like the wishbone from the chicken.

'So nice,' Kitty said.

'What were Dylan's parents like?'

'It was just his mum and her boyfriend. They were so sweet, you would really like them. She was great, the sort of person you'd be friends with.'

She didn't tell her mother about the pot smoking or the sleeping in the same room as the boys, because she knew she wouldn't understand that it was all done with innocence.

'What does she look like, Mrs Dylan?' her mother asked.

'Pretty, but in a different way to you, and much older than you are.'

Her mother smiled, and her face lit up from the inside like someone had turned on a light.

'Is it nice to have the youngest mummy?' she said.

Dylan was normal with her at school, and Kitty felt confused. It was as if the week had never happened. She stared at him, trying to find answers in his eyes, but they were not forthcoming. He teased her, and his voice was as it had been before Wales. Sharp, and shooting up at the end of sentences, so each one sounded like a question. He ignored her in front of other people, and stopped writing her funny notes in English. He laughed at her in tennis practice. She began to wonder whether it had been a dream. She stared at Nicky's hands instead.

Her telephone rang late in the night, and she thought that it was Jenkins, stating his intention to come home.

The voice on the other end of the line sounded at first like a little girl's, and it was crying.

'Kitty,' the voice said.

'Yes? Hello?'

'It's Dylan. It's terrible, Kitty, I've done something really bad.' He sobbed.

She said what her mother would say. 'Hush, darling, it's all right. What's happened?'

'Shone and I got arrested in Leicester Square, for buying ganja. We're in the police station, my mum's gonna be so mad at me,' he wailed.

Kitty did not think this was romance as she imagined it. Boys weren't meant to cry.

'Are you drunk, Dylan?' she asked.

'Yeah, wasted. I love you so much, Kitty, I love you.'

She heard Shone in the background, saying, 'Shut up, Dylan, give me the phone, you sound like a dickhead.'

'No!' Dylan shouted like a petulant child through his thick sobs. 'I love her!'

There was a tussle for the phone, the sound of it being dropped on a cold hard floor, painful retching and then a click.

It rang again.

'What?!' Kitty said.

'Kitty, it's the magician.'

'Sorry, I thought you were someone else. Hi.'

'Hello to you. I want you to meet Tex, he'd be your best friend in the world. He's so great, my boy. You're both so great. Destined for all good things. Just think, you could be brother and sister or husband and wife . . .'

'Can he play Scrabble?'

'Like a champion. But your mummy's the best at Scrabble, the best at everything. She has the most elegant feet I've ever seen.'

'Jenkins, please come back; we need you.'

'I wish I'd been your father – your real father. I could have been so good if I was the real thing. Shall we pretend?'

'Yes, we can pretend,' she said.

'Good, now I can go to sleep. You're a tonic. The magician is rendered somnambulant through the emotive powers of Miss Magpie Jenkins *née* Larsen-Fitzgerald of Clapham SW11.'

She knew he would hang up.

'Promise you'll call Mummy? Please?' she said quickly.

'Oh I promised so many things. But I love her, God, do I love her.'

'Could I lie with you?'

Her mother was curled, in a sleepy half-ball.

'Of course, my baby. Are you all right?'

'Yes. I miss Jenkins a bit, that's all. I can't sleep.'

'Oh Kitty, I'm so sorry. It's wretched. I miss him too, more than I could ever explain. I feel like my heart is wandering around the desert on its own, lost. We'll be all right. We'll always be all right as long as we have each other.'

'Mummy? Do you think if you hear someone throw up on the phone it can put you off them?'

'Absolutely,' her mother said. 'Without question.'

Her mother came to the first night of the school play. Kitty looked for her in the audience. She was sitting in a fur coat, next to Nora in the middle, and she gave Kitty a little wave. During the play, she watched her mother's face that was like a lighthouse guiding her in the dark, every smile bringing her closer to shore, a laugh inspiring her to sing louder, or wiggle her bottom with extra vigour.

As they sang the resounding finale, her mother clapped heartily, and called out 'Bravo!' Kitty didn't mind that the other parents were staring at her mother, because she was beguiling, and her hair fell in glossy curls over her white fur, and she knew that the question on everybody's lips was, 'Who is that woman?'

'Your mum is really fit. I'd do her.' Nicky sidled up to her, a lopsided smile on his face.

'Fuck off. You're disgusting,' Kitty said.

Her mother glided over, a bunch of white lilies spilling from her hands.

'Darling, I thought I could take you and your friends out to celebrate. You were an utter triumph. You can really dance too. I'm so proud of you, my beauty.' She registered Nicky. 'Hello,' she said. 'Would you like to come to dinner?' She touched his arm, and he jumped back like he'd been burnt.

His face was red, and he stuttered.

'No, he's not invited,' Kitty said. 'My REAL friends are over there.' She felt the warm stab of revenge, and it was sweet.

Taking her mother by the hand she guided her through the crowd, leaving nothing but a snaky trail of Mitsouko and some wobbly-looking fathers.

That weekend it was raining, the house terse and claustrophobic. Kitty couldn't think of anything to do, and everyone was busy. Honor was at an Amnesty International symposium, and Candy was in the country at a French revolution party. Her mother was holed up in her room with a migraine and there was a sign on the door in her writing begging 'Please do not disturb at all, please! Love Mummy.' The writing was shaky, as if it had been written by an elderly Victorian widow, scratches of ink on her headed writing paper.

Kitty could hear her crying. She went downstairs to make some toast with strawberry jam. She decided to make her mother some porridge, and on it poured the top of the milk, and honey, a thick cloud of a spoonful.

She made a tray, and took it up. She opened the door very carefully and slid in. Her mother was sprawled out like a baby horse, in her long white nightdress with pansies embroidered at the bosom, hands covering her eyes.

Kitty knelt on the floor, because she knew any movement on the bed could cause a ricochet of pain to scissor through her head. She took her hand.

'Is that my big girl?' Marina said.

'Yes. I wanted to see if you were all right,' Kitty whispered.

'Yes, no, yes, no. No, I don't think I am all right. I've done something very awful.'

'What?' Kitty said, her voice louder, watchful.

'If I tell you, you have to promise not to tell anyone; it has to be a secret.'

'I promise,' Kitty said.

'I'm a horrible person; I don't know how any of you can love me . . . look what I've done to myself.' Her mother pulled up her nightdress and pointed to her legs. 'Look!' she said.

The skin looked obscenely naked because of the needle marks and bruises that spanned from the top of her thighs to her knees like a broken map. Kitty shrank back.

'What have you done?' she said. 'What is that?'

Her mother held her arms out and tried to pull Kitty to her. Kitty spun away and ran backwards into the bathroom. Her mother cornered her there, until she felt that her back was embedded in the wall, sconce-like.

'I didn't mean to,' her mother said. 'It was all from the doctor; I was just in so much pain – it was my headaches. You can't understand the pain.' She went to lift up her nightdress again as if to illustrate her point.

'Please, don't – I don't want to see again,' Kitty said.

'You must see, you must see how bad the pain was to understand, look what my pain has made me do to myself.'

She showed her once more, and Kitty retched.

'Please don't show me any more, Mummy.' Kitty began to cry.

'Shush, don't cry. Everything will be all right, I just need to go to the hospital for a few days and have a little rest. That's all I need, a rest. We won't tell anyone why, OK? But you have to promise me, cross your heart you won't tell.'

'I don't have anyone to tell,' Kitty said, and she realised this was true.

'You must not tell Nora or Bestemama or Honor or anyone.'

'I won't,' Kitty promised.

She made her mother a cup of tea, and helped her pack

her bag. They packed with purpose. Clean nightdresses, knickers, scented candles, and cold cream. Kitty put in a copy of *The Borrowers*, but she knew her mother wouldn't read it. They sat in the back of a cab, neatly, and when the cab driver asked how they were today, her mother said, 'I'm not very well.' Kitty squeezed her hand.

He dropped them off at a dark Gothic building in Chelsea, and took her mother's hand, saying, 'Feel better soon, love.' He looked at Kitty almost sternly and said, 'Take care of your mum, she's the only one you'll ever have.'

She helped her mother check in at the reception, writing her name and her date of birth, and in the column where it said 'Reason for seeking treatment', her mother took the pen and wrote 'GRIEF' in big black letters.

When Kitty left her mother cried out like she was homesick, until a broad nurse led her away. Kitty could hear her mother's thin cries in her ears, and in the cab home she rubbed at them fiercely, to banish the sound from her head.

In the letter her mother left for Nora, she said she'd decided, on a painful whim, to seek treatment for her migraines at a special clinic that used bio-feedback.

'What is a migraine anyway?' Nora said. 'When I was young it was just called a headache. I tell you, she's something your mother – always got to have one better then everyone else. Why did she decide to suddenly go today?'

'I don't know,' Kitty said. 'It was a really bad one.'

'Well, at least Violet and Sam will go to bed on time. Now it's just boring old me.'

Kitty buried her face in Nora's neck.

'You're not boring. Don't ever say that. You're the best.' She felt like crying.

'Oh Pest,' Nora said. 'It's not easy, is it?'

'No, it's not,' Kitty answered. 'I don't know why.'

The doorbell rings, and Violet catapults down the stairs with Little Dorritt calling a symphony behind her.

'God, that dog is noisy,' Ingrid says, laughing on the doorstep.

'She's not, she's just excited,' Violet says. 'She leads a quiet life.'

Ingrid scoops Little Dorritt up into the grey downy nest that is her coat and the dog collapses on her back, offering her stomach up in blissful surrender.

'She's such a slut,' Sam says.

'Don't call my dog a slut, Sam.' Violet swats him. 'You'll hurt her feelings.'

'She's not your dog, she's Mum's dog.'

Kitty comes down the narrow stairway, carefully holding on to the banister.

'Please don't fight,' she says warily.

'It's how we express our love for one another. Calm down.' Violet points to Kitty's stomach. 'Look, Ingrid, Kitty's had sex.'

Ingrid takes Kitty into her arms.

'Not my eldest niece. As a doctor, I can tell you for sure

it was an immaculate conception. Hello, my love,' she says. 'Are you tired?'

Ingrid has to go home to Barnes to put her children to bed.

'I'll go and see her in the morning,' she says, getting into her Volvo. 'What a bloody mess. Will you do me a favour, Kitty? Don't mention it to Bestemama when you see her. She's fragile, and she's got enough on her plate with Dad's stroke. I don't think she could take it. They have become very old suddenly. I want them to have peace. They both deserve it. God, the order of life is so strange, isn't it? One's parents who have spent their lives caring and protecting are almost overnight reduced to vulnerable children who need looking after themselves. But I suppose you know all about that.'

'Different,' Kitty says, kissing her aunt goodbye.

Chapter Nine

Candy called and offered to take Kitty swimming. She said she was lonely.

'I need to keep fit, darling,' she said. 'My bum is starting to hang. I don't like it. I walk out of the room backwards when there's a man in my bed, which is rare these days, to be perfectly frank.'

She was a member at a ritzy health club in South Kensington, and she could take a guest for twenty pounds. Kitty liked the thought of being on Candy's health plan.

Candy wore a white string bikini, and her belly button had a diamond in it. Kitty looked at her bum to see if it truly was hanging, but to her it looked perfectly round and high.

'Do you want to know something I do?' Candy asked.

They floated lazily on their backs in the empty pool, looking up at the ceiling which was a pastel mess of cherubs. If you stuck your head under the water, music played. Kitty wondered if Candy thought she looked awful in a swimsuit.

'What do you do?' she asked.

'If there's no one else here I go over to the jets, open my legs and I make myself come.'

'Oh my God, that's so sick!' Kitty said. 'How?'

'Have you never read Nancy Friday?' Candy said. 'It's so funny; it happens really quickly. Do you want to have a go?'

'What if someone sees us?'

'Who do you see, darling?' She laughed. 'Don't be frightened, there's nobody here.' She was right. There were two jets next to each other. 'Move up,' she said. 'I have to get the angle right. One, two, three, go.'

Kitty kept her eyes wide open in case someone was watching. The feeling she had was deeply impersonal; she felt removed from it, and how quickly it happened.

'I can't believe you beat me,' Candy said, splashing her as the cherubs looked on. 'Oh that was lovely. Let's go out tonight, but don't tell your mum.'

'She's away anyway,' Kitty said. She saw her chest was flushed.

'I wondered why she hadn't rung me. Normally she rings me for a chat?' Candy said like a question.

'Can you lend me a dress? I don't feel like going home. Where do you want to go?' Kitty didn't want to talk about her mother; she wanted to revel in having Candy to herself. In those brief moments it was like normal life was suspended, and by talking about them, real things would break the spell.

'I'm Rusty Lude.' He held out an elegant hand. He had long fine fingers like a painter. He was very old, but he wore it well. He looked distinguished.

Kitty felt excited. Maybe she was being discovered. Maybe he was a talent-spotter. She tried to make her eyes look tragic.

'My name's Scarlet,' she said.

He had kind eyes. Kitty looked over at Candy who was kissing a boring Swedish student from the LSE with straight teeth. The nightclub passed them by like a carnival. She sighed.

'People aren't going to understand you till you're older. I bet boys your own age don't get you. I bet that it's primarily older men who chat you up. Am I right?' He gazed at her intently.

'How do you know that?' Kitty said. She felt quite giddy and drunk. 'Are you psychic?'

'Yes, I am. You should be drinking champagne. Shall we order a bottle?'

'Can it be pink?' she said.

'You're adorable. Yes, it can.'

The waiters were cleaning up around them. Rusty Lude lit her cigarette.

'I don't know whether your girlfriend's going to be going anywhere with you.'

Candy was in a banquette with the Swede, who had his hands in her knickers. She arched her back and bit his neck. The waiters muttered excitedly. Kitty felt ashamed for her.

'Do you think we should go home?' she asked Candy. 'Everyone's left.'

'No. I'm having a really, really, really good time. I'm going back to mine. You can come home with me if you like, in a bit.' Candy's lipstick had slid around her face.

'I'll take her home,' the Swede leered.

'Who is that man, darling?' Candy squinted at Rusty Lude. 'He's ancient.'

'He's really nice,' Kitty said severely. 'And he's giving me a lift.'

The lights of Albert Bridge shone on the water so it glinted and danced like there were mermaids in it.

'What a beautiful view to have. If I were you I'd never stop looking out of the window,' Kitty said.

'Yeah, it's great. Shall we smoke a joint?'

'I don't know. I get paranoid and hungry. I don't know if I really like the way it makes me feel.'

'It's good stuff. You won't get paranoid. We'll relax.'

'You could go out with my mother.'

They sat on the floor listening to Cat Stevens. Rusty Lude made a face.

'I don't know about mothers,' he said.

'You should. She likes Cat Stevens too. She's really pretty, and young.' Much younger than you, Kitty thought.

Rusty's Siamese cat wove around her legs. He had his eyes shut.

'My daughter doesn't speak to me,' he said. 'I really miss her.' He passed her the bottle of champagne. Kitty took a greedy gulp and it went up her nose.

'Why?'

Tears ran down his long cheeks.

'Says I was a bad father. I bet you speak to your dad.'

'I don't, actually. He's dead. I didn't know him,' Kitty said.

'That's the saddest thing I've ever heard.' He reached for her hand.

His hands were soft, like a woman's. He traced an invisible line up her arm, and she squirmed. A memory as wispy as old leaves tried to struggle through her foggy head.

'I want to know you,' he said.

'I have to go to the loo,' Kitty said.

His bathroom belonged to a seventies film. Brown carpet, smoked brown mirrors, and misty photographs of a little girl with serious dark eyes. He had a lot of hairspray and Badedas. Kitty imagined him getting ready for a night out and she felt a bit sick, then guilty, because it wasn't his fault he was old and lonely.

The sitting room was darker, and Barry White lowed from the stereo. She looked down at the floor, where a pair of leather trousers lay like dead slugs in the rain. Rusty Lude, pale and blue as skimmed milk, was naked, clutching his flaccid penis in his long fingers.

'Oh my God,' Kitty said. 'What are you doing?'

'Waiting for you, baby. Can't you feel the sex magic? Scarlet, baby, please?' He sounded like he was begging.

'That's not even my name,' she said.

'Rusty Lude, Rusty Lude, penis in hand, pallid and nude. Rusty Lude, Rusty Lude, jailbait in his house and he wants to get rude.' Tommy gave a lascivious wiggle at the end of the rhyme, which he sang all the way to Clapham on the night bus.

'You're lucky I was around,' Tommy said. 'I could have been with a girl and I might not have answered the phone. Then where would you be? Stuck with no money outside a naked elderly man's house wearing hooker shoes, that's where.'

'Shut up, OK? It was a traumatic experience. Don't mock me.' Kitty glared at him.

'You're such a fool. Some octogenarian with a ponytail picks you up in a nightclub, tells you that you have STAR stamped all over you, and you go HOME with him? What's wrong with you?'

'I thought he was interested in my mind,' she said tightly.

'Your mind! Ha! That's brilliant. Brilliant.'

Honor and she were walking down Kensington High Street, their heels clacking companionably like horse shoes. Kitty was trying to merge her two groups of friends.

'You'll love Tommy, now you're meeting him properly,' she said. 'And Ollie and Naim. They all go to college together, they're so funny. You and Tommy are my best friends.'

They linked arms and she pulled up the collar of the Afghan coat she had bought that morning at Camden Market. She felt like Julie Christie in it.

Honor's mum laughed at them as they got ready.

'Why don't you wear blusher? You look like you have moon faces, with all that pale foundation. Kitty, does your mother mind if you go out in a dress that short? I don't think it's safe. It sends a message. I don't know how I feel letting you leave the house in a dress like that . . .'

'She says it's fine as long as my coat covers the dress.' Kitty smiled.

'Oh Mum, you couldn't possibly understand,' Honor said. 'We look wildly glamorous.'

Naim and Ollie eyed Honor up.

'All right?' they said.

'Yes.' She looked around the room.

'What do you want to drink?'

'Sea breezes,' they said in unison.

The first taste was syrupy sweet, and then you got used to it. Her mother said Kitty had a predilection for Essex-girl drinks. Her mother was a considered drinker of serious drinks, gimlets and Martinis. Kitty liked things with childish frivolous names – fuzzy navels, sex on the beach – or peach schnapps with fizzy lemonade, which made her eyes burn.

She stood and tried to look bored, her lips thrust forward. Honor and she spent many hours practising their pouts; Honor thought a pout was crucial to looking both truculent and alluring.

'Why are you making that stupid face?' Tommy asked.

'Other people may not find it stupid,' Kitty said mysteriously, pointing her finger to a group of suited bankers who were looking her over with some vague muttering interest.

'They're not looking at your face; they're looking at your tits, which are hanging out for all to see.' He pointed to the top of her scarlet dress, festooned with roses.

'Can you just stop it for one minute?' Kitty hissed. 'You may not find me sexy but other people miraculously do sometimes. You make me feel really bad, like I'm dirty or sluttish and you disapprove of me.'

'Sorry,' Tommy said.

'You should be. Honestly.'

'I think we should have a fashion show, or a play,' her mother said lazily. She was in bed wearing a silk peignoir, and her hair curled damply around her face. 'If you're all going to come rattling in here in the middle of the night, the least you can do is entertain me. I could report you to Major Nora. Then you'd be in trouble.'

The others laughed, but she said it in a mean way. Her pupils were very small.

'I bet you've got some grass, Tommy. Why don't you make a big joint?'

'Mummy!' Kitty said.

'Oh come on. Don't pretend you've never done it. I thought you all longed to be grown-ups. Well I'm inviting you to a party in my bedroom, and we're going to have fun at the party. Come on, Honor, don't look so disapproving.'

Tommy's eyes were on Kitty, as if he were asking her permission. She nodded. From his pocket he took the bag and a packet of Rizlas.

'Bingo,' her mother said.

Kitty had only smoked pot three times before. It made her mouth buzz, and her head feel like it belonged to another body.

'Your mum is so cool,' Ollie said.

'I am cool.' Her mother laughed. 'Now I think we should all dress up, and do a play. Honor, you can be the director. I will be the make-up artist, and the audience.'

Tommy had velvet red lips, Naim striking bronzed cheekbones, and Ollie black-ringed eyes; he looked like Balthazar. Standing at the end of her mother's bed, the boys were no longer scuffed teenagers, they were beautiful. They began to walk differently, like peacocks.

'Can you all remember *Hamlet*? Kitty, you are Ophelia;

Ollie, you are Horatio; Naim is Hamlet and Honor, you're no longer the director, you're the grave digger. I'm the director now. Tommy, you can be the joint maker.'

'Fine,' Honor said. She rolled her eyes at Kitty.

Kitty was wearing her mother's long linen nightdress, and her hair was down.

'Action!' her mother said. 'All right, Kitty, the carpet is the river, and you're going to kill yourself. You're in despair . . .'

She turned the lights off, and the room was lit with scented candles. Kitty came out from behind the bathroom door with a tormented expression on her face, and walked slowly over to the edge of the carpet. She looked around at their faces, strangers in the light, and she felt the joint coursing through her, filling her with laughter. She began rocking with it. The boys and Honor all laughed too.

'For goodness sake,' her mother said. 'That's not very suicidal. I'm going to have to relinquish my role as director and show you myself.' She ran into the bathroom.

Kitty went to sit on the floor with the others.

'Your mum is so funny,' Naim wept. 'She's completely mad.'

Her mother had powdered her face until it was like a kabuki doll's, and her eyes burned out through the white. She wore her wedding dress, but it was too big, and the layers of tulle seemed like they would swallow her. Her eyes were half shut, and she sang a song, in a clear voice. She knelt at the river, looking at her reflection, and she trailed her fingers through the water. Tears ran down her powdered face, and it looked as though she was melting. Then slowly and deliberately she lowered herself in. She lay still on the carpet river and her breath fluttered from a rasp to a stop.

The others had stopped laughing, and the room seemed to move with the heaviness of wax and water.

'Is she OK?' Naim said in a whisper.

Tommy looked frightened.

Marina pulled herself out of the river, quite suddenly, jumping up, and gave a long sweeping bow. They applauded in relief.

'Your mum is a brilliant actress,' Ollie said.

In day's slatternly light, her mother's bedroom looked like a group of wild hijras from Bombay had been dancing there, dropping scarves and belts, cigarette butts, hats and rouge, scraps of paper scratched with poems and notes, as they surrendered to night.

Now they were gone, and lying in the storm's eye was her mother sleeping, still wearing her wedding dress.

'I'm going to an artist's colony in Italy. They've invited me and I thought it would do me good to go. I can't sit around and be maudlin. I have to work, and get inspired. Don't you think it would be good for all of us? I do . . .' Her mother was listening to Willie Nelson singing 'Always On My Mind'. Her lip quivered.

'What do you mean, us?' Kitty said.

'Us. As a family. I think it would be good for us as a family if I go and figure some things out while I'm working. I'll come back and it will all be right again.'

'Why do you have to go away to make things right?' Kitty said.

'I just do. That's what I have to do. I wish you could

come with me, Magpie, but you've got the dreaded school. I'd also rather you didn't see Candy while I'm away – I don't know how good she is for all of us. Please don't make me feel guilty, I beg of you.'

'I wasn't,' Kitty said. 'I was just asking you a question. Why can't I see Candy? She's my friend.'

'I can't answer questions right now, about anything. Do you want to go shopping? Oh look outside the window, there are doves . . . a couple. Do you see them? They're cooing at one another, they're in love.'

'Those aren't doves,' Kitty said. 'Those are pigeons. And they're screwing on your windowsill – it's revolting.'

Life became monotone, black-and-white. Honor and Kitty went to Fanelli's on the Fulham Road, which is where they met Romeo the Russian. He had an incongruous mop of shaggy curls, and a underbite that gave him the look of a very old Jack Russell. He was surrounded by a group of thin, very blonde girls. Their eyes were glazed as if they had had too much cake at a tea party. Romeo was having fun, though. He danced vigorously on the table, shaking his corpulent hips. The girls laughed politely.

Honor and she laughed impolitely. He sent them over a bottle of Cristal which they drank, leaving their twenty pounds of Saturday pocket money crisply virgin.

'Well, now we won't be on the night bus,' Honor said.

'Hurray for us and our teenage appeal,' Kitty said.

Romeo the Russian came over.

'I'm Romeo, like *Romeo and Juliet*. I'm a lover, not a fighter. Any time you want to go out, call me. I'll take you anywhere you want to go and send you home with my driver. Tramp, Hanover Grand, Iceni . . .' He listed nightclubs like he was reciting verbs.

'Thank you so much for the champagne. It was very generous,' Kitty said.

'Nice manners.' His eyes were moist. 'I love English girls. I love all girls but especially English ones.' Then he asked with great hope, 'Do you go to public school?'

For once they didn't have to lie about their ages; Kitty realised their illegality was the whole point. She felt like she was on the brink of discovering some vital truth about life, that she was participating in a huge social experiment.

'Why are we meeting up with those girls AGAIN?' Honor asked her. 'I don't like them, they make me feel weird. My mother would be furious if she knew we were going out with a man in his sixties. I don't like lying.'

'You're not lying, Hon, you're withholding information. We're not doing anything wrong – she just wouldn't understand. It's not harmful. It's interesting. We're seeing all walks of life. It's anthropology. It's one night.'

'I don't want to be like those girls,' Honor said, and she sprayed lily of the valley on her ears, tossing her shiny hair in Kitty's direction.

She half wanted to be like them. They were so polished and hard. Laetita was Romeo's favourite. She was fourteen. She was the only one who wasn't blonde. She looked like Ava Gardner's baby sister.

She told Kitty that on Saturday mornings, every weekend, Romeo gave her his platinum card and she went to Sloane Street and bought whatever she wanted. Kitty was repulsed and jealous at the same time.

'Do you have to have sex with him?' she whispered, fascinated.

'No. He just likes me to wear my school uniform and call him Daddy.'

'Doesn't that make you feel sick?'

'A bit, but then we go to Cartier and I feel better.'

Kitty had stumbled upon a group of baby women, and she was completely enthralled. It wasn't like going out with boys her age, because everything you could ever want, and what you had yet to discover you wanted, was paid for. There was a Bentley with soft leather seats, and buckets of champagne.

She and Honor went to Iceni and had a table that was roped off, and their own security, because Romeo didn't want any other man to talk to them. She perfected dancing at the table with a look of vacancy, sexy as the others. It was easy, in a leather bustier she borrowed from Charlie, the hardest of all his girls. Charlie had the biggest bosom Kitty had ever seen, golden skin that she maintained at the Electric Beach, and people looked at her with a mixture of envy and disdain. Kitty didn't know girls like this existed outside of pulp fiction. Nice girls didn't accept presents from strange elderly men with a penchant for rap music. By association did this mean she wasn't nice either? Dancing and winding, hands reaching up through her hair, touching the others, because everyone knew men liked to watch girls touch each other when they danced. She knew the curve of Charlie's waist like her own because she held it as Charlie moved against her. Her fingers felt the heat of skin through the moulded rubber Charlie wore. Her sweat was sweet, and her hair as it brushed against

Kitty smelled of American shampoo and cigarettes and bleach.

Kitty was scared of her, because she seemed numb inside.

Kitty made Romeo the Russian laugh. He said she reminded him of his English nanny.

'So strict! It's spectacular.' The others rolled their eyes.

One evening she found herself sitting next to him, and he was serious for the first time.

'You know, you are going to be a great beauty when you're older,' he said. 'You're going to get better with age.'

'So everyone keeps telling me,' she said. 'I wish it would hurry up and happen soon. I feel like a wine.'

'It will.' He smiled at her kindly. His eyes began to gleam and his face was vulpine. 'You know, I could set you up, give you everything you ever wanted. You'd have earrings that matched your eyes, and a flat in Belgravia. You wouldn't have to worry about anything. You should be looked after, have an easy life.'

Kitty thought about it: no school, shopping at Joseph, long lunches on Sloane Street and the blind adoration of a buck-toothed dilettante with hairy hands. Her inner harlot, of whose existence she had been until now unaware, piped up in a horrid baby voice, which whistled through her head, 'You'd look lovely in sapphires and you'd never have to take the tube again.' Kitty was horrified, and prayed that the dark inner workings of her soul were not transparent. 'Go away,' she told her. The harlot disappeared in a sliver of scarlet satin with a pout.

'Thank you, Romeo,' she said, 'but the thing is, prostitution has never been that appealing to me. I can see how it would be for some people, but I want to get married and have babies and have a garden.'

He stroked her hair.

'Ah. But you wouldn't be a prostitute, you'd be a mistress. There is a world of difference between the two.'

'I don't think mistresses have very happy lives. I think they're probably very lonely.' It was an unimaginable conversation, and she felt worldly and morally upright, now the hoyden was gone.

'You're a good girl,' he said. 'But oh! To romp with you, what fun that would be.'

'I'm too old for you really, Romeo,' Kitty said, patting his arm, and she knew that this was true.

Honor shot her a look.

'What are you talking to HIM about? I feel sick when we're with these people,' she whispered. 'It makes me feel awful. Everyone's looking at us. They think we're prostitutes.'

'Stop being silly,' Kitty said. 'Of course they don't. Would you rather be at some stupid school party, drinking snakebites in the corner with a bunch of midgety boys? This is glamorous. I was talking about the importance of being a morally intact woman, for your information.'

'Can we go, old man? I want to dance.' Charlie fixed her black eyes on Romeo and kicked Kitty under the table.

'Kitty?' She heard Ruth's voice. 'Kitty you have to get up. Honor's gone to school. She did try to wake you. Oh God, what's that?' She stumbled on the bucket Kitty had thrown up in.

Kitty froze in shame under Honor's Laura Ashley sheets.

'I think I got food poisoning,' she said.

'Well, you need to go home to your mother,' Ruth said. 'She's going to have to phone the school and tell them that you aren't well. I can't do that. Come on, poppet. Do you have any clean clothes?'

'I can wear what I wore last night.' Kitty's voice sounded louder than usual. It sounded wrong in Honor's tidy room.

'I'll give you a pair of Honor's jeans and a jumper. I've got the WI coming here for elevenses but Roy can give you a lift home.'

'I can get the bus,' Kitty said.

'No, at least let us do that. Why don't you have a quick shower?'

She crept down the corridor in Honor's dressing gown. The sun was shining, the house smelled like Pledge and warm bread. She heard Ruth say in a loud angry voice from the kitchen, 'I can barely clean up my own children's vomit, let alone someone else's child's. She's meant to be at school. Where is the mother? What about the grandparents? This isn't right, Roy.' Kitty didn't want to hear Roy's response so she locked herself in the bathroom.

'I bought you a bagel.' Roy passed her a tinfoil package. 'Radio One all right?'

'Anything. Thank you so much for driving me home. You really don't have to. If you want to drop me off at the tube, that's fine.' She folded her arms over her chest.

'Listen, Kitty, it's no problem. None. You're a blessing in disguise. I don't want to have to hide from the biddies from the WI – you've saved me. No problem, chook.' Kitty heard him call Honor this when he was affectionate.

'What's wrong with you?' Nora said. 'Why aren't you at school?' She stood at the door with her arms crossed. She looked terrifying.

'I was staying with Honor and I threw up in the middle of the night, so her dad drove me home.' Kitty couldn't look Nora in the eye.

'Well, why did you throw up?' Nora grabbed Kitty's chin in her hand.

'I was ill,' she said.

'Do you think I was born yesterday, Kitty Larsen? You were out. Jaysus, but you're a disgrace. And if you think I'm calling your school to say you're sick, you've got another think coming. I will not lie for you. I will not encourage this sort of thing. It's un-AC-CEPTABLE. Do I make myself clear?' Nora said, her voice low and quiet.

'Yes,' Kitty said. 'I'm sorry.'

'Well, I'm not sending you to school in that state. You look like a dog's dinner. You can sit there and don't speak to me for at least an hour, after which you're going to make me lunch, and then we're going to pick Sam and Violet up from school and take them to the park. Got it?'

'Yes,' Kitty said.

'Higher!' Violet said.

'I can't push you any higher – my arms hurt.' Kitty felt like she was going to throw up again.

'You have to. Nora says you have to play whatever we want.' Violet was unrepentant.

'Fine,' Kitty said. 'Can we go in the tree house?' She thought about lying in the cool oak darkness, the sounds from the playground far below her.

'No. Not today. Next we're going to go on the roundabout.'

'As fast as the Concorde!' Sam shouted.

On the park bench Nora looked up from her John le Carré book and sniggered.

Kitty started to forget how bad she felt as they ran in the leaves, and Sam and Violet held her hands, and they asked her questions like she knew the answers.

'Was it as bad as all that?' Nora patted her leg over the covers.

'No,' she said. 'It was quite nice, except for the shouting, and the roundabout. I liked us all having supper together.'

'I want to be able to trust you, Kitty; we didn't bring you up to lie.' Kitty wanted to embrace her, but she held back.

'I know you didn't,' she said in a small voice. 'I do try to be good.'

'Well, try harder,' Nora said, and kissed her softly on the forehead.

Kitty saw Honor in the lunch queue.

'Can you meet me outside the library after school?' she said. Her hair was done in a French plait, and Kitty knew Ruth had done it for her that morning, in the kitchen as they chatted, and it made her feel angry.

'Of course. Do you want to go to Camden?'

'I can't today; I just need to talk to you.'

'About what?' Butterflies began to bat their wings in Kitty's stomach.

'I'll tell you when I see you.' Her voice was high and clear like her singing voice.

Honor sat on the library steps, listening to her Walkman.

'Hi,' Kitty said. 'What are you listening to?'

'Desirée. Listen, we need to talk.' Honor was nervous, tracing circles on her tights with her clean baby nails.

'What is it?' Kitty looked at her and saw her lip beginning to flutter.

'This is not really a conversation I want to have, but um, I've thought about it, and I don't think I can be friends with you any more,' Honor said.

Kitty took a step back.

'Why? What have I done? Are you upset about Romeo and those girls? We don't have to go out with them again if you don't want to . . . What is it?'

'It's bigger than that. It's sort of everything. It's not necessarily things you can help. I think, because of circumstances, it's beyond your control. It's like how you spend time with that weird woman who lives in a hotel, who you think is so glamorous, but really she's depressing, and how you actually like Romeo the Russian, and those girls.' Honor sounded robotic, like she was repeating something.

'I don't understand what you mean!' School was empty, and it was getting dark.

Honor stared down at her feet.

'Do you not like me any more?' Kitty said.

'I do – it's just – my parents don't want me to be friends with you, they think you're a bad influence. They're really worried and upset, and I don't want to upset them any more. It's not your fault. I think we're interested in very different things, I think you'd agree.'

'We like the same things,' Kitty said. 'We both like reading and going out . . . We talk about everything.'

'You're making this difficult. My parents think your mother is irresponsible.'

'Your parents don't even know my mother. They don't know anything about her!'

'Kitty, it's obvious. They don't need to know her. Your house is not normal.'

'What's normal? It's completely normal. Maybe not compared to your house but yours is extraordinarily normal. Why are you being so judgemental?'

'I'm trying not to be. I'm trying to tell you it's not going to work.'

'I feel like you're breaking up with me. I still don't understand what I've done wrong.'

Honor started to cry.

'Please, Kitty. You haven't done anything wrong. We're not the same. I feel bad about myself when we go out and do the things we do. It used to be fun when we just went to the cinema, and you stayed the night, and we went to the market. It's not fun any more.'

'So should I ignore you when I see you, and that's it? Should I forget we were friends?'

'I don't know,' Honor said. She hid her face in her hands. 'I'm sorry. I don't know what to say.'

'I think you're boring,' Kitty said, 'and I think your parents are really boring. My other friends are far more adventurous then you, anyway. I'll have much more fun without worrying about you sitting there glowering at me all the time, making me feel self-conscious. Don't worry about it. I'll see you around. And by the way, Candy thinks you sound really prim and dull, and I have far better conversations with her than I ever have with you: proper adult conversations, and we laugh about your stupid boring life and how often you wash your hair!'

'Kitty, please!' Honor said as Kitty ran.

Outside school she kicked the bus stop so hard her heel came off and fire shot up her leg.

'Fuck you, Honor!' Kitty said at the top of her voice.

'Language!' the lollipop lady on the other side of the road muttered, thrusting her eyes at Kitty through the dark. 'Language!'

'Oh leave me alone,' Kitty said.

She hobbled up the hill, looking as dignified as she could, with her skirt flying up in the wind, as flimsy as a handkerchief, one crippled patent stiletto tapping an angry war march against the cold pavement.

Kitty interrupts Violet and Sam who are shouting at each other.

'Do you mind if I lie down for twenty minutes before we go? I can't move all of a sudden. I promise I'll be twenty minutes.'

'It's fine,' Sam says. 'We're in no urgent rush to go – we're bonding.'

Violet half smiles, but decides against it. Instead she nods, pointing her elegant little foot in the direction of Sam's balls. She narrowly misses.

'Oh for God's sake,' Kitty says.

Her mother's bed is soft, and there are many layers of sheets, blankets and duvet. Through the window she sees the Thames moving in the dark, as though it has breath. Kitty presses herself between blanket and duvet. Next to the bed is a photograph of Marina, young and laughing, in the orchard at Hay, with Kitty gazing up at her and Sam and Violet crawling in muslin nappies, out of the frame. Kitty doesn't remember who took it, but she recalls the feeling of the sun on her face, and how her mother laughed when she told her she was going to build a tree house and live at Hay until she was very old, at least fifty-three.

'But what about your husband, little Magpie? And your babies?' her mother said, stroking her hair out of her eyes. 'What about what they want?'

'They're just going to have to like trees,' Kitty had answered.

'And Bestemama and Bestepapa,' her mother said. 'Don't forget them.'

Chapter Ten

She was at Alice's Wonderland with Tommy. Jake and Con Brown were half with them. They were Tommy's friends from tutorial college, cousins who she felt merely tolerated her presence because of Tommy. Kitty was in love with Jake.

She told Tommy this and he said very seriously, 'Jake's a real fuck-up, Kit, and he's weak.'

He didn't look weak. He looked like a film star. He was broody and silent. She felt maybe if she tried hard enough she could make him fall in love with her.

Her mother had called her earlier to find out where she was.

'Oh my God,' Kitty said. 'You're so neurotic. I'll be home at one, OK?'

'You're at Wondering Alice's though, yes?'

'It's Alice's Wonderland, Mum. Yes, that's where I am.'

Tommy and Kitty were standing by the bar doing shots. 'Playing with Knives' was vibrating from the speakers. She kept sneaking looks at Jake, who was chatting up a girl who looked like Kate Moss.

Tommy was boring her with the story of the German girl

who'd broken his heart. He always did this when he was drunk.

'And so then she gave me the Leonard Cohen album . . .'

'Yes,' Kitty said testily. Jake was getting the Kate Moss girl's phone number.

'And then . . . Oh my God, I think your mother's just walked in.'

Kitty burst out laughing, but she looked up and saw it was true.

Her mother was standing at the top of the stairs with Naim and Ollie holding an elbow each. She was laughing. Her hair was in her eyes and she flicked it back with impatient hands. Every man in the room looked up, or so it felt, and looked again.

'Oh my God! Mortification,' Kitty hissed at Tommy. 'Why is she here? I am so embarrassed.'

Her mother saw them and walked slowly over.

'Hi, Marina,' Kitty said. She didn't feel like calling her Mummy.

'Hello, darling. I thought I'd drop in for a drink. Why don't you introduce me to your friends?'

Con Brown leapt to attention.

'How do you, Mrs Fitzgerald. I'm Con Brown. Can I get you a drink?'

Suck-up, Kitty thought.

'Actually, I'm not married. It's Larsen. Call me Marina. I'm too young to be a Mrs, don't you think?' She looked at him mockingly, and he seemed very young.

Jake looked through her and mumbled, 'Jake,' then turned away lazily. Kitty loved him for it.

Her mother stood in her Armani dress and they fought for her attention in droves. Whenever she reached for a cigarette a thousand lighters were flourished. Kitty sat sulking, and held her B & H which was bitterly unlit. Yet her mother was so funny that night, funny and alive, and everyone was so clearly entranced that Kitty was proud that she belonged to her.

Looking straight at Con Brown her mother said, 'So – who can get me some coke?' Kitty looked at her incredulously and she shrugged, gave a throwaway smile.

'I can handle that for you Mrs – Marina.' Con was sure and smooth and cocky all of a sudden. Kitty didn't know how he could possibly be related to Jake.

'Yes, I thought you could,' her mother said.

A look passed between them and Tommy elbowed Kitty. Watching it made her feel as though an army of ants was crawling in her skin.

At 3 a.m. they went to the flat the Browns shared in Soho. Kitty had been there once before to an after-hours party. The flat was squalid. But tonight her mother cast her Lux glow on everything she touched. She made the flat look bohemian and intelligent.

'What a sweet little flat,' she said generously.

Con positively blushed under her gaze.

'Oh well . . .' he said modestly.

Kitty's mother followed her to the bathroom.

'You don't mind, do you?' she asked Kitty anxiously as Kitty crouched over the loo seat.

Kitty looked at the bath. That's where Jake lies naked, she thought in wonder.

'What?' she said.

'Do you mind?' Her mother said.

'Oh . . . No; it's all right. I was just a bit surprised, that's all.'

Kitty rubbed the eyeliner from under her eyes.

'I like your friends,' her mother said.

In the sitting room her mother racked out lines of coke expertly, chopping them like a surgeon, and everyone sat at her feet, the lost boys to her Wendy. Kitty couldn't take her eyes from her.

Her mother did it so smoothly. Kitty waited for black hailstones to come pouring through the ceiling, but none did. The world didn't stop. Her mother passed the tray to her. Kitty bent over it, and Tommy grabbed her hair back as she leaned into it. She was glad the straw had only been up her mother's nose. It didn't seem sanitary sharing. She followed what her mother had done. The powder smelled acrid, like a household cleanser, something to get rid of rings round the bath, and it made her nose feel very empty inside.

When Kitty was finished she looked up to see if her mother was staring. She wasn't. She was in the middle of a story, gesticulating and making Con laugh.

'Thanks,' Kitty said, as she passed the tray on.

No one stopped talking, so she thought she must have looked natural, and she was pleased for that. She took a sharp swig of her drink to make the chemical taste go away.

Con fussed about her mother like an old maid. Dispensing drinks, offering omelettes, anything, anything just to keep her there, the only spark in that dark little room.

Con's girlfriend Suzette didn't like it. She began to whine and rub up against him.

'Con?' she said. 'Con, I'd like an omelette.'

'Shut up, will you. I'm listening to a story.' He nudged her away from him.

Her mother stood up.

'Thank you for having me, but I really should go.'

Kitty half stood, her eyes questioning.

'I've got to go and see someone,' her mother said apologetically. 'You stay, have fun.'

Kitty sat down heavily.

'But do TRY to go to school tomorrow, darling.' Her mother kissed her goodbye.

'Bye, Marina,' Kitty said casually.

When she'd left the room, there was the sound of a collective exhale.

'Your mother is a brilliant woman.' Con Brown smiled at Kitty for the second time in her life.

'Yeah, I know.' She bathed in this reflective glory.

'You look a bit like her. The eyes . . .'

Suzette rolled her eyes at him.

'No, she doesn't. They look totally different. Katie's more interesting,' she smirked.

'It's Kitty,' Kitty said.

Jake sat smoking, half looking at her. When she dared to look back he had dropped his eyes. If I can just wait, Kitty thought, for everyone else to go, we'll be alone. Minute by hour, she willed them, leave.

At 7 a.m. as the cruel dawn crept in and she was beginning to despair, Tommy, the last man standing, said, yawning, 'I've got college. Kit, shall we share a cab?'

She gave him a pointed stare.

'Oh. Right. Bye.'

He stumbled out, and she was alone, with him.

Jake and Kitty sat on the sofa like wooden matches. Con had run off after Suzette, who had left with a face threatening tears.

They sat, the silence unbearable.

'Do you want me to give you a massage?' Kitty asked, her voice sounding alien in the empty flat.

'Yeah, OK,' Jake said.

She rubbed his back under his shirt. It was smooth and warm. Awkwardly, he grabbed her face and kissed her, eyes squeezed shut. His mouth dry, their teeth mashing together.

I'm kissing Jake, her brain said triumphantly. He held her in a stiff embrace that had potential.

'I should go to school,' Kitty said, wanting him to say, No, don't, skive, we'll go to the park and have a picnic.

'Yeah, I need some kip,' he said. 'Do you want a jumper?'

She looked down at her dress: her breasts were more suited to a nightclub than a classroom. She felt cheap.

'Get one from my bedroom,' he said.

His cupboard was the only place in the flat that was tidy. Kitty found a blue jumper that looked replaceable. Her eyes were drawn to a stack of *Playboys*, a safe and a big hunting knife. She shut the door quickly, pulled the jumper over her dress. Jake was on the sofa, asleep. His fingers twitched a bit.

'Goodnight. Sweet dreams,' Kitty said.

Wardour Street was grey and drizzly, but the light was forgiving. She walked all the way to school, early for once, too elated to be paranoid or tired. She had kissed Jake

Brown, essentially stayed the night with him, and taken drugs with her mother and her friends. This was life, Kitty thought.

When she got home her mother was taking a nap.

'She's got a headache,' Nora informed her.

Kitty was desperate to wake her mother and go over the night, reliving it, detail by detail. She kept pacing loudly past her bedroom door, coughing like an old harridan.

Violet passed her.

'You look like a dead fish,' she said. Violet gave her a suspicious look and marched into her bedroom.

'I thought we could have a little dinner party.' Her mother lay with a packet of frozen peas on her face. 'On Friday, with those friends of yours. Maybe Con could leave that annoying girlfriend at home.'

'Maybe,' Kitty said distractedly. The thought of Jake at the kitchen table was foreign and frightening. She'd never seen him eat.

'I'd have to get Tommy to ring them,' she said. 'I mean, I don't know them that well, to ring them, you know.' She felt worried.

Her mother lifted the peas up and smiled.

'I think that Jake really likes you, Magpie. He kept looking at you.'

Kitty telephoned Tommy immediately.

'My mother wants everyone from last night to come to dinner,' she said, 'and she wants you to call the Browns.'

'Your mother is a real weirdo. Why would ANYONE want the Browns to come to dinner? They're really uncivilised people. The Browns don't have dinner, they just go to nightclubs and cane it . . .'

'Well, they're your friends. Just do it, please?'

Tommy thought for a moment, as Kitty bit her nails.

'Fine,' he said darkly. 'Weirdo.'

Her mobile rang at eleven o'clock. She didn't know the number, but she knew in her tremulous heart it was Jake. She let it ring three times, as her mother taught her, holding her breath until she picked up, blushing.

'Hellllooo?' Kitty breathed low into the phone like Marilyn Monroe.

'Kitty, it's Con Brown.' Her heart swam down to her feet like a bottom-feeding fish.

'Hi, Con,' Kitty said, trying to keep the defeat from her voice. 'Hi.'

'So – yeah, we'll come to dinner,' Con said.

Kitty told him the address. She felt nauseous. Who was the WE he spoke of?

'By the way, Kitty,' he said in a hushed and silky voice. 'I know you like Jake.'

She felt the panic bubbling in her like a pan of milk about to spill over.

'Jake knows too. And here's the thing – if you put in a good word with your mum, I'll sort you out with Jake, OK?' He laughed a little bit. 'See you on Friday – bye!'

She tried to sound cheery as she hung up.

Her mother walked into her bedroom. She didn't look remotely hungover. She looked wan and charming.

'So are they coming?' she asked smugly as one who knew they were.

'Yes,' Kitty said. She started to cry.

'What is it?' her mother said. 'I thought it would be

good if they came. I thought I was doing you a favour, inviting Con and Jake.'

'It doesn't matter,' Kitty shouted. 'And Con Brown fancies you.'

'Don't be silly, Kitty,' her mother said. 'He's a young boy.' But her eyes glittered. 'I'll cook lamb,' she said. 'That's good boy food.'

'I don't care!' Kitty wailed. 'I'm a fucking vegetarian! Please turn the light off on your way out.' She buried herself under the covers. After a while she heard her mother leave, saying sadly again, 'I thought it would be good . . .'

Kitty could not sleep. Her side of the bed was too hot and close, the other side achingly empty.

The memory of Jake's kiss, so real an hour ago, had shaken away from her, now shadowy like paper, something that was not hers to begin with.

Marina gave Kitty the day off school the night of the dinner party. She also gave Nora the weekend off, and dispatched Sam and Violet to a schoolfriend's.

'So it's just us girls,' she said, her tone suggesting that Kitty would know what she was talking about.

She called a beautician named Julie who came and painted both their nails, Kitty's blood red, near black, and her mother's a soft baby pink.

'I think you should wear your hair up,' her mother said. 'It looks so beautiful when it's up. And I think you should wear that little pink knit dress I got you from Ralph Lauren. Con left a message to say Suzette can't come. She's busy. It was so sweet, he sounded so gruff and grown-up on the phone.'

Jake never arrived. Con kept saying, vaguely, 'Yeah, I spoke to him earlier – he said he's definitely on his way.'

But when he hadn't shown up by three she knew he wasn't coming. She had made a chocolate mousse for him. It sat uneaten in the fridge. The sight of it depressed her. The next day, Kitty wanted to ring Honor and tell her, but as she dialled the number she remembered that they weren't friends any more.

Her phone rang but it was never the voice she wanted. Jake eluded Kitty, like the night creature he was. She went to all the old familiar places and saw glimpses of him in other people, the curve of his nose, a glint of burnished brown hair, the quick smile, but they were all imposters. Con, she saw everywhere. It made her hate him more than she had previously. In his smirk, Kitty saw a million judgements, conversations she had not been privy to. She hated him for knowing the secrets of her heart.

When she was on her own, in her room at night, she thought that someone else's fate had entered her like an incubus. Crept up in the night, and stolen into her soul, breathing badness through her blood. Sometimes she washed her face with her mother's holy water from Lourdes. She wanted to be a good sister and take Violet and Sam to Ed's Diner for chocolate milkshakes on a Saturday morning, but she could never wake up in time. They knocked on her bedroom door and Kitty pretended she couldn't hear.

She borrowed twenty pounds housekeeping from Nora. They sat on the train from Clapham Junction and outside it was grey and the houses all looked the same. Violet and

Sam chattered to her about a book they were reading called *Stig of the Dump*.

'Can you just be quiet?' Kitty said. 'I'm taking you out, aren't I? You're giving me such a headache.'

She sat in silence with her arms crossed. Their eyes became round and watchful, and they were guarded and very polite, each quiet please and thank you a jab in Kitty's heart.

'I don't mean to be cross; I went to bed really late,' she whispered.

'Isn't that a treat?' Sam asked, in a hushed voice.

She wanted to ask, Why do you both trust me? Why do you both trust me when I don't trust myself?

They sat, such little perfect people, the thoughts in their heads left dangling with nowhere to go. They looked silently out of the windows at the people going by, and Kitty thought her heart might break.

She wished they were back in New York playing spy games, or climbing trees in the orchard at Hay, a lone hot-air balloon sailing across the sky, as they played at guessing where it was destined.

Chapter Eleven

'I have a new friend who's a princess.' Her mother lay back in the bath, blowing smoke rings.

'A real princess? With a castle?' Violet watched her intently from the floor as her rabbit ran around the bathroom.

'Yes. A real-life princess. She's an artist, she was at my colony. She has a castle in Italy. Violet, your rabbit is chewing on my Clarins face cream . . . Please pick him up.'

'It's a she,' Violet said.

'My friend is BISEXUAL,' Marina mouthed to Kitty. 'She's coming over for tea tomorrow.'

Kitty had never met a princess, or someone who boasted about being bisexual. She wondered whether she could glean either thing by just looking at Marianne.

Marianne was not a real princess; she was a raven-haired beauty from Surrey who had married a louche Italian prince whose peccadillo was opium and transvestites.

'You can't imagine what it was like, living in exile in Siena. The family had cut us off, the roof was falling in, and Oberto was nodding into his risotto as young boys wearing MY jewellery flitted in and out,' she said loudly. 'It was where I discovered painting. It was my only outlet. I started selling my paintings to tourists and as soon as I had enough money I got the bloody hell out.' She pushed her fringe back from her doll face. 'It was ghastly.'

Kitty stared at her, with her mouth open.

'Poor thing,' her mother said sympathetically. 'Would you like a biscuit? Stop staring, Kitty.'

'No, darling. Can't. I shall be fat, and no one will want me.' She pondered the Jaffa Cakes with rue.

Marianne and her mother whispered and giggled like schoolgirls. They had inside jokes and locked the door to her mother's bedroom. They constantly praised each other's merits and talked of nothing but men and parties.

'I don't like Marianne. She's rude, and she makes Mum be silly,' Violet said to Kitty, on a locked-door night.

'I agree.' Kitty thought that she would be a phase, but Marianne had become a stalwart fixture.

Violet finished painting her nails acid green. It looked like she had a disease spilling from her fingertips.

'Sam doesn't like her either. He says her eyes are like a witch's. They are, if you look, they're yellow and wicked. She pretends to be nice, but you can tell she's not.'

Nora was watching *Doctor Who*, sitting tidily in her old crimson armchair. They couldn't see her face: her back was to them. A plume of smoke rose with her voice, and she said, 'I don't like her either.'

Nora was the master of objectivity. Kitty sat up in surprise.

'Marianne must be really bad then, because Nora likes EVERYONE.' Sam pointed his fingers like a gun to his head.

In the shadows of Kitty's room, hangmen loomed, the oak outside became a lynching tree.

Her mother locked her bedroom door again and she and Marianne sat inside, talking of hushed things in careful hushed voices.

Kitty knocked on the door, trying hard not to sound plaintive or desperate as she said, 'Mummy, can I come in?' Her mother said if you played hard to get people wanted you more.

'I'm having grown-up time, Kitty. Come back later.'

'We're telling our secrets!' Marianne shouted, as though it was a joke.

'I tell you all my fucking secrets!' Kitty shouted.

There was a silence, after which she heard her mother say, 'Teenagers!' in a tone that was both patronising and bored.

She went to her room, covered her mouth with a pillow and screamed. She decided she would have her own grown-up time. In her jewellery box she had a two-gram wrap of coke, which Charlie had left in her handbag the last time they went to Iceni. She racked out two long lines on her dressing table, and put 'Killing in the Name' by Rage Against the Machine on her CD player. She turned the volume up as loud as it would go. She lay on the floor, her head splintering with words, and realised with frustration she had no one to talk to. Her feet were numb.

She decided to do a fashion show for herself and pulled out everything from her wardrobe and put it on the floor. She tried on an old Alaia dress of her mother's that was too small and she sucked in her cheekbones and her stomach. To her reflection Kitty said, 'Hello, princess.' She didn't know why she said this but she said it in a cockney accent, which made her laugh at herself.

Kitty knew Rosaria would think it was funny too so she rang her.

'Are you coming to my birthday party this weekend?' Rosaria asked.

Kitty had forgotten it was her birthday.

'Yes, if I can get enough money for the train. I spent my allowance,' she said.

Rosaria sounded like she was going to cry.

'Mummy says she'll buy you a ticket, Kit. Are you all right? You sound so weird.'

'Cool. Then I can come. I'm fine. I'm having a fashion show on my own in my bedroom. Everything's great.' She spun again.

'What's that ghastly racket in the background? Are you at a festival with the beardy weirdies again?' Rosaria liked the Bangles and Right Said Fred.

'Rage Against the Machine, man. So I'll come up on Friday evening 'kay?' Kitty said.

'All right, babes. Are you sure you're all right?' Rosaria asked.

'Yup. Fine. Wicked,' Kitty said.

'Wicked indeed. You have got to go back to public school.'

Kitty heard Rosaria's brothers in the background.

'I have to go,' Rosaria said. 'Mayhem here. Love you.'

'I love you too.' Kitty truly meant it.

Her mother screamed outside the door. 'Will you turn that fucking music down?!'

'I'm sorry.' Kitty said. 'Speak up. I can't really hear you.'

'Turn it DOWN!' she said, rattling the doorknob. 'You're giving me a headache!'

'Why don't you call the doctor?' Kitty shouted through the door. 'Isn't that what you do when you have a headache?'

'What are you doing in there?' her mother said, and she sounded lonely.

'I'm having grown-up time. That includes loud music and self-expression.' Kitty twirled around in her dress, crazily.

'Why are you punishing me?' her mother asked forlornly. Marianne had clearly gone home.

'Because that's what you get,' Kitty whispered.

Rosaria's house smelled like Christmas. Her room was on the top floor and they listened to Massive Attack while they got ready. Kitty sat in the bath, reading a Jilly Cooper book while Rosaria blow-dried her hair, a complicated process that involved heated rollers and a lot of hairspray.

'Marcus Chapman's coming tonight,' she said wistfully. Rosaria had nurtured a crush on Marcus Chapman for six years.

'Why don't you just get royally pissed and jump on him?' Kitty said.

'I can't. It would ruin our friendship. I'll just have to continue loving him from afar. What on earth have you done to your pubes, Kitty?'

'I put Immac on them while I was on the phone, and forgot it was on, and then there was this horrid burning smell, and I ran to wash it off, by which stage it was too late and all of my pubes had been burnt to a crisp, so now I look like a bald egret,' Kitty said.

'You have the pudenda of a ten-year-old,' Rosaria cackled.

'I know. It's really revolting. Good thing no one's going to be investigating down there any time soon. Will you dry my hair like yours? It looks lovely.'

'Yes. If you'll do my make-up,' Rosaria said.

'Do you want to do a line of coke? I've got some,' Kitty said, nonchalant.

'Kitty!' Rosaria's mouth made a big curly O. 'Where did you get it?'

'From a friend,' she said. 'Actually that's a lie. My mother told me if I took Violet and Sam to school she'd give it to me. She wanted to lie in, and it was Nora's day off.' She laughed to show Rosaria that it was all right.

Rosaria handed her a towel.

'How long has your mother been doing coke?' she asked quietly.

'I think she just does it occasionally. Like if she's going to a party or something. I don't think it's a big deal. A lot of people I know do it.' Kitty shrugged.

'But your own mother doing it is different,' Rosaria said.

'Your mother smokes dope.' Kitty stared at her.

'Yes, but she's a hippy. And dope is different somehow.'

'Well, we don't need to get into the semantics,' Kitty said. 'Do you want to try it or not?' She felt like a nasty drug pusher.

Rosaria set her lips defiantly.

'I'll try it,' she said. 'But you can't tell anyone. My friends would really disapprove.'

'That's because your friends are prudish and boring. I'm your fun friend,' Kitty said.

Rosaria raised a thick black eyebrow at her.

'You'll have to show me what to do,' she said.

Kitty made two neat lines and chopped them smooth with Rosaria's Barclaycard. She bent over one.

'So you hold your hair back, stick the note up your nose, and snort, hard,' she said, and proceeded to do it, theatrically.

'It's not working,' Rosaria said a few minutes later. 'I don't feel any different.'

Kitty started to have a creeping feeling that her mother had supplied her with fraudulent coke, but she didn't want to share this thought with Rosaria.

'Maybe you've just got a high tolerance. Maybe you're Chichester's answer to Tony Montana. Let's get pissed instead,' she said.

Rosaria's friends were sweet and warm. They clustered around Rosaria like chicks, shiny-haired and clean-skinned. Kitty stood and talked to Rosaria's mother, wanting to be a part of them.

'You've got so glamorous, Kitty. You look like a woman,' Mrs Nivolla said.

'Not really.' Kitty shifted her weight from one hip to another. 'Do you still make lasagne?'

'God, I'd forgotten how much you used to love my lasagne. I'll make some tomorrow if you like. How's your mum?'

'Oh, she's well. The same, but sort of different too. I can't explain,' Kitty said.

'I think we all change a bit as our children grow up,' she said kindly.

'So you're Rosaria's famous Kitty.' Marcus Chapman

smiled at her. He had very straight white teeth and he smelled like the beach.

'I suppose so,' Kitty said, smiling. 'We've known each other since we were little, but she was always cooler than me.'

'She's pretty cool,' he said.

'I feel a bit like I'm at someone's wedding. And I don't really know anyone.' She feared that he might think her a social leper.

Instead, he took her around the room and introduced her as Rosaria's best friend from London. He was attentive and her glass was always full. He lit her cigarettes.

'You shouldn't smoke,' he said.

'I hate the word shouldn't,' Kitty said. 'It always makes me want to do the thing more.'

'So you're a bad girl.' He grinned.

She felt the lovely oozing warmth of alcohol trip down through her body. Everything felt soft and feathery, and she felt as though she were made from down.

'How old are you?' he asked.

'I'm fifteen,' she said.

'You seem older.'

'Thanks,' Kitty said sarcastically. 'Maybe it's because I'm bad. I seem older. Worn. I used to be good. But somehow now, badness just befalls me.' She thought she sounded like a fifties starlet from Shepperton Studios, bleached with innuendo. She disgusted herself. Why can't I have a normal conversation with a boy? she thought.

'Aren't we meant to be leaving to go to the club soon? I have to find Rosaria,' she said desperately.

'Come back. I'll be lonely without you,' he said.

The club was cavernous, far bigger than anywhere she'd been in London. Girls danced in cages, their stomachs enviably taut like sailors' knots, belly buttons flashing with semi-precious stones. Rosaria was dancing slow in the middle of all of the fastness, and she was happy and drunk and beautiful.

Kitty watched them from the floor above.

Hands were over her eyes. It made her jump. Marcus Chapman stood laughing.

'I want to kiss you,' he said.

'I can't kiss you. Rosaria's my oldest friend,' Kitty said, her eyes still looking below to the dance floor.

'So? I'm not, nor have I ever, gone out with Rosaria. She's a great friend,' he said.

She thought about this. He was right. Rosaria had never even let him know her feelings. She had no prior claim to him. He was as much Kitty's as he was hers.

'Fine,' she said, deciding. 'But kiss me somewhere secretly and promise you won't tell anyone.'

'I promise,' he said solemnly.

Her adrenalin started pumping with guilt and risk, but it was not an unwelcome feeling. She felt alive.

He pushed her up into an alcove. They kissed, and she coursed with heat and want.

'Come back to my house,' he whispered in her ear, pressing himself against her, hard. She thought that an imprint of him might leave itself on her skin like a scar.

'I can't, I'm staying with Rosaria.' Suddenly she was

sober. They were not star-crossed lovers, they were strangers, and she had stolen a moment that belonged to someone else.

Guilt made her greedy. Kitty devoured a packet of digestive biscuits and sat on top of the Aga.

'Did you have fun, Kit?' Rosaria asked dreamily, rubbing her feet where her shoes had bitten into them.

'It was amazing,' Kitty said, avoiding her eyes.

'Was the club all right? I know you're used to London clubs, but the DJ was really good, no?'

'London clubs are rubbish,' Kitty said heavily. 'Everyone's too cool to dance. I promise, you had a great party, I could tell, everyone had a fantastic time.'

'Oh good. Weren't we wild though, doing coke and everything?'

'Wild,' Kitty said.

'Did you have a wonderful time, my darling?' asked her mother innocently from the sofa. She was lying with her feet up, listening to old scratchy jazz records.

'No,' Kitty said shortly. 'What was in that coke you gave me?' Her mother flashed a serene smile.

'Crushed-up arnica tablets,' she said smugly. 'I was looking out for your health, and I didn't want you to poison little Rosaria Nivolla. Plus, because of its anti-inflammatory properties, you now have bruise-free insides.'

'My insides are most certainly not bruise free,' Kitty said furiously, as she ran from the room.

Her mother came to her bedroom later.

'I'm sorry,' she said, sitting on the bed. 'It was a shitty

thing to do. I should have given you twenty pounds like a normal person. I think Marianne is a bad influence on me. Did you have a horrible time?'

'I had the most horrible time, and I'm the most horrible disgusting person in the world,' Kitty said, and she told her mother everything.

'Oh sweetie pie, it's not the worst thing in the world. I understand your upset though. Just don't ever tell Rosaria. And don't do it again. The problem with life is, we often do things that will ultimately be self-destructive and make us unhappy, yet in that moment it seems like the best idea in the world. You have to be very careful of moments – they're very tricksy things.'

'I wasn't a moment, was I?' Kitty asked after a while, as they lay in companionable silence.

'My darling, you were, and are, a lifetime. Nothing momentary about you, I promise,' her mother said.

'You bitch, Kitty! You utter bitch!' Rosaria's rage shot down the phone and pierced her. Marcus Chapman clearly did not believe in secrets.

'Look, it was nothing,' Kitty said. 'We were both pissed. I kissed him for two minutes at the most. It really isn't a big deal. He didn't even like me, I could tell.'

'It is a big deal. It's a huge deal. My best friend and the boy I've been obsessed with for six years. He's my next-door neighbour! Why did you do it?' Rosaria was crying.

'I don't know,' Kitty said slowly. 'I'm sorry.' She didn't know whether she was sorry, or sorry Rosaria had found out. She decided both were true.

'I can't speak to you for a while. I'm too angry. My other friends think you're a terrible person, and I would feel too stupid to speak to you. Do you understand?' Rosaria said.

'Yes,' Kitty said.

Chapter Twelve

Alice's Wonderland was empty, it was Wednesday night. She sat at the bar and ordered a vodka and cranberry, hoping to look wistful and mysterious. Her hold-up stockings kept falling down, and she tried to adjust them surreptitiously. Her lips were red, sticky glossy red, and her dress, she felt, was appropriately coal black to match her character.

The barman presented her with another drink.

'I've still got one,' she said.

'Yeah, I know, but the bloke over there sent you one.'

Jake smiled at her from the end of the bar. He lifted his glass to her.

'Who are you here with?' he said, as Kitty rearranged herself next to him.

'Oh, my friends are late,' she said lamely. 'You?'

'I had to see a man about a dog.' He winked.

'Oh,' she said again, like she understood.

'You look pretty tonight,' he said. 'Really pretty.'

'Thank you,' Kitty said. Her hand trembled.

'Do you want to come out tonight with me?'

Trying to conceal her excitement, she reached into her bag and put on another coat of jammy lip gloss.

'Yes, I would,' she said.

'What about your "friends"?' he said mockingly.

Smoke machines, the tart taste of cranberry slicing against her teeth, her hands in the air, Jake's fingers finding the space where her stockings ended and her thigh began, his sharp intake of breath, drum and bass at Subterania hitting her in the groin, could this be love, everybody smiling, their teeth ivory white in the dark with the strobes, so the whole night is like a living breathing Polaroid picture.

'I want to be an actor!' Jake shouted above the music.

'What?!' Kitty couldn't hear or wasn't sure she heard him properly. He handed her a key, and together they snorted coke off it, right there in the club, right there in front of everyone.

'You're a good girl, do you know that? You're a good girl. I'm the same as you – I can see it in your eyes. We're not like the rest of this scum. I think your mum and Con are wrong, but we're not going to talk about that because it makes me feel strange, we're going to talk about what's real and now, what's important. I'm going to get the hell away from all these people and I'm going to live on the beach in California, breathe the sea air, and make everything right. I've done some bad things, that aren't really me, and I need to get away. Did I tell you I think you're a good girl?' He ruffled her hair.

'Yes,' Kitty said. 'I think you're good too.'

He introduced her to everyone he knew, all the fast, sharp-suited night people, and they seemed to think she was funny, and they flirted with her, and Jake looked proud, with unfocused eyes, proud to be with her, and she spun with delirious happiness.

The Soho flat was cold and empty, but they were high on drugs and drink and each other so it didn't matter, nothing mattered.

She fell with him for what seemed like miles, cocooned in laughter, whispers and clumsy apology down on to the stained futon.

'I'm a virgin,' she said, but she wasn't frightened like she'd always thought she would be.

He reached over her, kissing her neck, and took a condom from a drawer. When he entered her it hurt, a searing pain right through her, like she was breaking in half, but she did not tell him. She just said I love you, and when she looked at him it was as if Kitty was seeing him for the first time.

Con and her mother were laughing on the sofa, and they didn't move away from one another when she walked in.

'Where are Sam and Violet?' Kitty asked angrily. It was half term; Nora was visiting her family in Ireland. Her mother giggled girlishly.

'They're outside playing cricket with Con's friends.'

'Have they had tea?' she said.

'Yes, Kitty, they've had tea.' Her mother rolled her eyes at Con.

'Jake said to say hi.'

Con laughed, and her mother followed. They were spectacularly annoying. Kitty hated them.

'Con is going to take a photograph of all of you for my birthday,' her mother said, as though this were reason for great celebration. 'He's a very talented photographer, you know.'

'Well, I'm not going to be in it,' Kitty said. 'You can put

a blank space where I'm meant to be. Can I talk to you in private, Marina?'

'Oh OK,' her mother said. 'Though I don't see why we can't share things out in the open.' She followed Kitty into the hall.

'I don't think you should let Violet and Sam be around these people, I don't think it's good. Please make them go home,' Kitty said.

'Darling, I think you're overreacting. They're having a lovely time with Con's friends in the garden. We're all just having a relaxed Saturday afternoon. Stop being such a control freak. Come and sit with us – I feel like I haven't seen you for ages. Come and tell us what you've been up to.' Her mother took her hand. Kitty snatched it away.

'Since when have you and Con Brown become an US? I don't want to sit with you and Con Brown and tell you what I've been up to. I hate Con Brown. He's using you – can't you see that? He's got no money, and he'll use you until he gets bored. Even Tommy hates him; he won't come over any more because of him.'

'They're your friends,' her mother said.

'What?' Kitty took a step back.

'You brought them into my life. I would never have come across them if it wasn't for you. They're your friends. Maybe you're a bit jealous.'

'I hate you,' Kitty said.

Shrugging, her mother walked back into the sitting room.

She calls Mark from her mother's bed. Violet and Sam are downstairs, sitting on the sofa looking at old photograph albums, friends again.

'It's me,' she says.

'Hey, you. How's it going?'

'All right. We haven't seen her yet; we're going in a minute. Tell me something funny.'

He proceeds to tell her about a conversation he's had with a Romanian poker-playing, carp-fishing, ex-lawyer taxi driver on the way to work.

'His name's Eugene. He's invited me to be his first mate in the Massachusetts shark tournament. I've got his email; I think we should fix him up with my cousin. Great guy . . .'

'Mark, I'm frightened,' she says.

'I know, honey. I can tell. You have your wobbly voice.'

'I don't know how to be. I know how to be for Sam and Violet, I know how to be for everyone else, because I can be myself; I don't need armour. But I don't know how to be for her. It's like I've built a wall and I'm numb, and I can't remember any more.'

'Kitty, I will never know entirely what this is like for you, because it hasn't happened to me. I know an inch of it from loving you, and understanding through that. The only thing I can say is just try to remember that above all your mother is sick, she has an illness. You've done your best, you need to know that. It's like that poem, shit, how does it go? What will abide with us is . . . Fuck, what is it . . . ?'

'"What will survive of us is love?"'

'That's the one.'

'Thank you,' she says.

The damp, which she has forgotten after living in America for so long, seeps into Kitty's bones. She shivers. Violet notices and puts her scarf over Kitty's shoulders. They walk through the car park towards the hospital, which is lit up like Harrods at Christmas. There is something comforting about the antiseptic glaring light. They are walking into a world of the orderly, of timed meals, temperature-taking, lukewarm baths and honest-faced nurses.

Kitty looks at Sam and Violet. She takes a deep breath. 'Ready?' she says.

Chapter Thirteen

The doorbell rang long into the night, and soon the sitting room was filled with the sharp reek of weed, which even her mother's scented candles couldn't dissipate. Sam and Violet were asleep, in their bunk beds, a storyteller tape speaking of lions, witches and wardrobes as they slept.

Downstairs they were playing spin the bottle, and Kitty sat to the side, smoking, one cigarette after another. Con had many people with him, boys that she didn't recognise, men really, with expressionless faces, and coats that they kept on. The girls were dressed in black, had tiny skirts and tiny handbags. They kept passing round a tray of coke; it was one of her mother's painted trays from the kitchen, one that Kitty remembered her painting in the studio at Hay long ago, when life was not so complicated. She wanted to scream at the intruders to stop it, and explain who her family was, not this, and what that tray meant, but her voice had gone away.

'Kitty, truth or dare?' Con was looking at her and smiling.

'I'm not playing,' she said.

'You have to, you're in the room.'

'Come on, Kitty,' her mother said. 'Everyone else is playing. It's fun.'

Marina didn't look like her mother any more, Kitty thought. A stranger had come and taken her away. Her silver eyes, Kitty's eyes, were black, and they frightened her.

'Truth,' she said.

'Did you or did you not screw my cousin?' Con asked in a silly falsetto voice.

Everyone laughed, the faceless men boys too. She looked at her mother in appeal, and she wanted to lie, but Con's smile froze her like a deer in headlights.

'Did you, Magpie?' he repeated.

Kitty moved away from her nickname sliding with ease from his lips.

'Did you?' her mother asked, and she sounded surprised, and a look went over her face that was something like hurt.

Kitty looked down at the floor. It needed to be cleaned. Precious could have used her magic orange polish on it, she thought.

'I think we can take that as a yes.' Con leaned back, satisfied, his hand on her mother's thigh.

'That is so sweet,' her mother said. 'Darling, we should open some champagne.'

Kitty shut her eyes.

'Oh my God!' Con guffawed. 'He really did, didn't he? I was guessing! He wouldn't tell – prides himself on some fucking old-fashioned gentleman's code. My cousin popped your daughter's cherry! This is all just so fucking modern! Let's call Jakey. You can speak to him. Pass me the phone.'

'Don't! Please don't!' It was the first time Kitty had spoken, and her voice sounded loud and thick.

'Come on, Con, don't tease Kitty.' Her mother spoke tenderly, as if they were siblings.

'I didn't answer your question. Give me a dare,' Kitty challenged him.

'Your non-answer was the answer, my dear,' Con said.

'I didn't say anything. Give me a dare.'

'Take your clothes off and run down the street naked.' His brown eyes swept over her dismissively.

'Fine,' Kitty said.

She kicked off her jeans, and the pink cashmere jumper that she loved, the one that her mother had been given by Bestemama when she was born. She shed them on the ground like skin that she had no use for. She stood in her bra and knickers in the room full of strangers.

'I'll take the rest off by the front door,' she said to Con.

'You'll never do it. You're a prude. A babyish prude. You hadn't done anything until you met us. You were a loser, always. I've seen the pictures of you when you were little – you had glasses. You wouldn't do anything.'

Kitty smiled at Con, at her mother, who was silent.

'I will,' Kitty said.

She welcomed the dark and the cool air, which slid against her nakedness like song.

The street compared to the house was blessedly

quiet, and the lights were off in the tidy row of houses. Her skin shone bright white, electric in the dark.

'"My mother said, I never should, play with the gypsies in the wood. If I did, she would say, naughty, naughty girl to disobey,"' she sang quietly, liking the neatness of the rhyme as she ran to the sign that began the street, and touched it with her hand, as if she were playing one of the nameless that children play, and she sailed to the other end, her bare feet slapping against concrete, tapping the crumbling brick of the last house's garden wall, the place where the street officially ended.

She was tired. Her bones felt chipped and dry. Kitty washed her face religiously and, sitting on the edge of the bath, scrubbed the street from her feet.

She put her clothes back on. She walked into the sitting room, where they huddled, frozen in the same places, snorting and talking over each other, as though time had simply stopped. The air had changed, thickened, and rounded with some dark intention.

'I'm going to bed,' Kitty said.

'Goodnight,' her mother said. She could not look Kitty in the eye.

She peered in to check on Sam and Violet, who both slept, arms open, as if to catch the snow. Their long eyelashes made shadows on their heart-shaped faces. Their room seemed to belong to another house, in which a fire died softly in the grate as the parents slept upstairs, warm from wine and conversation. The alarm set for 7 a.m. in time for breakfast-making, and the school run.

Kitty lay on the floor and watched them for a while, and imagined an angel with a wing-span of twenty feet shielding them with a great impenetrable wall of creamy feathers, which met in the middle as he spread his arms.

She got into bed, throwing the covers over her head, and curled up like a foetus.

'Kitty.'

Someone was sitting heavily on her bed, pulling her from sleep with an insistent voice.

'Kitty! There's something wrong with your mum. She's really fucked up.'

'What do you mean?' She sat up to see Con looking at her with wide and frightened eyes.

'She seemed to be having a really good time, and she asked me to call some chick at a hotel and get more stuff, but she's lying in the bathroom and I can't wake her up. I think she may have taken some pills or something.'

Kitty leapt up, away from him.

'Have you called an ambulance?' she said, as she ran down the narrow hall.

'No. I didn't want to. The house is loaded with drugs.' He started crying.

The bathroom door was open. Her mother lay on the floor and her eyes were shut. Her legs were crumpled to the side of her, carelessly, as if someone had thrown them away.

'Mummy! Mummy! Mummy!' Kitty shook her.

Her mother was heavy in her hands and Kitty couldn't move her properly. As she tried, her mother's head grazed the side of the bath with an almost comical thud.

'Help me,' Kitty said to Con.

He dragged her mother's feet, and her legs splayed, showing her white knickers. She didn't want Con to see, so she pulled her mother's skirt down and held it against her.

'Get the phone from next to the bed, the portable one. Bring it here.' Kitty cradled her mother's head in her lap.

'Mama, Mama, can you hear me?'

She called 999. The man on the phone spoke with a soft Scottish burr.

'What's your emergency?' he said in a voice trained with calm.

'It's my mother – I think she's taken an overdose, she's not moving, and we need an ambulance as soon as possible, please.' She told him the address.

'All right, love, we'll send someone right now. What's your name?'

'Kitty,' she said.

'Is she breathing, Kitty? And do you know what she's taken?'

'I can't tell if she's breathing. I know she took some coke, some cocaine, and I think she's taken pills as well,' she said.

'All right, my love, someone will be there very soon. Do you need me to stay on the phone with you?'

'No, just please tell them to hurry up. Please make them hurry!'

Her mother's eyes started rolling back in her head, like a scene from *The Exorcist.*

'Oh my God! Oh fuck, this is really heavy. I've got to get out of here.' Con Brown began to retch.

Then it was just the two of them, her mother and she, in the bathroom with the blue-and-white-striped wallpaper. There was a poster on the wall of some happy children dressed in woollen clothes on ice skates, heading home for some Ovaltine. Things she looked at every day, bath salts, her mother's skin cream, cold mundane everyday things.

'I love you, please don't die, Mummy.'

Kitty rocked her mother in her arms. Her skin was cold. She wrapped her arms around her, putting her mother's hands in the sleeves of her nightdress. She looked at the almond-shaped nails, the long painter's hands. There had been no paint on them recently, Kitty saw now. They were too white and clean. She missed the hands that were flecked with paint, which smelled of turpentine when her mother stroked her face, and danced with chips of colour when she told a story.

'You'll be all right,' Kitty said. 'I promise you. I'll make it all better, just please don't die. It will all be all right, I know it. I don't hate you. I'm sorry I said that, I didn't mean it. I love you. We need you.'

They took her away down the narrow stairs. It wasn't like television or a film: they put her neatly on the stretcher, and they spirited her away into the ambulance, the only sign of their visit the tube from the stomach pump, and the howling wail of departure.

Sam and Violet did not wake.

Her mother's bed was unmade. Kitty crawled in, trying to fit into the grooves that her body had left in the sheets, placing herself in them carefully like she was a piece from a jigsaw.

She buried her head in the pillows, the soft satin ones Ingrid and Elsie had sent from Frette in Paris, breathing in, holding the ghost of her mother's scent in her lungs, until it stung, each count of her breath willing her mother's breath to correspond from the hospital bed by osmosis, so they could take the rubbery oxygen mask away.

The sun was rising, a milky newborn thing, above the jagged roofs and aerials of Clapham. Outside the window in the rows of houses, in the massive grey tower blocks that hung spare in the distance, the curtains were shut, and she knew that people carried on, often without ever knowing who they shared breathing space with, as other lives were lived right next to them.

The number was tattooed in her brain. She waited as the phone rang. She knew they were asleep, his arm as always propped behind the crook of her neck, his nose inches from the shoulder where her silver hair fell in a thick cloud. Outside their bedroom birds would be just beginning to call each other to day, the window would be dulled by frost.

'Yes?' He sounded old, impatient. Kitty heard her grandmother murmur in the background, still dreaming maybe.

'Bestepapa?' she said.

* * *

Sam and Violet sat in the back of the BMW. Between them, Torty lay nestled in a bed of lettuce. Sam had said he would simply starve on the journey from London without it.

'I remember it here, Bestemama!' he said, as the car turned into the lane. 'That's the train bridge, and Kitty used to tell me a troll lived underneath there.'

'There isn't really a troll, Sambo,' Kitty said. 'I was making it up.'

'I know that,' Sam said. 'Obviously I was little when I believed that.'

Kitty smiled at Bestemama.

'It is sunnier here than where Mummy is working?' Violet asked.

'Oh about the same, I should think, darling,' Bestemama said. 'Now what shall we have for supper?'

'You buggers are enormous!' Bestepapa shouted down the garden. 'You could be a basketball team if there were a few more of you.' He stopped in front of Kitty. 'Hello, little Kitkat.' His voice shook. 'I'm very glad you're here, all of you, my rabble.'

Sam and Violet looked at him with interest.

'Now who's this fellow?' Bestepapa said, pointing at Torty. 'He looks a very wise beast. Is it a bird?'

'No, silly. It's a tortoise,' Sam said.

'Ah, a tortoise. Shall we take him round the garden and see whether we can find him a girlfriend?'

'He doesn't like girls. He's an old man,' Violet said, laughing.

'Well, as a very old man, I can tell you, he might have

the spirit in him yet. Come on, up we go, your sister can help your Bestemama with supper.' He held out his hands.

'How's Rosaria, darling? Gosh, you two can chat.' Bestemama was sitting by the fire, reading the papers, when Kitty came out of the study after being on the phone for an hour.

'She's well. She's got a boyfriend called Constantine.'

'How exotic,' Bestemama said. 'I do like her.'

'Her uncle is the headmaster of a boarding school in America, in Connecticut. It's meant to be a really good school.'

Bestemama stared at Kitty.

'You have a school, darling. You've just come back from America.'

'I think it might be better for me to go far away. They're going to send a prospectus. I'd like to sort of start again, and I know Connecticut isn't far away from New York, and I thought I could stay with Elsie some weekends if she doesn't mind, and come to you and Mummy for the holidays. I couldn't live at Hay if Mummy lived in London; it would be too strange, and I don't think I can live there with her.' She took a deep breath.

'You don't need to run away, Kitty,' Bestemama said fiercely. 'You haven't done anything wrong. I feel so angry with myself. I felt in my bones that things weren't right from the moment all of this began with that bloody woman and her bloody tambourine. I think Marina should move back here, to the cottage, with all of you. She was fine here. She wasn't doing any of this nonsense when she lived with us. It breaks my heart . . . I'm just so sorry – oh my Lord – to think of it.' She placed her hand on Kitty's cheek.

'I think . . .' Kitty said. 'I think it doesn't really make a difference where she is, because she always takes herself with her.'

Chapter Fourteen

The night before she left Tommy came over to say goodbye, and as he left he pressed a battered copy of his favourite book, *The Little Prince*, into her hands. 'I'm sorry if I ever made you feel bad,' he said.

'You didn't. I'll write to you. Come and visit and fall in love with an American girl so I don't have to hear about the Fräulein any more,' Kitty said, kissing his cheek.

'I'll come by and see your mother – I won't let anything happen.'

They stared at each other.

'I have to go. I'm crap at goodbyes,' he said.

She slept in her mother's bed. They played the alphabet game, and her mother made her laugh so hard her ribs felt like they had been broken.

Her mother cooked her breakfast, French toast with maple syrup, and she laid the table with snowdrops from the garden, and used her Irish linen napkins.

Nora, Sam and Violet slept, because it was early, early even for them, but she had said goodbye the evening before. Her mother carried her case downstairs, and on Kitty's head she placed her favourite hat, a tweed newsboy cap.

'Are you sure?' Kitty said.

'Yes. I need to know your head will be warm.'

'I'm not going to Antarctica, Mummy, I'm going to New York. The school's in Connecticut, they'll have central heating.'

'New York gets very cold,' her mother said. 'Don't you remember?'

As she stepped into the red beetle, Kitty looked up at the windows of the house. She saw Sam and Violet, their faces squashed against the glass. She waved, and in her wave she tried to convey everything she knew of love. Swallowing hard, she sat down and shut the door. Dusty Springfield sang from the radio.

'You don't have to go,' her mother said by the gate. 'Everything can be different, it can go back to how it was. We can ring Elsie and tell her that we've changed our minds. It doesn't need to be this dramatic. Why are you going so far away?'

A voice announced the flight to New York on the tannoy.

'I think I sort of have to go. I don't think I have a choice.'

Her mother started to cry.

'I'm sorry,' she said. 'Please know that I love you more than anything, that it is infinitely easier to love you more than I will ever love myself. Please know that always, that you are loved.'

Marina seemed to lose her words as Kitty kissed her and walked down the orange-carpeted tunnel, looking back at her mother silently watching her. She waved, mouthing 'I love you', until she disappeared from view, teetering long-legged towards her future.

Her mother lies in a ward full of other people who have tried to hurt themselves in irrevocable ways. They are all women, twelve of them. Kitty holds her stomach trying to fend off the communal despair of the room. Her mother's eyes are shut. She touches her arm lightly. She finds it miraculous that her mother bears no ravages on her face. She is, in her hospital nightgown with mascara staining her cheeks, still breathtaking.

'Hello, Mummy,' she whispers softly.

Her mother opens her eyes. Kitty doesn't feel the anger she thought she would; she looks at her mother small in the stiff white sheets of her hospital bed, amongst these sad strangers, far away from home.

Kitty looks at the faces of her mother, brother and sister, feeling the tiny little life beating inside her, and she is overwhelmed by compassion for all of them, including herself. She knows that tomorrow there will be another morning, and in that morning their lives will continue to muddle along, as lives do. She prays for the baby girl within her, she prays that she won't fuck it up, this all-consuming job that no one seems equipped for, however hard they wish and try.

'You all came.' Her mother's voice is small, but she smiles at them, and love burns from her. Turning her head, she shuts her eyes, and says quietly, 'I'm so sorry.'

'I know, Mummy,' Kitty says, taking her hand. 'I know.'

Acknowledgements

Thank you and biggest love to my family: Tessa and Julian, for their unerring support, humour and love. Maureen for her wings, wisdom and lentil soup. Clover, Luke and Ned, who share my history and make me proud. Bloomsbury's magic trinity of Alexandra Pringle, a paragon of patience and encouragement, Victoria Millar for her sense and eye and Mary Tomlinson for understanding the finer points of grammar and my writing. Ed Victor, my friend and agent. Felicity Dahl for letting me stay in the annexe whenever I needed a dose of England. Daniel Baker Sr. for opening his doors and letting me write in the bliss of his garden. Mary Conley for her cards, wit and love. Justine Picardie, heroine and surrogate big sister. And last but not least, Caitlin Blythe, for her letter, which reminded me why I wanted to write the book in the first place.

A Note on the Type

The text of this book is set in Linotype Guardi, which was designed by Reinhard Haus in 1986 following a visit to the Bibliotecca Marciana in Venice. The labels on the old picture frames there inspired him to develop his own letter forms based on Venetian Renaissance roman. The letters have the appearance of being formed by the stroke of a broad nib held at an angle. This is reflected in the slanting axis, the minimum contrast between hairlines and stems and in particular the sloped bar of the small e.